PRAISE FOR THE ANNA STRONG, VAMPIRE SERIES

## LEGACY

"Urban fantasy with true depth and flair!"
—*Romantic Times* (4½ stars)

"As riveting as the rest . . . one of my favorite urban fantasy series."
—*Darque Reviews*

## THE WATCHER

"Action fills every page, making this a novel that flies by . . . Dynamic relationships blend [with] complex mysteries in this thriller."
—*Huntress Book Reviews*

"An exciting, fast-paced novel . . . first-rate plotting."
—*LoveVampires*

"Dazzles readers with action-packed paranormal adventure, love and friendship. With many wonderfully executed twists and turns, this author's suspenseful writing will hold readers spellbound until the very end."
—*Darque Reviews*

"Snappy action and plot twists that will hold readers' interest to the last page."
—*Monsters and Critics*

# BLOOD DRIVE

"A terrific tale of supernatural sleuthing . . . provides edge-of-your-seat thrills and a high-octane emotional punch."

—*Romantic Times*

"Once again Jeanne C. Stein delivers a jam-packed story full of mystery and intrigue that will keep you glued to the edge of your seat! Just like [with] the first book in the Anna Strong series, *The Becoming*, I could not put this book down even for a second. You will find yourself cheering Anna on as she goes after the bad guys. Jeanne C. Stein has given us a wonderful tough-as-nails heroine everyone will love!"

—*Night Owl Romance*

"I loved this book . . . hugely enjoyable . . . an exciting read and everything any vampire-fantasy fan could hope for."

—*LoveVampires*

"Jeanne C. Stein takes on the vampire mythos in her own unique manner that makes for an enthralling vampire thriller. Readers of Laurell K. Hamilton, Tanya Huff and Charlaine Harris will thoroughly enjoy this fast-paced novel filled with several action scenes that come one after the other, making it hard for the readers to catch a breather."

—*Midwest Book Review*

"A really great series. Anna's strengths and weaknesses make for a very compelling character. Stein really puts you in [Anna's] head as she fumbles her way through a new life and the heartbreaking choices she will have to make. [Stein] also introduces new supernatural characters and gives a glimpse into a secret underground organization. This is a pretty cool urban fantasy series that will appeal to fans of Patricia Briggs's Mercy Thompson series."

—*Vampire Genre*

# THE BECOMING

"This is a really, really good book. Anna is a great character, Stein's plotting is adventurous and original, and I think most of my readers would have a great time with *The Becoming.*"

—Charlaine Harris, #1 *New York Times* bestselling author of *Dead and Gone*

"A cross between MaryJanice Davidson's Undead series, starring Betsy Taylor, and Laurell K. Hamilton's Anita Blake series. [Anna's] a kick-butt bounty hunter—but vampires are a complete surprise to her. Full of interesting twists and turns that will leave readers guessing. *The Becoming* is a great addition to the TBR pile."

—*Romance Reviews Today*

"With plot twists, engaging characters and smart writing, this first installment in a new supernatural series has all the marks of a hit. Anna Strong lives up to her name: equally tenacious and vulnerable, she's a heroine with the charm, savvy and intelligence that fans of Laurell K. Hamilton and Kim Harrison will be happy to root for . . . If this debut novel is any indication, Stein has a fine career ahead of her."

—*Publishers Weekly*

"In an almost Hitchcockian way, this story keeps you guessing, with new twists and turns coming almost every page. Anna is well named, strong in ways she does not even know. There is a strong element of surprise to it . . . Even if you don't like vampire novels, you ought to give this one a shot."

—*Huntress Book Reviews*

"A wonderful new vampire book . . . that will keep you on the edge of your seat."

—*Fallen Angel Reviews*

*Ace Books by Jeanne C. Stein*

**THE BECOMING**
**BLOOD DRIVE**
**THE WATCHER**
**LEGACY**
**RETRIBUTION**

# RETRIBUTION

JEANNE C. STEIN

ACE BOOKS, NEW YORK

**THE BERKLEY PUBLISHING GROUP**
**Published by the Penguin Group**
**Penguin Group (USA) Inc.**
**375 Hudson Street, New York, New York 10014, USA**

Penguin Group (Canada), 90 Eglinton Avenue East, Suite 700, Toronto, Ontario M4P 2Y3, Canada
(a division of Pearson Penguin Canada Inc.)
Penguin Books Ltd., 80 Strand, London WC2R 0RL, England
Penguin Group Ireland, 25 St. Stephen's Green, Dublin 2, Ireland (a division of Penguin Books Ltd.)
Penguin Group (Australia), 250 Camberwell Road, Camberwell, Victoria 3124, Australia
(a division of Pearson Australia Group Pty. Ltd.)
Penguin Books India Pvt. Ltd., 11 Community Centre, Panchsheel Park, New Delhi—110 017, India
Penguin Group (NZ), 67 Apollo Drive, Rosedale, North Shore 0632, New Zealand
(a division of Pearson New Zealand Ltd.)
Penguin Books (South Africa) (Pty.) Ltd., 24 Sturdee Avenue, Rosebank, Johannesburg 2196,
South Africa

Penguin Books Ltd., Registered Offices: 80 Strand, London WC2R 0RL, England

This is a work of fiction. Names, characters, places, and incidents either are the product of the author's imagination or are used fictitiously, and any resemblance to actual persons, living or dead, business establishments, events, or locales is entirely coincidental. The publisher does not have any control over and does not assume any responsibility for author or third-party websites or their content.

RETRIBUTION

An Ace Book / published by arrangement with the author

PRINTING HISTORY
Ace mass-market edition / September 2009

Copyright © 2009 by Jeanne C. Stein.
Cover art by Cliff Nielsen.
Cover design by Judith Lagerman.
Interior text design by Kristin del Rosario.

ISBN: 978-0-441-01773-7

ACE
Ace Books are published by The Berkley Publishing Group,
a division of Penguin Group (USA) Inc.,
375 Hudson Street, New York, New York 10014.
ACE and the "A" design are trademarks of Penguin Group (USA) Inc.

PRINTED IN THE UNITED STATES OF AMERICA

10   9   8   7   6   5   4   3   2   1

*To my pop—who never really got it*

*And my family and friends who do*

*This one's for you*

# PROLOGUE

*I*T WAS TOO DARK.
*She couldn't see.*

*Her nose wrinkled. Something smelled bad. Smelled of urine and vomit and . . .*

*Death. She recognized it, though she shouldn't have been able to. She wouldn't have been able to twenty-four hours ago.*

*She was afraid. He was supposed to be here. He promised to be here.*

*She stepped closer to the wall, away from the door. The dark clutched at her with icy fingers. She was too new. She felt vulnerable, exposed. Her blood, his blood, ran through her veins, but it offered no protection. Where was the strength he promised? The freedom from fear?*

*She began to shake. She was so hungry. She needed to feed. He said he'd be here to help her. To show her what to do.*

*A sound, the scrabbling of claws on concrete, made her*

jump. Her skin tightened at the base of her spine. There were rats in here. Rats. He didn't expect her to eat rats, did he? No, he'd have to let her feed from him again if that's what he had planned. She would not eat vermin. No matter how hungry she was.

She felt a thrill of excitement. She had done it. She had become vampire, one of the strong, one of the immortal. It wasn't exactly what she expected—the becoming. But she'd crossed the threshold and come out the other side. She was vampire.

So, why was she cringing here in the dark like a child just because he was late? Hadn't he said instinct would kick in when the time came to take her first human?

Maybe he had more faith in her abilities than she did.

Maybe he had decided to let her hunt on her own because he knew what she was capable of.

Maybe he was right outside the door, waiting for her to—

To what?

She peered into the darkness. There wasn't anyone here. There were no humans in the building, of that she was certain. She didn't smell anything except the putrid odor of decay. She didn't hear any hearts beating, nothing breathing or snorting or coughing.

She was alone.

With the rats.

She pressed a dial on her watch. The face glowed. She'd been here thirty minutes. She would wait five more.

She worked her way back along the wall to the door. There was no moonlight to break the gloom or cast a shadow through the broken windows. Irritation quickened her step. Why had he told her to meet him here? Was this some stupid initiation prank? If it was, she didn't find it funny. He'd know that soon enough.

She pushed at the door.

*It creaked open.*

*He was waiting for her outside, his features pale in the dim light.*

*"Where have you been?"*

*He smiled and raised his arm.*

*A shiver of uncertainty ran up her spine. "What is that?"*

*He took one step closer and fired.*

*The dart from the crossbow caught her just under her left breast. A prick.*

*Warmth.*

*Then . . .*


I SIT STRAIGHT UP IN BED—HEART POUNDING.

Christ.

What a weird dream.

# CHAPTER 1

THERE ARE SOME THINGS ABOUT BEING A VAMPIRE that come in handy in my line of work.

Tonight is a perfect example.

I'm a bounty hunter. The human I'm after is sitting at a bar ten feet away from me getting shit-faced on cheap beer and bad whiskey. She's leaning on the shoulder of her loser boyfriend, whose name is Hank. I know this because I smell the booze, see the drunken haze clouding her eyes, hear every word they're saying. Where they plan to go when they leave, who they're planning to meet, how much money they expect to have after they rob the neighborhood 7-Eleven.

She has no idea that anyone is listening. How could she? The noise in this dive is at jet engine decibels. But I hear. Everything.

She pushes herself off the bar stool and staggers to her feet. Her name is Hilda. She's wanted for three counts of aggravated assault. The boyfriend she's drinking with is one of the complainants. Seems they've made up. She's about five feet four inches, two hundred fifty pounds. She's dressed in low-cut jeans and a tight T-shirt.

Not a pretty picture.

Hilda gathers up what's left of a twenty—a fiver and some coin. The barkeep laid the change down five minutes ago with a smile after she'd called for the tab.

The barkeep's expression now reflects disappointment; he thought she might forget.

Hilda's expression says fat chance.

Hilda pushes the coins toward him but drops the bill down the front of her shirt and grins. "Want a bigger tip? Come get it."

Hank grabs her arm. "What are you talking about, bitch?"

The bartender takes a step back and moves away. The boyfriend is bigger than Hilda and mean-looking. I can see by the frown on his face that the barkeep thinks no five-dollar tip is worth the aggravation. He moves to the other side of the bar.

Hilda and her boyfriend argue all the way to the door. I slip out right after them. I already know where they've parked their car and while they lurch toward it, I take off ahead of them. By the time they get to me, I'm leaning against the driver's side door, twirling a pair of handcuffs.

"What the fuck?" Hank says.

"Yeah, what the fuck?" Hilda echoes.

"Hilda, Hilda. I got a call from your daughter this afternoon. She's upset. Do you know why?"

Hilda's eyes scrunch. "No. Why?"

"You must have forgotten that you had a court date this week. You didn't show up. Now if I don't get you to jail tonight, your daughter is going to lose her house. You really wouldn't want that to happen, would you?"

The boyfriend snarls and takes what I'm sure he imagines to be a menacing step toward me.

The fact that his eyes are crossed and drool spindles from the corner of his mouth takes the sting out of the threat. I hold my ground and snarl right back. Literally.

His eyes widen, but he places his hands on swaying hips and says, "Those are bullshit charges. You'd better get away from my car, little lady, or I'm going to have to take you over my knee."

He grins at Hilda. "That's pretty good, huh? We'll give this bitch a spanking she'll never forget."

Hilda grins back. For a minute, I think they've forgotten I'm here. Then they both turn around.

And start to run.

In opposite directions.

Hank picks the better route—toward the street. With surprising dexterity, he leapfrogs into the back of a moving pickup and peeks up over the gate. The driver doesn't realize he's picked up a passenger and continues on his way down the road.

Hank has no bounty on his ass, so I don't care. I take off after Hilda. She has a head start. Still, it's no contest. She's two hundred and fifty pounds of couch potato. I don't need to tap into vampire strength or speed. I'm on her before she makes it to the end of the parking lot.

I push her to the ground and jump on her broad back. She bucks under me like a bull. I yank both of her hands behind her and snap on the cuffs. It happens so fast, she doesn't realize she's trussed until she tries to push herself up.

She starts to yell. For Hank.

"Save your breath, sweetie," I whisper in her ear. "The last glimpse I had of Hank, he was hopping in the back of a pickup. He's long gone."

I reach down and haul her to her feet. I use one hand, as if she weighs twenty-five pounds instead of two-fifty. "Looks like it's just you and me."

Hilda is looking at me bleary-eyed with confusion and alcohol. "How did you—? What did you—? Where did you—?"

I pat her head and push her toward my own car. "Don't try to figure it out, Hilda. You'll hurt yourself."

She stumbles forward. I've got one hand on the cuffs and one on the small of her back. We're just about at the car when my cell phone rings.

I dig it out of my pocket and flip it open.

It's my partner, David, on vacation in the Bahamas.

"Hey, Anna," he says. "How's it going?"

"Just peachy." I open the rear car door and shove Hilda down onto the seat. "Are you having fun?"

He laughs. "I'm laying on a beach drinking mojitos out of coconut shells. How about you?"

Hilda looks up at me and spits. Only trouble is, she's got the coordination of a drunk and the spittle dribbles down her own chin and settles somewhere in the vicinity of that five-dollar bill she'd shoved down her blouse.

I slam the door and take my place behind the wheel. "Actually, yes," I tell David. "I am having fun."

# CHAPTER 2

I DEPOSIT HILDA IN CITY LOCKUP AND HEAD TO the office David and I share on Pacific Coast Highway. It's just past midnight on a Saturday night and the restaurants in Seaport Village, our neighbor to the south, have already shuttered for the night. I take a beer out of the fridge, gather the day's mail from the desktop and step out onto the wooden deck that spans the rear of the building.

It's a cool, moonless, late April evening. Too cool for a human to enjoy sitting out on the deck the way I am now. For a vampire, temperature is irrelevant. Ninety degrees or fifty, makes no difference. However, the feel of a soft ocean breeze blowing off the water, the cool iciness of the beer bottle in my hand, the play of light on the water from Coronado across the bay, are human sensibilities I can still enjoy.

The beast is quiet within me. It's nice.

I place the bottle on the deck and sort through the mail. A couple of bills, a couple of checks. A postcard.

From France. The Eiffel Tower.

I flip it over, smiling because I know it will be from my niece. Trish's precise, graceful script fills the back. Her friend Ryan and his parents are visiting for spring break. They've traveled from my family's home in Avignon to Paris and her words sparkle with wonder and excitement. Her fourteenth birthday is next week and they plan to celebrate with fireworks at the chateau. Could I possibly fly over, too?

Oh, Trish, I wish I could.

She is having such a good time, learning so much. I can't remember ever feeling as optimistic or hopeful about the future as she does. It's a gift. I wish I could share it with her. If I were human, I might be able to.

As a vampire, I'm afraid that all I can bring to her life is the threat of danger. She and my parents are better off with distance between us. It's the reason they are now living on a winery in France and I'm chasing lowlifes like Hilda in San Diego.

I gather the mail and the now-empty beer bottle and go back inside. For the first time, I notice the message light blinking on the telephone. I lift the receiver and punch in the code for voice mail.

"Anna. It's Williams. This is the fifth message I've left. I need to talk to you, damn it. It's important."

I delete this message just as I have the other four. He doesn't seem to get it. I don't want to talk to him.

I slip the checks into a drawer to be deposited tomorrow, place the bills on the desk blotter and prop the postcard against my computer monitor. I'll call Trish on her birthday. I can do that. Talk to her. Let her know I love her.

And speaking of love . . .

I close the slider and grab my car keys. I have a date up the coast. It'll take me a while to go home, shower and get to Malibu but I know what awaits me is worth it.

* * *

LANCE MEETS ME AT THE DOOR OF HIS BEACH HOUSE wearing a smile and an open terry robe. He's tall, handsome in an edgy, bad-boy way and has blond hair that falls to his shoulders. The look he's giving me makes my blood heat and my heart pound. He's as happy to see me as I am to be here.

"What took you?" he asks, grabbing my hand and pulling me inside. "I've missed you."

"I can see that."

He pulls me over to the couch and lets me plop down before reaching for the opened bottle of wine sitting beside two glasses on his coffee table. He pours, I take one, and in another second he's beside me and I'm settling my head on his shoulder.

"This is nice," I say.

And I mean it. I met Lance right around Christmastime last year when everything in my life was going to hell. He was the one bright spot—a willing, energetic and quite enthusiastic lover who helped me forget my problems.

Amazingly, we became friends and that led to our becoming *real* lovers. He's an underwear model for Jockey. Do I need to say more about the body? He's also a vampire, which means I don't have to hide my nature or hold back in our lovemaking for fear I'll hurt him. We can bite, suck and fuck each other's brains out.

It's liberating. It's cathartic. It's an arrangement I can live with.

I release a breath, run a hand over his chest, down lean-muscled, rock-hard abs.

His human buddies have to diet and work out all the time to keep this kind of physique. The only diet Lance is on is the one we share—the liquid protein kind.

He's a female vamp's wet dream.

And for now, he's mine.

I let my hand roam farther, a feather touch, teasing.

He responds, staying my hand with his own, guiding my fingers so they encircle him, letting me feel him grow bigger, a pulse that's an invitation.

He shifts to take my glass out of my hand. He places the glasses on the table and stands up, drawing me with him. He lets his robe fall to the carpet.

In a heartbeat, I'm out of my clothes, too.

He lowers me to the floor, his mouth on mine, his own fingers exploring. Heat radiates from his touch, making me shiver with need. Blood sings. I'm ready. More than ready.

Time to get down to business.


THE BEDSIDE CLOCK SAYS THREE A.M. LANCE IS ASLEEP beside me. So why can't I fall asleep?

I kick off the covers and slide out of bed. His house is right on the beach, one of the perks of being a successful male model. The slider is open and the rhythm of the ocean draws me outside. I don't bother to take a robe or wrap a towel around me, but stand naked on the deck. At this time of morning, who is around to see?

The water is black under a cloud-studded sky. The surf advances and retreats from a white, sandy beach with comforting regularity. The smell of sand and sea is rich, teeming with life. Before Malibu was an enclave of the rich and famous, before there was a Los Angeles, before there were *people*, there was the ocean.

The concept of time changes when you're a vamp. Maybe that's why the sea draws me the way it does. If I'm not staked or beheaded or burned to death, I may live to see Malibu reclaimed by the ocean.

I used to be afraid of the idea of immortality. Had difficulty accepting the notion of never-ending life. Something is shifting inside me. I'm not so afraid anymore.

Not for myself. But when I lose my family, when I watch generations come and go without being a part of what makes human life bearable, when I have to constantly build new relationships to replace those I've lost—I may rethink the price of immortality.

Lance awakens. I hear his sleepy voice in my head. *Anna, what are you doing out there?*

I half turn toward him. *Contemplating eternity.*

# CHAPTER 3

JUST AS HAVING A MALIBU BEACH HOUSE IS A PERK of being a successful model, early morning photo shoots are a drawback.

Lance's alarm clock goes off at four thirty. I hear it before he does. I prop myself up on my elbows.

We're outside, on a chaise, with only his robe thrown over us. He'd joined me earlier to watch the ocean and one thing led to another as it inevitably does with us. We'd both fallen asleep after, our limbs tangled, my head on his chest. We've been asleep exactly thirty minutes.

I study his beautiful face, relaxed in sleep, brush a lock of long, silky hair out of his eyes and shake him gently awake.

He groans, stretches, kisses me and hauls himself up to go inside to shower.

I haul myself up to start the coffee.

About the same time the smell of fresh-brewed coffee has my salivary glands pumping, my cell phone rings.

The caller ID displays a number and area code I don't recognize.

"Hello?"

"Anna?"

"Culebra?" I almost drop the coffee mug in my hand. My Mexican shape-shifting friend has never called me. Never. It's no wonder I didn't recognize the number or that I blurt stupidly, "What are you doing?"

"I'm calling you."

"It's four thirty in the morning."

"Were you asleep? You don't sound like you were sleeping."

"No. Happens that I wasn't asleep. But it's still four thirty in the morning. What's going on?"

"Can you come to TJ?"

"You mean to Beso de la Muerte?"

"No. I'll tell you where to meet me."

It could be the lack of coffee, or the shock of having him call me, or the fact that it's four thirty. For whatever reason, my brain seems incapable of forming an intelligent answer.

Culebra waits a second before barking impatiently, "Anna. Wake up. I want to see you. Are you coming or not?"

I rouse myself with a mental thump to the head. "Yes. I'll come. What's this about?"

Lance comes out of the bathroom. He raises a questioning eyebrow at seeing me on the phone but takes my mug, pours coffee for both of us and hands mine back.

He's naked and smells of soap and shampoo and my thoughts drift to wondering just how much time we have before he has to go and what might happen if I follow him back into the bedroom . . .

"Goddamn it, Anna." Culebra's ire is escalating. "What the fuck are you doing?"

Lance moves back into the bedroom. Not fucking, which

is what I'd like to be doing. The bedroom door closes and the vapor lock in my brain releases. "I'm here, I'm here. Where do you want to meet?"

"I told you. Downtown Tijuana."

"TJ? Why?"

A pause. Then a noisy, impatient exhalation. "I have my reasons. Can you come?"

My turn to pause, impulse to grill him strong. But Culebra never asks favors. This must be important. I relent.

"Where?"

"Thirty-four Avenido Revolucion. In an hour?"

Crap. "Have to make it three. I'm not in San Diego."

"Where are you?" Then he laughs. "Let me guess. Malibu with that muscle-bound model. Am I right?"

There's no condemnation or sarcasm in his tone. If anything, he sounds pleased. "With Lance, yes."

"Okay. I have some things to attend to. I planned to do them after we met, but I'll take care of them before. Just don't get sidetracked. I'll be waiting."

He disconnects.

Lance is back, dressed. Too bad. No sidetracking now. He pours his coffee into a travel mug and leans down to plant a kiss on the top of my head. "Who was that?"

"Culebra."

"At this time of morning?"

I shake my head. "Don't have a clue what's up, but he wants to meet me."

Lance scoops his keys and wallet from the counter. "Have to go. Will I see you tonight?"

"Can you come to my place?"

He smiles and I'm suddenly counting the hours.

"I'll be there. Lock up when you go."

I see him to the door and wave him off. It's a small, comforting gesture, waving a lover good-bye in the morning. Normal. Human.

I like the feeling.

I get dressed and head back for San Diego. A quick stop at the cottage to shower and change clothes and I'm on my way again. When I hit the border crossing, I sail through. It's a little before eight on a Sunday morning. Too early for most tourists to be entering Mexico but the line coming back stretches a half mile.

TJ has changed a lot in the last twenty years. Especially the border crossing and the area right around it. Where there was nothing but bad road and vendors selling pottery and junk, there is now a mall. High-end stores, air-conditioning, trendy restaurants.

But go on into town, follow Avenido Revolucion to the end, which is where the address Culebra gave me is located, and you're back in the TJ of my youth. My mom hated coming here, but out-of-town visitors always insisted on seeing the real Tijuana.

Of course my family never made it back *this* far. Back through narrow streets lined with bars and brothels, a few dicey eating places and shops filled with fake turquoise jewelry and *authentic* Mayan pottery. Evidently the Mayans had forged a trade agreement with China. This is where the shows were, the infamous animal acts. Used to draw a lot of tourists until an attempt was made to shut them down. From the looks of the signs above the bars, the attempt failed.

I haven't been here in years. Memories flood back. As a teenager, armed with fake IDs and a wad of cash, my friends and I would sneak across the border for cheap booze and adventure. I was never afraid. Stupid, naive, but never afraid. When your brother is run over by a drunk on his way to a college class, your perspective on danger changes.

The bar where I'm to meet Culebra makes me wish I'd driven the car David and I use for work, a Ford Crown

Vic, instead of my Jag. I'm afraid if I park out in front of this dive, I'll return to a stripped hulk. What was Culebra thinking?

As soon as I pull up, a boy of about twelve steps from inside the bar.

"Are you Senorita Strong?" he asks in heavily accented English.

He's about fourteen, tall and skinny with a shock of black hair that curls like a comma in the middle of his forehead. He projects an air of hard independence. Hard *earned*, too, I suspect, looking around at the surroundings. He's wearing clean but well-worn jeans and a red Harvard sweatshirt.

I nod.

He holds out his hand. "Twenty bucks and I'll watch your car."

Must be Harvard Business School. I pull out my wallet and hand him a ten. "You get the other ten when I get back and my car is in one piece."

He accepts the bill and strolls over to lean against the passenger side door. "He's in the back room. Go straight through."

Reluctantly, I turn away from the car. My only consolation is that if I come back and something has happened, David has a friend with a good body shop.

Loud, grinding strip music suddenly starts up from inside. I push through the double swinging doors and the music intensifies. Bad sound system, like a seventies boom box, exaggerates the bass and warbles the treble. It might as well be amplified through tin. The smell of stale beer and overripe male is strong enough to wrinkle my nose.

I forget the smell and the bad music, though, when I look around the dingy interior and see what's going on.

Ten men in various states of inebriation slouch around a raised platform. A woman, a hard thirtysomething, struts in front of them. Grinning, leering. She's dressed in a halter top, breasts barely contained. And a miniskirt. She's wearing no underwear under the skirt. It's evident with every calculated step.

Behind her, there's a girl and a burro. She looks about twelve. She's dressed in jeans and a T-shirt. Her hands and voice are busy, coaxing the burro. Readying it for the performance.

My stomach lurches and I look away.

I think I'm going to be sick. Right after I kill Culebra.

# CHAPTER 4

I FLEE INTO A BACK ROOM AS DINGY AND BADLY LIT as the front, but it's a relief to leave the scene on the other side. There are four tables spaced on a sawdust-strewn floor. Culebra is sitting by himself at a table against the far wall. He doesn't look up when I come in. He doesn't sense my presence. Unusual. As a shape-shifter, he can read my thoughts and I his. Unless, like now, he's closed the conduit between us.

It allows me to use my voice. My loud voice. "Have you lost your mind? What are you doing here?"

His shoulders jump. He looks up. Even though I'm not able to read his thoughts, I can read what plays across his face just as clearly. He's startled, momentarily confused by my outburst, apologetic when he understands what's behind it. He pushes back his chair and stands up.

He gestures toward the other room. "God, I'm sorry, Anna. I should have picked somewhere else to meet. I've been distracted lately." He glances at his watch. "I know the manager here, and I had to see him. I have to be at the airport in an hour. But I am truly sorry for my thoughtlessness. Sit, please. I have much to tell you and little time."

When I don't immediately move toward the table, he adds, *I know it doesn't make the situation better, but that girl is sixteen and makes more in one week than her father makes in a month in the fields. She only cares for the burro.*

*Only cares for the burro? I saw how she was caring for the burro.*

Culebra winces at my anger. *She and her brother support a family of twelve.*

The brother must be the kid outside watching the car. *So who's the woman? Their mother?*

*It's an imperfect world, Anna. You know that better than anyone.* He lets a heartbeat go by before adding, *She isn't Trish.*

Bringing up my niece and the abuse she suffered at the hands of her mother's friends provokes a flash of anger. I narrow my eyes and stare back at him. *Not a good idea to be in my head right now.* Out loud I say, "I won't stay here."

Culebra has the good sense not to argue. He gathers the papers from the table. "There's a café across the street. We'll go there."

The music has stopped. The show must be over. When we step into the other room, men are staggering toward the door, no doubt off to find some other perversion. The urge to stop them, to break each of their necks and toss them into a Dumpster, is strong.

But stronger still is the urge to break the neck of the woman scooping scattered dollar bills and pesos from the stage. When she's finished, she says something in Spanish and tosses a dollar to the girl before disappearing into the back.

The girl is brushing the burro, crooning softly, ignoring

the crumpled bill at her feet. She's pretty in the Spanish/ Native American, dark-haired, dark-eyed way. She's slender, small-boned. Her skin has an unhealthy pallor. She spends too much time in this dump.

I fish my wallet out of my bag. I have two hundred dollars in twenties. I give it all to her. "Take the rest of the day off."

She looks at the money, then up at me. Her expression doesn't change. Her eyes hold neither warmth nor interest. She folds the bills out of my hand, slips them into the halter, and resumes grooming the burro.

*That won't alter her situation, Anna. I hope you didn't think it would.*

Culebra's tone is sad and disapproving.

Of course I didn't think it would, I'm tempted to snap back. But a part of me knows that's a lie. I was hoping it might alter her situation for at least a day. That she would take the money and go shopping or to a movie, do anything a normal sixteen-year-old girl would do on a Sunday afternoon.

Instead, there's a group of American teenagers, boys about seventeen years old, pushing through the doors, pointing with leering grins to the girl on stage.

My last glimpse of the girl is that she's grinning back.


CULEBRA IS APOLOGIZING, AGAIN.

We're settled in a booth in a café across from the bar. I can't get that last image of the girl out of my head.

*It's all she's ever known, Anna. She lives in a house, a real house, and provides food for her family. She has a chance to go to school . . .*

God. I don't bother to dignify that with anything other than a snort. *Don't bullshit me, Culebra. She's not ever going to school.*

I shrug out of my jacket and cast a glance around the café. While it is much cleaner and brighter than the bar, it does nothing to improve my mood. I slouch down on the bench.

"I hate it here. Why aren't we in Beso de la Muerte?"

Culebra's expression shifts to a look strange for him. Excited. Secretive.

"What's going on?"

He leans toward me across the table. "I'm going away for a while."

"Going away? Where?"

"I can't tell you. Not now."

"What will you be doing?"

"I can't tell you that, either."

He says it almost gleefully. Strange behavior for a shape-shifter whose expression normally spans the gamut from subdued to restrained.

So, I repeat, more forcefully this time, "What's going on?"

He fidgets, not meeting my eyes, sending off a gust of impatience. "I just need to get away for a while. I wanted to tell you personally."

"So why not tell me this on the phone or at Beso? Why drag me to this dump? There's got to be more."

He folds his hands and leans toward me again. "Sandra is going to be watching the bar for me."

"Sandra?" I sit up straight. "She's back?"

The last time I saw Sandra was four months ago, right after she won her battle against Avery. Avery, my Avery, the one I fought and staked only to find out he hadn't died after all. He used powerful black magic to take over Sandra's body and will. In a fight that almost killed her, Sandra accomplished what I had not. She sent Avery to hell, for real this time.

"She told me she would never come back."

"She came because I asked her."

"Why did you ask her?"

"I needed someone to watch the bar."

My stomach is contracting into a barbed-wire ball of aggravation. This is like talking to a three-year-old. "Sandra turned down my offer to take over Avery's estate. She said she was returning to her home to be with her own kind. Her pack. Now, suddenly, she's here tending bar? You couldn't think of anyone else? What about all your human employees? What about me?" It comes out a petulant howl of protest.

Culebra is in my head. I don't care. I want him there. I want him to know that I'm more than a *little* upset that he didn't think I would have done him this favor. Instead, he called on a stranger.

*I'm sorry, Anna. You have your own business to run. I didn't think you'd have time—*

*How long are you going to be gone?*

*I'm not sure. Two weeks, maybe.*

I start to slide out of the booth. "Have a good time."

"Anna, wait."

He holds out a hand to stop me.

"Why? Are you going to tell me the reason you brought me to this shit hole?"

"I did."

"No. You didn't. You didn't tell me a fucking thing you couldn't have told me on the phone."

He glances to the papers on the seat beside him. There's a map on top. He shuffles them together so the map is hidden in the middle.

"I didn't want you to be surprised if you went to Beso de la Muerte and found me gone and Sandra there. That's all."

Bullshit.

If that was it, he could have met me in Beso de la Muerte.

He picks that thought out of the ether. "Sandra is uncomfortable with seeing you. She asked if you might stay away until I get back."

It's the aha moment I've been waiting for. "Sandra doesn't want to see me? That's why we're here?"

He drops his eyes.

"Why would she not want to see me?"

He looks up at me again. "She hasn't gotten over what happened at Avery's."

"Wait a minute. She blames me for that?"

"It's not rational. I know. *She* knows. But she lost Tamara. It's complicated."

No. It isn't. I'm staring at Culebra, waiting for him to say something else. Something that makes sense. Something like Tamara was going to kill us both and her death was self-defense.

But he doesn't. And his mind is closed.

Guess I'll have to get answers from Sandra.

*No. Please, Anna. Honor her wishes. Honor my wishes.*

I stare at him. *You're actually asking me to stay away until you get back?*

*Yes.*

He's not looking at me. I feel agitation, it's emanating from him like heat from fire. His lined face is creased with worry. It tempers my aggravation. I love Culebra like family. I put a hand over his. *Tell me what's wrong.*

He pulls his hand back and smoothes the concern from his face. In its place is a frown of exasperation. *What's wrong is that I've asked you to do a simple thing. You fight me as you do anyone who will not cater to your whims. It's unfair, Anna, and insulting.*

The vehemence behind his words stuns me. The rebuke is unfair and insulting. Face hot, I snatch up my jacket and slide to the end of the booth. Hesitate as I wait for him to stop me.

He doesn't. He makes no move to stop me. He doesn't look up or even call a good-bye as I walk away.

The kid is still leaning against my car when I cross the road and the music has started up again in the bar. I shove the ten at him. I can't get out of here fast enough.

I don't know where I'm going until I'm back behind the wheel of my car and heading out of TJ. Culebra's evasiveness about the why and where of this trip distresses me. What distresses me even more is the idea that Sandra holds Tamara's death against me. I have a right to set her straight.

I don't care if she wants to see me or not. Culebra is off to catch a plane, winging his way to some mysterious destination. How is he going to stop me?

Fuck it. I have nothing better to do today. I'm going to see Sandra.

# CHAPTER 5

EVEN TO THE SUPERNATURAL COMMUNITY, BESO de la Muerte is a mystery. It takes me almost as much time to reach it from Tijuana as it does from San Diego, mostly because it's forty miles of bad desert road. The town is not on any map, and if a mortal happened to ignore the inhospitable surroundings and take the unmarked turn off from the main highway, it would not be long before he realized he had made a mistake and quickly head back.

He would not be able to articulate *why* he knew he had made a mistake. He would simply know that he had.

With one exception. If he is a mortal coming to Beso de la Muerte to be a host.

Culebra has been the sole proprietor of this ghost town turned supernatural hangout for as long as anyone can remember.

The first time I came here I was tracking down the vamp who turned me. I was hunting him because I thought he had kidnapped my partner, David, and burned down my house. Turns out, I was wrong. Avery had done those things. Just as he had laid the false trail that led me to Beso de la Muerte in the first place.

The one good thing that came from the whole debacle was meeting Culebra. I need human blood to survive. Culebra offers humans with an inclination for adventure the opportunity to make money as well as experience the best sex imaginable while providing that blood. He protects both vampires and their human hosts. Keeps vampires off the street and off the radar of those who would hunt us. No bodies left suspiciously drained of blood to attract unwanted attention.

The system works.

More important, Culebra became my friend.

At least, I thought he had become a friend.

I push the biting sting of his parting remarks from my head. Along with the guilt that I'm doing exactly what he asked me not to. A whiny little voice justifies it. Don't I have as much right to be in Beso de la Muerte as Sandra?

It's not yet eleven o'clock in the morning. Not surprisingly, there are only two cars parked in front of Culebra's bar when I pull up. Most of the action takes place after dark. The cars are a big Cadillac SUV and a silver Porsche Boxster. I park behind the Cadillac and send out a mental probe.

I detect three vampires and one human.

The human must be Sandra. She's a werewolf, but werewolves in human form do not give off a supernatural psychic signature. Two of the vampires are bemoaning the fact that they came all the way from L.A. and are starving and there's no one here to eat. The third vampire is emitting no telepathic signal at all.

I push through the double swinging doors.

The two vamps griping about the lack of service are sitting at a table in the middle of the room. They each have a beer in front of them. They are young, dressed in open-neck polos and jeans. Both are male, both have carefully coiffed hair and both have an L.A. chic look about them. Probably belong to the Boxster. They look up expectantly when I walk in, then wilt in disappointment when they realize I will not be on the menu.

Newly made, I'd guess, judging from the clumsy way they try to shield their thoughts from me.

The third vampire is at the bar. His back is to me but I sense his reaction when he recognizes me. Because he does recognize me. Immediately. His back becomes rigid. His thoughts draw in on themselves like a noose tightening around a neck.

He doesn't turn around.

Williams.

For an instant, *I'm* tempted to turn around and get the hell out of here. He's the last person I want to see.

Sandra, however, is a different story. She's the reason I'm here. If I can ignore Williams' phone calls, I can ignore him in person, too.

Sandra is arranging glasses against the back of the bar. When she hears the door, she turns and without looking up, says, "Take any table—"

She raises her eyes and the words die in her throat. She still has a glass in her hand. It remains suspended in air for the second it takes her to replace a look of irritation with one of resignation. She sighs and places the glass on the bar. While the words she speaks are, "Hello, Anna," her attitude says, "Fuck."

She looks good. She's tall and slim and has eyes that aren't quite green and aren't quite blue, but flash of both. Her dark hair has grown since I last saw her, it skims her shoulders. Her skin is sun-kissed and glowing. She looks healthy. She looks alive.

What she doesn't look is happy to see me.

"Hello, Sandra."

I step up to the bar and place both my hands flat on its surface. I know why she's reacting the way she is. Culebra made that clear. It's the reason I came.

For the moment, though, the more urgent problem is the vamp to my left. His negativity flares, burning into my subconscious, demanding response.

So much for ignoring him. Without turning, I say, "Hello, Williams."

The negativity is momentarily suppressed by a flicker of satisfaction. He was waiting for me.

He was *waiting* for me.

Son of a bitch. Did Culebra set this up?

Sandra's expression, though, hasn't wavered. Her reaction seemed real enough.

So what the fuck is going on?

Next moment, all my questions are washed away in the flood of nonverbal communication Williams sends my way.

*If you'd answer my calls, your friends wouldn't have to resort to trickery.*

*I do answer my friends' calls. I didn't—I don't want to talk to you.*

My gut churns in frustration and anger. Williams has played enough dirty tricks on me to bring out the animal instinct for self-preservation. The beast rises close to the surface.

Williams is in my head, probing for any hint of a threat. He quickly relays his own intention to keep this meeting a civil one, and politely inquires whether I can do the same.

The vibes we're throwing off must be explosive because the two vamps at the table get up and beat it out of the bar.

The roar of the Porsche engine is still rattling the windows along Main Street when Sandra ends our head game.

She isn't privy to what's going on between us, but her own animal instinct for preservation senses the hostility. She slams a glass on the bar with enough force to shatter it.

"Great," she says. "They left without paying for their beer. Which one of you big, bad vampires is going to pick up their tab?"

# CHAPTER 6

WILLIAMS REACHES FOR HIS WALLET, SLAPS A
twenty on the bar.

He turns on the bar stool and looks me over. "You look
well," he says.

Small talk? And out loud? I know he's doing it for Sandra's benefit, to diffuse the tension, but the time for bullshit
between us is long past. He's here. If he insists on talking,
we will. But what I have to say to him is better said in
private.

*We have unfinished business.*

He eyes flick to Sandra. "Do you mind if we go in
back?"

I see the uneasiness in her eyes. I can't read a werewolf's
mind and vice versa, but I imagine she's wondering what
she'll tell Culebra if we trash the place.

"Don't worry," I say. "We'll play nice."

If we don't, and Culebra did set this up, anything that
happens is his responsibility.

Sandra looks from me to Williams and back again and finally jerks her thumb in the direction of the back. Her expression says she'd rather risk us destroying the place than be alone with me.

A worm of irritation crawls over my skin. First Culebra with his mysterious vacation bullshit, and now Sandra and her revisionist history. "When I'm done, we'll talk," I tell her.

She doesn't answer.

Williams pays no attention to the friction between Sandra and me. His thoughts reflect bored indifference. He figures I've alienated yet another acquaintance as I have him. He shakes his head in our direction and hoists himself from the barstool.

My indignation ratchets up another notch, but I follow him to the back.

Williams picks the first room. It's a feeding room so there's a bed and a couple of chairs. He glances around, then shuts the door behind us.

Warren Williams is an old-soul vamp, and the ex–police chief of San Diego. When I first met him, he was a friend of Avery's, and eventually that led to him becoming an enemy of mine. Time and circumstances altered our relationship from adversary to mentor to meddler. I dislike him intensely. He manipulated the situation that led to my family moving out of the country. I allowed it because I feared what I am might put them in danger, but I haven't forgiven the manipulation.

This is the first time Williams and I have come face-to-face since I learned that he was behind my parent's inheritance—a winery in France. Avery's winery in France.

Williams is watching me, on high alert. He may be bigger than I am and older by about two hundred years, but he's tasted my wrath before and isn't letting his guard down.

"You shouldn't have interfered with my family," I say.

His expression remains cautious, his thoughts cloaked.

"You had no right."

A tight smile. "That's a matter of opinion."

"Whose? Yours? You continue to operate under the delusion that you know what's best for me. For me. It didn't work before, it's not working now. It's never going to work."

Williams' cool gray eyes don't flicker or look away. "That's only because you continue to operate under the delusion that you can take care of yourself without—"

Whatever he intended to say, he bites it off. "You are changing, Anna. You must feel it. Your power is increasing; your appetites will, too. It's inevitable."

"Once again," I reply, bitterness rising like bile, "you underestimate me. I'm doing just fine on my own. I come here when I need to. I have someone in my life. We're developing a real relationship."

"Lance? He's a model, for Christ's sake," Williams blurts, cutting me off. "He's not strong enough or bright enough to hold your attention past the fifteen minutes it takes to make you come. A big cock—"

The punch catches him square on the mouth. It spins him back and around and he trips on the corner of the bed. He wasn't expecting the attack but a vampire's reflexes are quick. He recovers his balance, whirls toward me and lunges.

My reflexes are just as quick. I sidestep and he slams into the wall, knocking one of the chairs aside. The plaster crumbles where his fist makes contact.

There's a yelp from outside. "What are you two doing?" Sandra yells.

Neither of us answers. Williams is angry, his mind a tornado of conflicting emotions he's unable to conceal. He wants to kill me, but he can't. He needs my help and it's

eating a hole in his gut. But there's a promise and a warning jumbled in there, too. A promise that when I'm no longer needed, we'll do this dance again.

It's that promise that calms him. His hands are still
balled into fists, but his shoulders lose some of their rigidity. He knows I'm aware of his thoughts and he waits for
my reaction.

I have none. The feel of my fist connecting with his jaw
gave me tremendous satisfaction. I'm not afraid of Williams, I'm not afraid to finish this anytime he wants.

I return his stare. *What are you doing here?*

*I have come to warn you.*

He says it like he's doing me a favor. After what happened a few minutes ago, it makes me laugh.

*This is serious, Anna.*

*It always is. You weren't surprised when I walked in.
You and Culebra set this up?*

Williams is massaging his right hand—the one that hit
the wall—with his left. I doubt he's aware he's doing it,
but it gives me a great deal of pleasure to know he's hurt.
When he picks up on that, he drops his hands to his sides.

*I asked you if Culebra brought you here?*

He kicks one of the chairs away from the wall and drops
into it. *Culebra doesn't bring me anywhere. I asked him to
arrange a meeting with you. I told him it was important. I
told him you wouldn't return my calls. Yesterday he called
me and said to be here this morning. That you'd show up
to see Sandra.*

Son of a bitch. But why such an elaborate charade? Why
not just tell me to meet him here?

Williams' smile is derisive, mocking, as he reads my reaction. *He knows you, Anna. You'd walk in, take one look
at me and walk back out. I don't know what's going on
between you and Sandra, but obviously he used that to get
you here. What did he say? Don't come? And what did you*

*do? You came anyway. Right on schedule. Right after he asked you to stay away. Jesus, Anna, you are so fucking predictable.*

Predictable? If I were so predictable, I'd give in to the anger scorching through the tissue of my control and have Williams' head through the wall. Culebra tricked me. He sent me here to see Williams and made sure he was elsewhere when I found out so I couldn't take it out on him. Did he really leave town? Or is he hiding out somewhere, waiting for me to go back to San Diego?

I don't know whether to feel angry or hurt. Instead, I suck in a breath and let it out slowly before saying, "What is so fucking important? Oh yeah. I forgot. You came with a warning. Deliver it and get out."

A flash of dark rage sparks the depths of his eyes. For an instant, I read that he doesn't want to tell me—that he would love to let me become the next victim.

*Victim? Of what?*

His anger still seethes, fighting to surface. He looks down and away, swallowing back his emotions, regaining control. When he looks at me again, his eyes are flat, hard, expressionless.

He says, "Someone is killing vampires."

# CHAPTER 7

THIS IS THE BIG NEWS? I BARELY CONTAIN THE snicker.

"Someone has been killing vampires since the dawn of recorded history. Tell me something I don't know."

My sarcasm is not well received. Williams has the look of a spoiled kid ready to take his ball and go home. At the same time, I pick up on the vibe that he's not being over-dramatic in his concern.

"Okay, okay. Tell me. What is this about?"

Williams' thoughts darken. *Vampire corpses are showing up drained of blood. There have been six in the last week alone.*

It's not easy to kill a vampire.

*The Revengers?* I ask. *They're a group of human vampire slayers.*

He shakes his head. *No. The Revengers don't leave corpses. They don't want to attract attention to themselves any more than we do. This is something else—something*

*different. These corpses are left in plain sight, for the
human community to find.*

By the human community, I know Williams is referring
to the police. I also know Williams was recently forced
to resign as chief of police—a position he held for many
years until a case I was involved in turned public opinion
against him.

It wasn't my fault and it wasn't his.

He follows my train of thought. It diffuses some of his
anger and when he comments, it's surprisingly without bitterness. "It was time I resigned. The position was too high
profile. It's not the first time I've found myself in this situation. It won't be the last."

Vampires, like humans, are creatures of habit. Williams
has been in law enforcement of one kind or another for two
hundred years. He'll undoubtedly follow that same path
when it comes time for him to move on from San Diego.

"You know how the police are handling it?" I ask.

Old habits *are* hard to break. He goes into cop mode to
answer.

"So far, the vamps have all been young females newly
turned. Exsanguination is the cause of death. A small
wound at the jugular made by a weapon of indeterminate
origin. The bodies have been found in different jurisdic-
tions throughout the county. The only reason we know they
are vampires at all is because our contact in the coroner's
office recognizes what the total absence of food in a diges-
tive tract means."

He doesn't expound on any of these things, but I understand. Especially that the vamps are all newly turned.
If a vamp is destroyed by stake or fire, he leaves nothing
behind but ash. If he is killed any other way, by draining,
for instance, his body reverts to its human age and an au-
topsy would reveal nothing but intact human organs. They

no longer function, which would not be obvious, but neither do they shrivel or disappear. A newly turned vampire would appear normal.

"I haven't seen anything in the newspapers about bodies turning up."

"Not yet," Williams replies. "The police are playing it quiet. So far, the victims all seem to have been young people who have fallen off the radar. No missing reports filed, no families have come forward to claim the bodies. Whoever is doing it is choosing his victims carefully. That will change the first time he fucks up and a victim turns up who has been reported missing."

Williams stands up. "I've done what I came here to do," he says. The civility is gone from his tone. "I thought you should know what's been happening. You may be in danger. You are slightly older than the others, but you fit the profile. You are newly turned and you have a penchant for pissing people off."

"You're telling me to watch my back?"

"I know your partner is out of town and your family is gone. I'd like to think you'll live long enough to get over your childish refusal to integrate into your real community. Maybe you will, maybe you won't. Frankly, I don't care one way or the other." *But there are others who do.* The thought is squelched the instant it forms in his head.

He watches to see if I caught it. I did. Same tune, different song. He puts his hand on the doorknob and twists. "You know where to find me."

He walks out and I'm right on his heels. I'll think about what he's told me later. Right now, it's one pain in the butt down, one to go. Time to find out what put the bug up Sandra's ass.

There's a human behind the bar—a guy I've seen here before. One of Culebra's gofers.

"Where's Sandra?"

He shrugs. "Errands. She told me to tell you not to wait. She didn't know when she'd be back."

Terrific.

# CHAPTER 8

THE ONE BRIGHT SPOT IN A SHITTY DAY IS THAT Lance is at the cottage when I get home.

He senses my mood the minute I walk in the door.

"So what's up? Trouble with Culebra?"

He's sitting on the couch, a magazine open on his lap. He's dressed in a pair of jeans, no shirt, no shoes, and must have just come out of the shower because he smells of my soap and shampoo. Only Lance could make the citrus of my favorite Chanel fragrance, Chance, smell masculine and sexy.

I sit down next to him. "You smell good."

He drapes an arm over my shoulder. "And you smell like cigarette smoke and stale beer. You've been in a bar?"

Two in fact. An image of that girl in TJ and her dead eyes makes me squeeze my own shut in exasperation.

He reads my reaction and the reason behind it. "Must have been hard, seeing that girl. I'm surprised Culebra would have chosen a spot like that to meet you. Why not Beso de la Muerte?"

I let him pick the story out of my head. "He set you up?" he asks in surprise. "With a story about Sandra?" Lance and I had just met when Sandra arrived in town the first time. He's heard the whole story. He's one of the reasons I made it through that period without going crazy.

"What did she say?"

"Never got the chance to talk to her. Williams took over."

I replay the episode for him through the lens of my aggravation. He listens with quiet concentration until I get to the part about Lance not being bright enough or strong enough to hold my interest.

"That guy is a jerk," he says. Then he starts to laugh. "Did you really clock him?"

I pantomime a right hook to the jaw.

"Wish I could have been there to see it." He takes a sip of his wine, tilts his head, studies me. "I think he's jealous."

"What?"

"I think he has the hots for you."

"He hates me," I reply with a snort. "And he's married."

Lance's turn to snort. "He's a male, isn't he? He's got a dick. Why else would he disrespect a guy he doesn't know?"

He tightens his arm around my shoulders. "What do you think about the rest of the story? The vampires turning up drained?"

I shrug. "I don't know what to think. I don't know why he came to me with it. I don't know what he expects me to do."

Lance interprets my chagrin. "Do you think he wants you to come back to the fold? Help him track whoever or whatever is doing this?"

I snuggle against his chest. "If he thinks I'd work with him after all we've been through, he's delusional. He's got the Watchers to figure it out." I let my hand slide to the bulge between his legs. "I don't want to talk about it anymore. There must be something more pleasant for us to do."

He laughs and gives me a nudge. "Let's get you into the shower. Wash away the bar stink first. Then we'll see what comes up."

He doesn't have to ask twice.

SOMEBODY SAID THE SEXIEST ORGAN IN THE BODY IS the brain. Must have been a vamp. It isn't possible to explain how much of a turn-on it is to be able to *feel* your partner's desire and react to it without relying on words. Lance and I don't have to tell each other what we want. We feel it. We anticipate it.

The air around us becomes charged. First in the shower, then after, again, in bed, the shock of him runs through me like a current. I welcome him into my body, into my head, and it's more than sharing a moment of physical need. It's allowing him into my soul.

It's the second bright spot in an otherwise dreary day.

ONCE AGAIN, LANCE IS GONE WITH THE FIRST LIGHT of day. This time he's leaving for New York. Abercrombie & Fitch tagged him for their new winter catalog and the shoot will last a week.

I start to miss him before the door snicks closed.

With his departure, exasperation comes flooding back. Exasperation that Culebra could pull such a dirty trick. Exasperation that Sandra wouldn't even talk to me. Exasperation that Williams still thinks he can jerk me around.

I look around for a distraction.

The Sunday paper is spread out on the coffee table. I

never got the chance to go through it yesterday. I have a
mug of coffee in my hand so I settle my butt on the couch.
Lance's lingering scent is still in the air and that's enough
of a distraction in itself that I'm only paying half attention
as I leaf through the pages when an article in the business
section catches my eye.

The article is about a local cosmetics firm about to
make a big splash. But it's not the product that catches my
eye, it's the picture of David's ex, Gloria Estrella, standing beside the president of the firm, a woman named Simone Tremaine. Gloria is to be the spokesmodel for the new
product Eternal Youth, a revolutionary antiaging cream
(according to the article), and the launch party is in two
weeks at Gloria's restaurant.

It makes me smile. How appropriate for the queen of
vanity to be involved in something like antiaging. She's
probably already ordered a lifetime supply.

I take a closer look at the picture. Gloria looks good.
Evidently, she's recovered from her brush with the law. The
last time I saw her she had been charged with the murder
of her business partner, Rory O'Sullivan. My dad and I
helped to get those charges dropped by pointing the police
in a different direction. O'Sullivan sold the rights to a formula for an AIDS cure right out from under the noses of
his board of directors. Bad move. One director in particular took exception to being cut out of a billion-dollar deal.
He hadn't read the fine print in his contract. O'Sullivan
owned the rights to the formula and when a foreign gov-
ernment offered him a huge amount of money, he took the
quick and easy way out. Unfortunately, being greedy had
a price. His life.

So far, I haven't received a thank-you note from Gloria.
But to be honest, she has lived up to part of the bargain. I
agreed to investigate if she'd agree to cut David loose.

Given that David is right this minute vacationing on

Paradise Island with a hot real-estate developer he met while looking for investment property, I'd say it's worked out pretty well.

I've finished the paper and my coffee and since it's a cloudy gray Monday and Lance is gone and I can't think of anything better to do, I fall back on the last thing I ever want to do—cleaning and laundry.

The vacuum is sitting in the middle of the living room floor, my laundry is divided into whites and colors and Creedence is blasting on the CD player when my cell phone rings.

I dive for the remote to mute CCR and flip open the phone.

This time I recognize the number—from yesterday.

"Culebra." Coldness creeps into my voice, anger at him for yesterday bubbling to the surface. "That was a fast trip."

"No. It's Sandra."

Sandra? I draw a quick, sharp breath. "What are you doing calling from Culebra's cell phone? Is he back?"

There's the briefest hesitation before she replies, "Yes. You need to get down here, Anna. Culebra is ill. I think he's dying."

# CHAPTER 9

IN ONE HOUR, I'M PARKED IN FRONT OF THE BAR.
Everything I did to get here—getting dressed, getting in
the car, racing over—was done in a haze. I kept hearing the
sound of Sandra's voice when she said Culebra was dying.

All the rancor I felt yesterday, all the anger and disappointment is forgotten.

Culebra can't be dying.

The street is empty. As soon as my feet touch the ground,
I'm hit with a curious flutter of energy. Not positive. Not
negative. Stinging my skin like pinpricks of electricity.

It gets stronger when I step inside the bar. There's a
sound now, too, a hum. It settles in the middle of my chest
and makes my heart race. I press my hand to my chest,
fighting the urge to turn and flee.

Where is everyone?

There's no one behind the bar. It's littered with empty
glasses and a few beer bottles. Most half full, scattered
randomly, as if discarded in a hurry.

No customers. No Sandra.

I call her name.

No answer.

I go all the way to the back door—open all the feeding room doors, and still, I find no one.

Uneasiness slithers up my spine.

Could they be in the caves?

There's a path that leads from the bar to an outcropping of rock about half a mile away. An easy run. I've been here before and know what to expect. The rock hides the entrance to a warren of tunnels—living quarters for the inhabitants of Beso de la Muerte.

I peer inside. The interior is lit with a string of electric lamps. I listen. I don't hear or sense anyone but the inexplicable hum I first heard in the bar. I hug the wall, following it until there's a fork, about a quarter of a mile in. The whine is louder and the feeling of static on my skin is stronger. Pressure in my chest builds.

"Sandra?" I call again, panic very close.

This time, I hear a scuffling of feet. A man appears. I recognize him. He took care of David when I brought him here after Avery's attack. He's an American—a doctor whose license was stripped in the States—human, blond, thin. Thinner than the last time I saw him. He was a junkie then and from the looks of him, is a junkie still.

But he helped David. I hold out my hand. "I'm Anna."

"I remember." He shakes my hand and gestures for me to follow him. "Culebra is back here."

I follow him deeper into the cave. I don't detect any other presence. Since there are usually human and supernatural criminals of one type or another granted sanctuary by Culebra, it's unusual.

"Are we alone?"

"Sandra sent everyone away. She thought it would be safer."

He says it over his shoulder, still walking back into the bowels of the cave. He stops finally and gestures me inside. Into a ward set up like a MASH unit with stainless-steel gurneys and IV racks. There's a cabinet along the back wall, a refrigerator and a makeshift lab counter with a centrifuge and a couple of beakers. No monitors. No fancy equipment.

Culebra is laid out on one of the gurneys. He is pale, barely breathing. When I try to get into his head, to read what happened to him, I get nothing but faint static, like a radio signal too far from its transmitter.

What is coming through is a stronger vibration, a louder hum emanating from his body and centering in my own chest. My heart thumps with disturbing irregularity against my ribs. My hand presses against my sternum as if to ease the pounding, but there's no pain.

"You feel it, too, don't you?"

The voice at my shoulder makes me jump. Sandra has joined us.

"Do you?" I ask her.

She shakes her head. "No. But Culebra complained about pressure in his chest before he collapsed."

I look up at the doctor. "Did he have a heart attack?" Am I about to have one?

A shrug. "I don't think so. His blood tests don't indicate heart problems. Frankly, the tests I performed don't indicate anything wrong at all."

I glance back at the granite slab that serves as a lab bench. Can't imagine any tests performed here would be inclusive or extensive enough to rule out much of anything. "Should we take him to a hospital?"

Sandra answers before the doctor. "No hospitals. Culebra was very clear about it. Before he lost consciousness he said to tell you that, Anna."

I turn back toward Culebra, lying pale and still on the

cot. "He said he was catching a plane. How did he get back here?"

Sandra places her hand on the edge of his cot. "I found him this morning when I came to open the bar. He was lying outside on the street. I don't know how he got there. He couldn't tell me."

"Did he say anything else?"

"Only a name," Sandra answers. "Belinda Burke."

Only a name. My insides recoil.

He wasn't lying about going away. He was lying about what he was going to do. He was going after Belinda Burke, a powerful witch who killed an innocent in retaliation for our stopping one of her rituals. He must have located her. If he found her, why didn't he tell me? We'd agreed to go after her together. I have my own powerful reasons for exacting revenge. Culebra knew that.

Why wouldn't he tell me?

Accepting the fact that he didn't want my help is bad enough. Worse yet is the realization that if Culebra found her, what he is suffering from is likely no human illness at all. It's the result of a spell. Burke practices black magic. Modern medicine will be useless against it.

The doctor has been listening to Culebra's heart through a stethoscope. He is frowning and shaking his head. When he catches my eye, he says, "His heartbeat is erratic. I don't know how long he can last."

His words galvanize me into action. I grab my cell phone. "I know someone who can help."

Daniel Frey picks up on the second ring. He's a teacher and when I explain why I'm calling, he doesn't berate me for calling him at school or interrupting his class. He simply asks to speak with the doctor.

I hand the phone to the doctor and listen as he describes Culebra's symptoms to Frey. When he's finished, he gives the phone back to me.

Frey says, "I have to line up a substitute. Then I'll take a cab home and get what I need. Can you pick me up in ninety minutes?" Frey doesn't drive.

"I'll be there."

I've learned a lot since becoming vampire. One of the most surprising is how close-knit and supportive the supernatural community is when it comes to caring for its own. There are exceptions, Williams and his animosity toward me for one. And yet, even he came to Beso de la Muerte to warn me about the vampire slayers. I'm sure he regrets it now.

So when I pull up, I'm not shocked to find Daniel Frey already waiting, standing at the gate to his condo unit. He's dressed in jeans, a T-shirt. He's fortysomething, has salt-and-pepper hair, a good smile, a lean build. He's carrying two large tote bags. He lays them carefully on the backseat, then joins me in the front.

"Tell me," he says without preamble. "Has there been any change?"

I gun away from the curb and fill him in. I also tell him who and what I believe is responsible.

Frey, a shape-shifter like Culebra, was with me when we had our run in with Burke. In fact, she shot him and came close to killing him. He has an extensive library of books on the supernatural. I called him because I know that if he doesn't have an idea himself how to help Culebra, he will know which book to consult.

He listens carefully, then reaches into the backseat and does pull a book from one of the totes.

"I can't reverse the spell," he says, thumbing pages. "But I can arrest the symptoms. For a while."

"How can we break it?"

"*We* can't. Only another witch can."

Shit. How do I find another witch?

Frey is still looking through his book. Unlike Culebra, I can't read his mind. I broke our psychic connection when I bit him once. Dumb mistake with long-term consequences.

I give him a few minutes before I ask, "What do you think?"

He releases a breath. "I think we'd better find a witch."

Culebra didn't tell me where he was going. When we met yesterday he had papers with him. Are they at the bar? Did he tell Sandra? I remember seeing a map but I was too aggravated at the time to take note of what it was for. Could he have marked his destination? Can I retrace his trail back to Burke?

I'll have to ask Sandra if Culebra had anything with him when he reappeared in Beso de la Muerte.

If not . . . "How do we do that?" I ask. "Where do I find a witch?"

Frey throws me a sideways glance and says, "Go see Williams."

My shoulders bunch. "Why?"

"Because he has witches on his payroll. You should know that."

Shit again. I don't tell Frey about my last meeting with Williams. Besides, what difference does it make? Saving Culebra is the important thing. If I have to see Williams to help him, I'll see Williams.

As soon as we're back at Culebra's bedside, Frey gets to work. He's brought potions and candles and some kind of crystal that he shatters against the floor and places in fragments around the cot.

As he sets up, I turn to Sandra. "Did Culebra have anything with him when he got back last night? Papers? A map?"

She shakes her head. "No. He had nothing with him."

The sound of Frey's voice draws us both to Culebra's bedside. He's mumbling an incantation in a language I don't understand. As he speaks the words, the pressure in my own chest subsides. After a few minutes, he motions for the doctor to check Culebra's heart.

The doctor listens, then nods. "Much better. How long can it hold?"

Frey slumps into a seat beside the cot. "As long as Burke doesn't realize what we've done," he says. "When she does, she'll adjust the magic and I'll have to start the counter-spell all over again."

I've been so intent on Culebra, I hadn't noticed the change in Frey. His face is pale, drawn.

"Are you going to be all right?" I ask.

"Magic always exacts a price," he says. His hands tremble in his lap. He interlocks his fingers and looks up at me. "Go see Williams. Find us a witch."

"I don't think I should leave you."

Frey shakes his head. "I'll be all right. The sooner you get to Williams, the better."

I search Frey's face. I know he's right. The way I left things with Williams yesterday, I doubt he'd take my phone call. He'll want to see me grovel. And if that doesn't do it and I need to *persuade* him to use his supernatural connections, in person would be best.

"I'll be back as soon as I can."

# CHAPTER 10

AT LEAST I KNOW WHERE TO FIND WILLIAMS. Since he's quit the human police force, he's gone to work full-time for the supernatural one. His headquarters is underground in the middle of one of the country's most popular tourist attractions, Balboa Park, in the middle of one of the most popular tourist destinations, San Diego.

I know because I used to come here as a Watcher. Back when I was learning what it meant to be vampire. Back when I thought Williams was a friend who had my best interest at heart. I wanted a mentor; he wanted an enforcer. Someone to help keep the supernatural bad guys in line. He thought I was perfect for the job. And his way might be easier—find a rogue and eliminate him—but at least what I do as a bounty hunter doesn't involve being judge, jury and executioner.

It's late in the afternoon and there are lots of people around. I still get a little nervous when I attempt to access the place, even though it's protected by powerful magic. I don't understand how it works, I probably wouldn't be able to understand it if it were explained to me, but I'm standing across from The Natural History Museum and I take one step past a stone bench into some bushes and suddenly I'm not visible to the throngs passing by on a sidewalk ten feet away.

I've disappeared. Through a veil that feels wet and cold against the skin.

The door in front of me is locked. I fish a big brass key out of the depths of my purse and fit it into the lock.

I turn it.

Nothing happens.

At first, I think I must have turned the key the wrong way so I try it again.

Nothing happens.

I pull the key back and examine it. It looks the same as it did the last time I used it. Why won't it work now?

After the fourth unsuccessful attempt, a thought dawns on me. You need to be invited to access this place. Williams, in a fit of anger or resentment, may have revoked my invitation.

Damn him.

I step back onto the sidewalk, barely avoiding a toddler walking on unsteady legs a few feet in front of her parents. The adults don't notice that I've just materialized out of nowhere but the kid does. She plops down on her bottom and starts to cry, which garners me dirty looks from her parents. I step gingerly around them and head for the fountain in the center of the quad a few yards away, yanking my cell phone out of my handbag.

The first time I ring through, predictably, the call goes to voice mail.

I picture Williams reading the caller ID and refusing to answer. I leave a curt message, telling him it's important and to take my call.

I don't add that if he doesn't, I'll find a way in and rip his head off. My hand is shaking with impatience. I wait two minutes and call again.

This time Williams does answer, his tone cold. "What do you want?"

"A witch."

There's a moment of silence before he asks why.

When I tell him, some of the antagonism drops from his tone. "Where are you?"

"Outside by the fountain. Seems I've been locked out of the clubhouse. My key no longer works."

"Try it again," he says, disconnecting.

The kid and her parents are still hanging around the bench. I'm not sure what to do. If I walk right past them and they watch to see where I go, how will they react when I disappear? Always before it's been early in the morning or late at night when I've shown up here and nosy humans have not been a problem.

I can't wait. Not with Culebra's life at stake.

I sidle past them, pretending to be interested in the flora, touching the bushes as I walk. Williams always said supernaturals could access this place without attracting attention. Damned if he isn't right. This time, the three don't so much as glance my way as I pass right by them and disappear again through the magic portal.

Now the key works. The door opens and I'm in a small windowless room equipped only with a desk and a computer. I punch in a few keys, and the room becomes an elevator that whisks me downward.

Williams is waiting. No exchange of pleasantries. He gestures for me to follow him, leading me away from the busy command center in the middle of the room to an area off to the side—an area I've never seen before.

He opens a door. "Inside," he says.

It's a small room with a circular table and five chairs.

Three women are seated around the table—each as different from one another as is humanly possible—for they are humans. No supernatural emanations.

Williams makes the introductions quickly, pointing as he goes. "Min Liu." A small Chinese woman with piercing eyes and waist-length black hair. "Susan Powers." Middle-aged WASP with a quick, bright smile, chin-length bob of salt-and-pepper hair. "Ariela Acosta." The youngest of the three, midtwenties, I'd guess, Latina, pretty, dark eyes and hair drawn back into a ponytail.

He finishes up with a jab of the thumb in my direction. "Anna Strong." *Pain in the ass,* he adds, for my ears only.

It's his only diversion. "Tell them what you need."

*They are witches?*

*Isn't that what you asked for?*

He is still pissed over what happened yesterday. His tone resonates with it. Well, I am, too. It's surprising he took my second call.

Quickly I explain about Culebra—his symptoms, who I suspect is behind the spell. They listen with careful attention. Williams listens, too. He knows of Burke. He remembers what she tried to do, how close Frey came to dying at her hand.

When I'm done, Min speaks first.

"We know of Belinda Burke. She, alone, is more powerful than we are working collectively. We cannot reverse her spell. That would take an equal."

"But we may be able to locate her," Susan adds.

Ariela is nodding. "We can follow her telekinetic trail. To cast a spell such as the one you described involves creating a psychic bond between victim and witch. We can tap into that trail and follow it to its source."

Susan must read the question on my face because she says, "It's like a GPS system. We follow the signal to its point of origin."

"You said you couldn't reverse the spell," I say. "What would happen if Burke was to die? Would that break the spell?"

Min frowns. "It would be dangerous to attempt to kill this one," she says. "She has a powerful protective glamour. You must tread carefully."

"But would killing her break the spell?"

She nods.

That's all I need. I have some pretty powerful glamour myself—vampire strength and if that's not enough, a nice .38. Witch or no, Burke is human. Once I have her in my sights, I'll know what to do. "How long will it take to locate her?"

The three exchange calculating glances. "If we can do it, an hour." Ariela says. "Maybe less."

"*If* you can do it?"

Another exchange of glances. "If she's on this—an earthly—plane we can find her. If not—" Ariela's shoulders raise in a shrug.

Williams touches my arm. "We'll let you get to it. We'll be in my office."

Great. Bad enough that I may be wasting an hour of Culebra's life, but the idea of spending that hour alone with Williams sets my teeth on edge.

*I don't like it any better than you do,* he snaps. *But something else has happened that you should be aware of. It affects the vampire community.*

When I don't respond fast enough, he bristles with indignation. *You can't choose to be a part of this community only when it suits you. I've made my resources available to you. The least you can do is hear me out.*

He's right. I lift my shoulders in a half shrug of resignation and reluctantly follow the lion into his den.

# CHAPTER 11

GUILT GOT ME HERE. BUT ONCE WE'RE SEATED in uncomfortable silence around Williams' desk, I'm reminded of my conversation last night with Lance—and what happened after. I smile, letting some of the good stuff through.

"My boyfriend says hello."

Williams acts like he doesn't hear me, but the coil of his antipathy tightens. He pretends to ignore me, shuffling papers around his desk as if searching for one in particular, but a muscle at the base of his jaw jumps, betraying his agitation.

After another minute of thumbing through the piles on his desk, he finds what he's looking for and shoves a sheet toward me.

The first thing I notice is the letterhead: "SDPD Headquarters." Then, in bold letters: "Internal Memo."

I glance over at him. *Are you supposed to have this?*

Again no reply, concentration focused instead on arranging the discarded papers he'd shoved aside in search of the one I'm holding.

I take that as a no.

His mind is shut so tight, his jaw muscles strain with the effort.

That must hurt.

I barely suppress a smile as I start reading.

The memo is the summation of three police reports filed during the last twenty-four hours. Both involve males attacked by females who cut their victims with knives and suck at the wounds. The men describe their attackers as in their early thirties, attractive, seductive. Not the same woman, though the MO is the same in all three cases. The men meet the women in bars, the women agree to go home with them but instead of engaging in sexual activity, the women attack. They don't appear to want to kill their victims, the wounds are superficial, on the arms or legs, and the men easily subdue the women once they get over the shock. The women seem to just want to suck their blood. All three women have managed to escape before the police arrive.

*Weird,* I say, handing the report back to Williams. *They're obviously not vampires. Newly made vampires are still stronger than the strongest human.* I pause a second before adding, *Are you getting information from Ortiz?*

Ortiz is a vampire. Also, a member of San Diego's finest. He worked for Williams before the shake-up.

He nods. *Ortiz is keeping me in the loop. He's assistant to the new acting police chief. Gives him access to information pertinent to our community.*

A hint of wistfulness comes through. He misses his job. I wish I could muster some sympathy.

Instead, I gesture to the report.

*Sounds like a weird cult to me. No one has been killed. No one has been seriously hurt. So why is this important to the community?*

*I'm not sure.*

Three words I never thought I'd hear from the supreme know-it-all. He tents his fingers on the desk in a deliberately casual movement and looks at me.

And looks at me . . . until I get it. This is the favor he wants in return for lending me the witches.

*So what do you want me to do? Work with Ortiz? Question these guys again? What can I find out that the police haven't?*

A shrug. *I don't know. You fancy yourself a smart cookie. Come up with an angle. All three victims have been picked up in bars around the Gaslamp district. You know the area. Maybe you can stake it out, catch one of these women in the act. Find out what the game is. Between real vamp corpses showing up and these wannabes out there attacking men, it won't be long before the Revengers involve themselves. We don't need that.*

Especially if the Revengers get it in their heads that one of these human women is a vampire and decide to take her out. Killing a mortal would bring the worst kind of attention—to them and to us. Still—

*I can't promise to do anything until I know Culebra is safe.*

*Agreed.*

I stare at him. Too quick.

There's a knock on the door.

Ariel pokes her head in. "We have a location," she says.

I'm on my feet before she's finished the sentence.

Williams and I follow her back to the room. The table has been pushed to one side, a pentagram chalked on the floor. Crystals wink from each of the star's five points. In the middle, three candles burn. Under the candles, a map is laid out.

It's a detailed map of the city.

"She's in San Diego?" I ask.

Susan points to a tiny diamond on the end of a silken rope. The gem rests on a street in National City, a suburb to the south of San Diego.

"How could you—?"

Min smiles. "We started out with a bigger area," she says. "A map of the U.S. Working such a powerful spell would require proximity. When we were shown the way, a map of California. Finally, the energy led us right here. She's close."

She hands me a piece of paper with an address written in neat script. "But I must warn you, Anna, the same energy that led us to her location may have warned her that she was being sought."

My thoughts jump to Frey. "I have a friend who is working his own spell to counteract Burke's magic. What happens if Burke becomes aware of our interference?"

The three exchange anxious looks. Min speaks first. "He is in danger," she says shortly. "The sooner you find and deal with Burke the better."

Ariel holds something out to me on the palm of her hand. "Wear this."

I hold it up. It's a charm, a filigree ball, on a silver chain. Light reflects off the surface like sparks from a pinwheel. "What does it do?"

"It's an amulet. For protection and guidance." She helps me slip it over my head. "It will tell you when you are close."

"How?"

"You'll know."

I drop the charm inside my shirt, between my breasts. It's warm where it touches my skin.

"Don't take it off," Susan says. The seriousness in her eyes is mirrored in the expressions of the other two. "Promise us."

I don't believe in charms but neither did I believe in vampires until about nine months ago. Besides, what could it hurt?

"Sure," I reply. "Promise."

# CHAPTER 12

I CAN'T WAIT TO GET GOING. WILLIAMS FOLLOWS me back to the elevator, droning on about how I owe him. All I can think about is getting to Burke and I mumble a "yeah, yeah, I know" as the doors slide shut.

When I'm alone, I look at the paper.

The address is in an industrial park on the outskirts of National City. I'll head there directly after making one stop—I keep my gun in our office safe. When I've retrieved it, and it's reassuring weight is snug against the small of my back, I'm ready.

The exact address is a warehouse with a sign on the side that reads "Second Chance Products." The name means nothing to me. The way the building is situated, though, does. It's located below street level and surrounded by a parking lot and chain link fence. It's the last building in a string of utilitarian, prefab warehouses, the nearest neighbor a half mile to the west. To the east is a vacant lot.

It's perfect for surveillance. I pull onto the shoulder of

a frontage road where I have an unobstructed view of the entrance.

I touch the amulet through the fabric of my blouse. I don't know what magic it possesses, but I won't need it to recognize Belinda Burke. I remember the first time I saw her with Culebra at Beso de la Muerte. Remember the dark hair and eyes, the belligerent way she stared at me. She was arguing with Culebra in rapid-fire Spanish, standing over him, thin face drawn with anger. I see that face in my mind now, features burned into my memory.

I won't need an amulet to recognize her.

It's close to noon. The parking lot is full, trucks and workers streaming in and out. It's what keeps me from taking the direct approach, barge in, guns blazing. I'm not detecting any supernatural signatures. Only human. I don't know yet if Burke is inside.

At one p.m., a limo pulls up to the entrance. The driver disappears through the main entrance.

A few minutes later, he returns with a woman. He holds open the rear passenger door for her and stands aside. The woman is tall, slender. She's wearing a charcoal pantsuit tailored to accentuate broad shoulders, a small waist, narrow hips. She has red hair, fair skin. She pauses outside the limo and her gaze sweeps upward.

Directly at me.

I have the absurd impulse to duck. I resist. I know there's no way she can possibly tell that there's anyone sitting in a car so far away. Besides, this is a busy frontage road and there are two other cars, one parked in front and one, behind me.

Still, she is looking only at my car.

Then, a strange thing happens.

The amulet around my neck begins to burn.

# CHAPTER 13

I YELP AND PULL THE AMULET FREE. IT'S GLOWING red.

What the hell? If this is what Ariel meant by telling me the amulet would let me know when I was close to Burke, she could have warned me.

I start to yank it off, but the image of those three women and the promise I made to keep it on stays my hand. I let it fall against the outside of my blouse. It still smarts through the fabric, but not nearly as much.

By the time I look again at the parking lot, the limo is gone.

Shit.

The amulet's glow diminishes.

It takes me a second to regroup. There's only one egress from the warehouse. If it didn't come by me, the limo must have gone the other way.

Burke must have been in the limo.

I hang a U and take off.

The limo is a quarter mile ahead. I hang back and follow. They jump on 805 North and proceed up the coast. At
the junction with 52, they head west, into La Jolla.

La Jolla is a wealthy enclave of the rich and famous. It
attracts lots of tourists—so forget about finding a place on
the street to park. But people try. As a consequence, traffic
along Prospect, the main drag, is usually stop-and-go. At
lunchtime, it's stop and stop and stop before a short go. But
it gives me plenty of time to watch the limo as it pulls up in
front of La Valencia hotel.

The driver doesn't get out this time. Instead, an extremely big, extremely burly guy in a cheap black suit that
strains across his chest gets out of the driver's passenger
side door, scans the street, then opens the rear door.

The redhead steps out and goes straight into the hotel.
Burly guy slams the door, scans the street once again, then
slaps the roof of the limo. It pulls off and he follows the
woman into the hotel.

So where is Burke? Is she meeting the redhead inside?
The damned amulet is throwing off heat again. Whoever the
redhead is, she must have a powerful connection to Burke.

I know this hotel. Unless the redhead is staying here,
she's probably on her way to lunch in one its four restaurants. I can narrow her choices further because one of
those restaurants, the Sky Room, is open only for dinner.
I'm hoping she'll go for one of the two places that open
onto the patio. That would make it easier for me to check
her out.

First though, I have to find a parking spot. Not valet.
Not with this crowd. If I have to beat it out of there in a
hurry, I don't want to stand around with my thumb up my
ass waiting for a kid to find my keys. That burly guy in the
bad suit is probably not a date.

There's a parking structure across the street on Girard.
I leave the Jag there and jog back to the hotel. I realize I'm

taking a chance, assuming Burke is meeting the redhead. What if she's not? What if she left with the limo? Too late to worry about that now. Besides, the amulet is still glowing. If Burke is not inside, my backup plan will be to keep tailing the redhead.

It wouldn't be smart to walk into the hotel and start scoping out the restaurants. If she's here, Burke will recognize me. Instead, I go around to the back. The hotel is built to take advantage of an ocean view. Prospect sits above Coast Boulevard and a green ribbon of park that snakes along the shore. The hotel is built another twenty feet or so higher. There is a terrace along this side that two of the restaurants open onto. It's not a pretty day, cloudy, cold with an ocean breeze dropping the ambient temperature another ten degrees. Since anything below seventy-two sends most San Diegans scurrying for winter coats, no one will be eating outside today.

Which works to my advantage.

The base of the hotel is ringed with evergreens and bougainvillea. Perfect cover for a person scurrying like a lizard up the wall to the deck. Thorns tug at my clothes and tangle my hair, but at the top, I slide over a wooden railing and hide myself behind stacked tables.

So far, so good.

There is a buffet being served in the Mediterranean Room, the restaurant in my direct line of sight. It's crowded. I don't see the redhead. I wonder if I'm going to have to go inside when a figure moves into my line of sight. A big, broad back holds out a chair and the redhead slips into it. Burly guy takes up a position near the table, his back to the sliding glass door, scanning the crowd.

I wait to see if anyone joins the redhead. She's already begun to eat. Rude, if she's with another party. Finally, after five minutes, I come to the exasperating conclusion that she's alone.

Shit.

Was I wrong? Did Burke leave with the limo? So much for letting a superstitious relic determine my course of action. I finger the thing, tempted to take it off and throw it into the bushes.

Instead, I squat down behind a big potted plant. Superstitious or not, I made the witches a promise. Stupidly maybe, but I did it nonetheless. Nothing to do now except follow the redhead. Or go back to the warehouse and start over. Patience is not my strong suit. The urge to grab the redhead and shake information out of her curls my hands into fists.

Serves me right for putting my faith in a damned charm. Burke is nowhere in sight.

I don't have time to waste.

I'm climbing to my feet when the redhead slips her jacket off and hands it to the bodyguard. She's wearing a sleeveless silk tee. It's cut to reveal her shoulders and lean-muscled arms.

My stomach lurches at the same time the amulet emits another blast of white-hot heat.

The redhead has a tattoo on her right shoulder. A skull with a crimson rose where the mouth should be.

I've seen that tattoo before.

On Belinda Burke.

Reason is telling me not to jump to conclusions—that there could certainly be more than one woman in the world sporting a tattoo like that.

But the amulet is blazing away, trumping reason. If this isn't Belinda Burke, it's someone close to her. It has to be.

I'm not going to waste another single minute with Culebra's health hanging in the balance.

The redhead has headed back for the buffet. I use the opportunity to sneak into the restaurant through the un-latched sliding glass door. The people at the table nearest the door, an elderly couple, look puzzled. I'm in jeans and a leather jacket. Not exactly lunch attire in La Jolla.

I put a finger to my lips and whisper, "It's my mom's birthday. I just got in from London to surprise her."

They give me the once-over but don't call for security. After all, I might be a rock star with my shaggy hair and faded jeans. You never can tell anymore.

I make my way toward the redhead. Her bodyguard is with her. She's looking over the dessert table. He's looking over the crowd. He watches me approach, but doesn't react with anything but bored indifference.

The amulet is so hot now, I think it's going to catch my clothes on fire. I reach for the .38.

The redhead's back is to me. She has a plate in her hand. I'm no more than ten steps away when she puts the plate down and turns around.

The world stops.

Literally.

Everyone around us freezes in place.

Everyone except the redhead and me.

The unfamiliar face looking at me smiles and the glamour falls away. I'm staring into Belinda Burke's amused eyes.

"Very good, Anna," Belinda Burke says. She points to the amulet. "Now wherever did you get that little beauty?"

I lunge for her, drawing the gun.

She flutters manicured fingertips and I'm trapped, too, in suspended animation.

I can't move. Not my limbs. Not my head or hands. My thoughts slow, become sluggish.

I can only watch helplessly while she steps close. She reaches for the amulet, but smoke and a tongue of flame shoot out. She snatches her fingers away.

"Cute trick," she says, shaking her hand. "From a witch,

am I right? I'll have to pay her a visit. Too bad it won't save Culebra. Or that pathetic shape-shifter with his derisory spells. I should have killed that one when I had the chance."

She's enjoying herself, enjoying the sound of her own voice. If I could break free, I'd wipe that smug smile off her face.

She cocks her head and watches me, as if privy to my thoughts. She's not afraid, though. Why should she be? I can't move a fucking muscle.

Her smile widens and she goes on. "Culebra's finding me was an inconvenience. I would like to have had a little more time to—" She lets her voice drop and sighs. "Well, we can't have everything, can we? It was good while it lasted. Life has a way of throwing you curves when you least expect them. The trick is to know how to adapt."

She leans her head closer and whispers in my ear. "I could kill you, too. Right now. But what fun would that be? I think we should play a little game. See how clever you really are. Then you can watch your friends die."

The hand flutters again and the bodyguard is released from the spell. He acts neither surprised nor shocked, but simply goes to the table, retrieves her jacket.

Burke slips into it. "Have a nice day, Anna," she says.

I struggle against invisible bonds, powerless to stop them as they leave the restaurant. For another ten seconds, nothing happens. Then, the world returns to normal. People revive and resume whatever they were doing without the slightest notion of what happened. I hide the gun down by my side, look around. I appear to be the only one who feels slightly off-kilter, faintly nauseated at being suspended like a bug in amber.

By the time I gather my wits and race for the exit, Belinda Burke is gone.

# CHAPTER 14

GRUDGINGLY, I GIVE THE DEVIL HER DUE. THE witch pulled off a good one.

Shit.

I'm looking up and down Prospect with no real hope of spying the limo and the sinking realization that it would make no difference if I did. By the time I retrieve my car, Belinda Burke will have vanished.

I run back to the garage to get the Jag.

Thoughts cascade through my head like white water over a dam. She knows about Frey. She knows about the amulet. Can she trace it back to the witches in Balboa Park?

I've got to warn them.

The first call I make is to Frey. He doesn't answer. I try Culebra's cell, hoping Sandra will pick up.

Once again, there's no answer.

I disconnect and, fighting off the fear that they are both dead, call Williams. He does answer. Before I can ask, he tells me that he talked with Sandra a few minutes ago. Culebra is hanging on. I fill him in on what happened with Burke, including her threat against the witches. He assures me they are protected as long as they stay at the headquarters. He asks the obvious questions and I give him as full a description as I can of Burke's new persona. He wants me to come in and give the description to a psychic artist who can render a sketch.

There isn't time.

Now that I know Burke's assumed the guise of someone else, my next task has to be to determine who that someone else is. And get to her fast.

We ring off.

I'm back on Prospect. Burke must know it was no coincidence, my appearing in the restaurant. She's smart enough to know I probably followed her from the warehouse, which makes it safe to assume she won't be going back there anytime soon.

Which also makes the warehouse the logical place to start.

I'm retracing my footsteps to National City. Worry about Culebra and Frey and sudden doubt about my choice to go back to the warehouse are unwelcome passengers in the car with me. What if I'm wrong and Burke is waiting for me at the warehouse? What protection do I have against her power? I was helpless in that restaurant.

I'm suddenly aware that I've got the charm clutched in my fingers.

This is my protection. The moment I feel its warning heat, I'll know she's near. This time, the moment I see her, I'll shoot the bitch no matter where we are.

The warehouse parking lot is still crowded. Trucks from a loading bay around the side come and go. I pull right up to the door and park in a visitor's space.

May as well.

I check the .38 and slip it into the pocket of my jacket.
Quicker access.

I touch the amulet.

It's cold.

A gun and a charm.

I'm not leaving anything to chance.

A glass door opens into a reception area. Simple, utilitarian, no fancy furniture. Only an oversized metal desk behind which sits a woman with a computer monitor in front of her and a telephone headset attached to her ear. She's in her twenties, stylishly dressed in a light wool pantsuit and silk blouse. She has dark hair and eyes. When she looks up at me and smiles a welcome I detect no threat. She's human. That doesn't mean she can't be a witch. Or that Burke hasn't assumed another disguise.

I touch the amulet to be sure.

Nothing.

She's not Burke and Burke must not be close.

The woman has not yet greeted me and I realize she's talking on the phone. She rings off and says, "Sorry about that. The phones have been crazy since that newspaper article appeared yesterday. Are you here to place an order?"

She pulls a clipboard from a stack on her desk and holds it out to me. "We've had trouble with the website. So many hits, customers have not been able to access order forms. I've been telling them to come in and do it in person if they're in the San Diego area. They'll get the product much faster that way."

"Product?"

"Eternal Youth." The smile dims a little when she sees I'm not reaching for the clipboard. "Isn't that why you're here?"

Eternal Youth? Why does that ring a bell? I let the name filter through the cogs. It comes to me in a lightning bolt of recognition.

Yesterday's paper.

Gloria and her new gig.

And something else.

The woman with Gloria. The president of the company. The redhead, Simone Tremaine.

One and the same. Belinda Burke.

The woman behind the desk has returned the clipboard to its stack as she takes another phone call. I'm processing possibilities. I could go to Gloria and see what she knows about Simone Tremaine. Good old Gloria, once again she's gotten involved with a less than scrupulous business partner.

Last resort. I'd rather not see Gloria again—ever. She'd likely use any opening to weasel her way back to David.

The second possibility is to find out what I can from the receptionist. I doubt she's going to give me Simone's address or home telephone number no matter how sweetly I ask.

That leaves two options. Go back to the cottage and do an Internet search. Most likely a waste of time since Simone Tremaine is probably unlisted.

Or come back tonight and go through Belinda's files. Behind the reception area is a door with a glass window. I mosey over and look in. There's a long hall with doors opening on both sides—offices, no doubt—and a door in the back. Through the one on the end is something that looks like the landing to a flight of stairs.

"Can I help you with something?"

The enthusiasm has gone out of the receptionist's voice.

I turn to her. "I'm not here to place an order," I say, stepping back to the desk. "But I am interested in the company. What can you tell me about Simone Tremaine?"

The silky smooth smile of the saleswoman returns. "She's wonderful. She discovered the formula for Eternal

Youth herself. Are you from the press? I have a press kit I can give you."

This time I take the offering. It's slick and glossy and the first page is a headshot of Simone. "Where is she from, do you know?"

"New York. She was in advertising there. Which is why she's so good with the media. They love her."

Yeah. That and the fact that she can hex people to believe anything she wants.

I flip the twenty or so pages contained in the kit. Every one has a photo of Simone along with before and after shots of middle-aged women transformed from drab to gorgeous. No cream could possibly—

The receptionist interrupts my train of thought with a laugh. "I can tell from your expression you're skeptical of those results. Most women are." She reaches for something at her feet and comes up with a handbag. She fishes out a wallet and flips to a driver's license.

"How old do you think I am?" she asks.

"I'm not good at that game," I say. Being a vampire puts you at a disadvantage.

She holds out the picture so I can read her date of birth.

I look from the license to the woman and back again. "Is this a joke?"

She laughs. "Nope. I'm an Eternal Youth customer myself. And I'm fifty-two years old."

I react the way she expects—with shocked appreciation at the transformation. I don't bother to tell her that she's probably under some kind of spell, that the woman she has so much admiration for is a cold-blooded killer who has to be working an angle that I'd bet is more complicated than rejuvenating aging skin. Belinda Burke is not a humanitarian.

Instead, I take the literature and, thanking her for her

time, leave. I'll come back tonight, when I can be alone with Burke's files and see for myself what's going on.

In the car, I call Williams. I tell him who Burke is pretending to be, and he promises to pass the information to Ortiz. Legally, we can't prove she's done anything illegal. Yet. So there can be no official police involvement. But at least Ortiz may be able to use his connections to track her down.

Then I call Frey. This time he answers. He sounds spent. Culebra's condition worsened once, about an hour ago, but he adjusted his counterspell and Culebra is resting again.

I fill him in on what I learned. Culebra's relapse would coincide with my confrontation with Burke in the restaurant. She knows now that we're working against her.

What I don't tell Frey is that she knows it's *Frey* who is keeping Culebra alive. May as well not add to his concern.

"Is there anything I can do for you?" I ask Frey.

"Yeah," he says. "Find Burke. Kill the bitch."

# CHAPTER 15

I DON'T KNOW WHAT TO DO WITH MYSELF. I GO back to my vantage point above the warehouse. It's midafternoon. There are still cars and trucks coming and going from the parking lot. Inactivity chafes. Williams hasn't called, which means he has nothing for me from Ortiz. My first plan—to break into the warehouse—seems the most logical.

I settle down to watch and wait, something I should be used to in my line of work. Stakeouts are part of the bounty-hunting business. Except I usually have David to help pass the time.

I'm alone here and this is very personal.

I spend some time leafing through the Eternal Youth brochure. Two things jump out: the dramatic results the cream seems to have wrought and the price for those re-sults. Burke is getting two hundred fifty dollars for a twelve-ounce jar . . . a month's supply.

Yikes.

I throw the brochure aside and start to pick apart what Burke said to me in the restaurant. She mentioned wishing she'd had more time.

More time to what?

And what "curves" did life throw her? Culebra's appearance? He must have recognized her. How? I certainly didn't. Was the entire story he told me about going out of town a lie? Was he here all the time?

Nothing makes sense.

The only thing that does is the threat against Culebra and Frey. No riddles there.

It's a fucking long wait.

It isn't until midnight that the place is finally quiet. By now, my skin is twitching with impatience. I watch as the last car pulls out of the lot. If there's a night watchman, he didn't drive a car to work. I sprint down the steep bank and head for the back of the warehouse.

I had plenty of time to decide how I'd break in. The building is about three stories high. The only windows are right below the roofline. They are the old-fashioned, pulldown windows, so there are no ledges. I circle the building twice before I find one that looks like it isn't completely shut tight. I'd rather not damage anything, which is why I'm not smashing the door and going in through the front.

I use my shimmying skills for the second time today. It's really rather fun. Like having invisible suckers on the palms of your hands. It's all upper body, my feet seek purchase like a rock climber's, but it's more pull than push. Idly, I wonder what I look like. Hope it's not a giant spider.

I hang down from the roof and work at the window. It groans and gives way and I slide inside. These vamp powers are becoming second nature and once I accepted what I am, they seemed to grow stronger. Not entirely unpleasant.

There's a catwalk that runs along under the windows.

I crouch here, waiting for any indication that I've tripped a security circuit. I don't hear the whir of cameras or see the glowing beam of a motion detector. There are no lights on, but I can see to the factory floor thirty feet below. No guards come looking. After a moment, I step off the ledge and land on my feet next to the assembly line.

No jolt, no shock. I pat at my hair. Not a strand out of place.

Cool.

The factory floor looks like any other mechanized assembly line. Ingredients are measured and combined in big stainless-steel pots at one end and the finished jars of cream emerge from the other. The conveyor belt is still but all the components are lined up and in varying stages of completion as if a switch was hit at the end of the day and the line stopped. I walk the length of it, picking up jars, sniffing, looking for—I'm not sure what I'm looking for—but nothing jumps out at me. I take one of the finished jars and open it. The contents are a pale pink in color and heavily perfumed. Under it all, though, I detect something that smells slightly of raw meat. It makes me draw back in disgust. I close the jar and slip it into the pocket of my jacket.

At the end of the factory, there are two doors. Both locked. I'm prepared. I fish my lock picks out of another jacket pocket and go to work.

I remember from this afternoon that there was a door at the end of the corridor leading from the reception area. I'm assuming that door opened into the factory or to stairs leading from it. The first door I open, though, is a locker room and employee lounge area.

The other is the one I'm looking for. It opens to reveal a flight of stairs. At the top, the door leading into the corridor I spied this afternoon. On each side of that corridor are office spaces, six of them, all with doors now closed.

My task is simplified, though, by the little brass plaques on each. I head right for the one that says "Simone Tremaine, President."

It takes me about twenty seconds to pick the lock. I slip inside. The office space is big, about twenty by twenty, but not as luxuriously furnished as I would have expected. There's a wooden desk and chair, a row of wooden file cabinets, a leather couch and glass-topped coffee table and two leather visitor's chairs.

The desktop is clear. Nothing on it, not a blotter or a telephone. The desk drawers are locked but yield to a little persuasion. That's all they yield. The only things I find are telephone logs. A quick perusal tells me business is brisk. Calls from area codes across the country. Paper-clipped together on the inside cover are the most recent. I flip through the stack. One customer has called three times in the last two days. Must be desperate for her miracle makeover. I replace the stack as I found it.

In another drawer, web-generated order forms. Lots of them. Eternal Youth has struck a chord with middle-aged women in a big way. No wonder I saw so many trucks going in and out. Must be preparing for the big launch the newspaper spoke of.

Now what?

The file cabinets.

Again, everything is locked. There are six cabinets, none labeled on the front so I have no choice but to start at one end and jimmy each open. As is usually the case, the last cabinet is the one I want. Personnel files.

One file is marked Personal. When I open it, I find info about Simone Tremaine. There isn't much—insurance forms, utility bills for an address in Coronado, an out-of-state telephone number printed on a piece of company letterhead. I memorize the address and number and return the file to the cabinet.

Then another file catches my eye.

Test Subjects.

It's thick. I take it to the couch and get comfortable.

There must be one hundred cases. I go through each one. All include remarkable before-and-after pictures as well as testimonials. They're from local women in all walks of life—including some with PhDs and medical licenses. Women in their fifties and sixties look thirty again. With no adverse side effects reported. In fact, just the opposite, women report renewed vigor and increased libido. A few add that their figures are fuller, their hair more lustrous and their minds sharper. They call the cream miraculous.

I pull the jar out of my pocket and look at it. Miraculous, indeed, if it's true. In fact, if I were still human, I'd be tempted to try the stuff.

No wonder Gloria wants to hook her wagon to this star. Besides the obvious, Burke would be richer than God in a very short time if the product lives up to its press. Too bad *she* won't live long enough to enjoy it.

I return the folder and walk my fingers through the other tabs. I'd like to find a formula to take to Williams. He could duplicate it and see if there's magic involved. I don't find one so I'll have to do the next best thing. I'll give him the jar I took and let him analyze the product itself.

I relock the cabinets and offices and head back into the factory. I leap up to the catwalk, slip out of the window and secure it behind me while I cling to the wall outside. Then I let go and drop to earth.

Next stop: that address across the bay in Coronado.

I'm halfway up the bank to my car when my cell phone rings.

"Anna Strong."

"Anna, it's Williams. Where are you?"

"In National City. Why?"

"Meet me downtown, the end of the Navy Pier. Another

body turned up, and if you get here quick enough, we can check it out before the police."

He disconnects before I can object. I glance at my watch. The navy pier isn't too far out of my way. I'll give him five minutes. That's it.

# CHAPTER 16

T HE WOMAN IS LYING ON A COIL OF ROPE, AWK-
wardly, her back bent, legs twisted. Dumped here,
probably, after dark. This is a busy pier during the day. Her
form and face are obscured in shadow. The only light reflects from the pool of blood ringing her head like a halo.

And that looks black.

The scent of her blood is heavy on the air. "She's
human," I say.

Williams is kneeling beside the body. "She's human. I
thought when the report came in it might be another vamp."
He stands and slips off the latex gloves he'd donned when
we arrived. Cop habit.

"Looks like her skull was crushed," he says.

Being around this much blood awakens the hunger always lurking beneath the surface, but I force it back and
stoop to take a closer look. The woman is dressed in good
linen slacks and a long-sleeved blouse.

"She's wearing Jimmy Choos," I say, pointing to her

pumps. "There's a good-sized rock on her finger, and I'd bet those earrings are a carat apiece. She wasn't mugged for her jewelry."

I lean in. The woman's hair has fallen over her face. Gingerly I brush it away.

She looks vaguely familiar. She's in her thirties, attractive.

The wail of far-off sirens distracts me.

Williams puts a hand on my shoulder. "We need to go."

Still, I hesitate. I know I've seen this woman before.

"Anna, come on. We can't be found here."

Reluctantly, I get to my feet. Williams motions for me to follow him, and we make our way quickly back along the pier to the parking lot. Flashing lights and sirens bear down on the pier. We turn to the right and head across the trolley tracks toward the Gaslamp district. There's a hotel with an outdoor patio still serving and we take a seat. We can see the pier from here.

The show starts as soon as the cops arrive. I recognize Ortiz in one of the lead cars. No surprise then, how Williams found out about the woman. A crowd forms, the media arrives, a coroner's wagon pulls up.

I know I should be out of here—check that address in Coronado. But something tugs at the back of my mind. I'm sure I've seen that woman before. I sift her face through the sands of memory, hoping to shake something loose.

When it hits, it's not *who* she is but *what* she is that does it.

Today. The literature I picked up from the receptionist.

I jump to my feet and leave Williams with an abrupt, "I'll be right back."

The Jag is parked down the block. The brochure is still on the front seat. I grab it and quickly thumb the pages.

She's there. On page five.

She was one of Eternal Youth's test subjects.

When I rejoin Williams, I thrust the brochure at him. "Look familiar?"

He studies the picture for a minute, then looks up at me. "A coincidence? One of Burke's test subjects turning up dead?"

I shake my head.

Quickly I tell Williams about the other women in Burke's files.

I hand him the bottle of cream.

"You'd better have this analyzed. She's using magic, I'm sure. Can't do anything about that. But if it turns out the product she's selling at two hundred fifty dollars a jar contains nothing but animal fat and food coloring, maybe you can get her for fraud."

He slips the bottle into a jacket pocket. Then he calls Ortiz on his cell and passes the information along.

He listens for a minute, hangs up.

I already suspect what he's going to say. He doesn't disappoint.

"Ortiz will join us as soon as he can, but the fact that this woman was one of Burke's test subjects is not sufficient cause to get a search warrant for Burke's warehouse."

Ortiz is standing by his patrol car and he turns and looks for us in the crowd now gathered at the restaurant.

I stare back at him, a troublesome wariness beginning to build. Burke said she wanted to play a game.

"I don't need a search warrant. I'll get the file of her test subjects."

For once, Williams doesn't argue. "Bring the file back here. Ortiz and I will wait."


FOR THE THIRD TIME IN TWELVE HOURS, I AM BACK at the warehouse. I perform my bat-woman routine and shimmy my way inside. It's two a.m. I'm trying to decide whether to copy the file or take it when the decision is made for me. I hear a car pull to a stop outside.

No time to waste. I grab the file and lock the office door. I peek out front, but the lot is empty. The car must be at the loading dock.

Shit.

I run back through the factory and leap to the ledge. From the windows, I can just see the front of a white van backed up to the loading dock. I don't hear any noise and the doors to the factory don't open.

What are they doing? Trying to break in? A competitor trying to steal the formula?

It's so quiet, I'm beginning to think whoever drove the van here left in another vehicle. Maybe it's a vendor waiting to be the first in line for his supply of Burke's miracle cream. I hunker down. I'll give it twenty minutes and then I'll take my chances and find another way out.

I don't have to wait that long. Ten minutes later, the van starts up and pulls away. It's a white Econoline with no markings and no tags.

I leap to the ground and look around. The loading bays are closed tight, no indication at all that anyone tried to get in.

I look in the direction of the retreating van.

Maybe I'm not the only one up to no good.

# CHAPTER 17

$B$Y THE TIME I REJOIN WILLIAMS, THE RESTAU-
rant and bar have closed. He and Ortiz are sitting in
the hotel lobby in big overstuffed chairs arranged around
a table. We have the lobby to ourselves. There's no one
behind the desk to eavesdrop. I see a clerk through an open
door in the back sipping from a mug and reading a magazine. He looks up as I come in but, besides a curious glance
my way, makes no move to intercept me. His eyes slide
back to the glossy pages.

Williams follows my gaze.

*It's all right. He's a friend of ours.*

His imperiousness provokes the usual reaction in me. I
snort. *Of course he is. What are you, the Godfather?*

*It's always the same with you two, isn't it?* Ortiz says
before Williams can reply. His tone is reproachful and impatient like a parent addressing squabbling children.

My fault, I know. Williams brings out the bitch in me.
And there isn't time. Embarrassed, I hand Ortiz the folder

and watch as he and a visibly aggravated Williams divide the lot. Soon their thoughts are centered only on the task of sorting through the files. I wait, anxious and uneasy. If this doesn't yield anything important, I'm wasting precious time.

I focus on the two men, willing them to hurry it up, marveling at how different the two are.

At some point, Ortiz changed into civilian clothes. I think it's the first time I've seen him out of uniform. He's wearing slacks with a knife-edge crease and a long-sleeved polo shirt. He's a vampire who looks a like a thirty-year-old human. He's about five feet ten inches tall and weighs a lean one-sixty. He has the darkly handsome look of his Hispanic/Native American heritage: an aquiline nose, dark hair and eyes and olive skin stretched over high cheekbones.

His expression is somber as he works. He's been a deputy under Williams for as long as I've known him, but there's more to their relationship. I don't understand it and I have no desire to. Ortiz is genuinely nice while Williams is decidedly not.

Finally, Williams separates one sheet from the stack and Ortiz, two. They look at one another.

*Here's one.*

*And two others.*

They're showing each other the pictures they've chosen from the file. The picture Williams is holding is of the dead woman we found across the street. She looks much better alive.

"Who are the other two?" I ask.

Ortiz reaches for a slim leather folder on the table in front of him. He retrieves two artist's sketches from inside. He holds the sketches next to the photos from Burke's files, turns them around so I can see.

The resemblance between sketch and photo are remarkable in both cases.

Williams turns to me. "Remember the men who reported being attacked by women who cut them for their blood?"

"These are the women?"

"You tell me. These sketches were made from the victims' descriptions."

I take the photos and sketches and lay them out on the table for a closer look. "I'm sold. Is this enough to get a warrant?"

Williams shakes his head. "A warrant for what? We still don't know what connection Burke has to these women except that they've used her product."

"That's not enough?"

He fans the thick file of photos. "Not when there are a hundred other women here who don't seem to have gotten themselves into trouble."

I pick up the two photos and look to Ortiz. "Can I take these?"

Ortiz nods. He makes a note of the names and addresses printed on the backs of the photos and slips the rest of Burke's file and the sketches back into his folder. "What are you going to do?"

"I'm going to Coronado," I reply. "To the address I found in Burke's file. If I'm lucky, it's hers. After I take care of her, I'll visit these two."

Ortiz frowns. "You're going to Burke's alone?"

I'm afraid Williams is going to insist on coming with me. I jump in before he can.

"It's better if I do. If I get caught, neither of you should be involved. Someone has to take care of Culebra and Frey. This is the address I found in her file at the warehouse." I send it to him telepathically, adding, "If you don't hear from me in two hours, *then* you can send the cavalry."

"I will." Ortiz' dark eyes flash. He writes the address in a notepad and slips it into his pocket. "Be careful, Anna."

Williams, for once, doesn't say anything.

# CHAPTER 18

THE ADDRESS I GAVE ORTIZ, THE ADDRESS ON J AV-
enue I took from a utility bill in Burke's office, is across
the bay in Coronado. I can't even claim gut instinct that it
belongs to Burke. All I can do is hope it's hers. If I'm wrong,
I've wasted more precious minutes of Culebra's life.

It's a quick trip across the bridge and straight down
Fourth Avenue to J. The neighborhood is old money—
wooden shingles, tile roofs. Multistoried houses with big
yards and picket fences.

Not what I expected. I expected a black magic woman
to live in seclusion behind high brick walls covered with
poison ivy.

Doubt starts gnawing a hole in instinct.

The street is dead quiet in the early morning hours. I
park half a block from the address and work my way on
foot to the alleyway that runs behind each house. When I
get to the right house, I leap the fence and crouch down,
watching, listening.

I've got my gun in my hand. Ready this time. But I know it's too much to hope that Burke will pass by a window. Too much to hope I'll get a clear shot without giving myself away or allowing her to escape. Again.

I see and hear nothing out of the ordinary. The house is dark. The only sound, the faraway ebb and tide of the ocean a half dozen blocks away. I don't feel anything, either. None of the strange vibrations I did around Culebra. A bad sign. Wouldn't I feel something this close to the place where a powerful spell is being cast?

I touch the chain around my neck. Wouldn't the amulet be sending a warning?

The windows along the back of the house are shuttered. I make my way closer and try to peek between the slats. It's no good. I sneak around to the front, staying low to avoid being seen from the street. It's three a.m., but you never know when some insomniac pain-in-the-ass neighbor might decide to walk the dog.

As soon as I find a window with the curtains parted enough for me to look inside, I know why I'm not getting any vibes from the place.

The living room is empty. So is the dining room beyond it. No couch. No tables and chairs. Nothing. An empty expanse of space that goes from one end of the house to the other.

Shit.

My handy-dandy lock picks let me in through the back door. I pause to see if there will be an intruder alert, but none sounds. Doesn't mean there isn't a silent alarm going off somewhere, but by the time a response team gets here, I'll be long gone.

I run through the house, just to assure myself it isn't a case of Burke not taking the time to go shopping for her new digs. But there isn't a piece of furniture anywhere in the place. Not a pot or pan in the kitchen. The closets are empty. I don't find so much as a scrap of paper. If she had been living here, she isn't now.

A dead end.

Fatigue washes over me. Fatigue and guilt. Culebra is still near death and Burke has eluded me once again.

I slip back outside, call Culebra's cell. Sandra answers. Frey is asleep. There has been no change in Culebra's condition. I can't bring myself to tell Sandra that I'm not any closer to helping them than I was this morning.

So, I lie. Tell her that I'll have news tomorrow. That I'm close to finding Burke. If the despair I'm feeling is mirrored in my voice, Sandra doesn't let on. She may be as good a liar as I am.

When I'm back in the car, I call Ortiz. Tell him what I found, that is to say, what I didn't find. I also tell him I'm too tired to do anything else tonight. Tomorrow I'll go back to the warehouse and start all over again. I'll grill that receptionist. She must be in contact with her boss. Either the human Anna or the vampire will get the information out of her.

But now, I'm going home.

He offers to call Williams. I quickly take him up on the offer and we say good night.


AS SOON AS I WALK THROUGH THE COTTAGE DOOR, I sense it.

Subtle as the drop in pressure before a summer storm.

Someone is here.

I pause, tasting the air, letting supernatural acuity take over from the human. It's female, human, and she's upstairs. In my bedroom.

The vampire reacts without prompting. I slip back out

the door, position myself under the balcony that leads from my bedroom and leap up. I land on all fours, silently, weightlessly, and look inside.

A woman is on my bed. She's gagged, bound hand and foot. In the quiet, I hear her labored breathing. I hear her heartbeat, frantic as she struggles against her constraints. I smell her fear, acrid and harsh as bitter almond. I smell something else.

I smell her blood.

# CHAPTER 19

THE SLIDER HAS BEEN UNLATCHED AND LEFT OPEN. I slip inside, so quietly she doesn't realize I'm there in the room with her. She's bleeding from a dozen shallow cuts on her arms and legs. It drips from the rope binding her, pools under her on the bed.

The call of it beckons. I take a step toward her.

She's naked, hands tied above her head, face pointed away from me, toward the bedroom door. She either detects movement, or some instinct sounds the alarm. She turns her head. The gag covers her mouth and chin. I don't recognize her. When she sees me, her eyes widen. Her breath comes in gasps, the thudding of her heart turns thunderous, sending the blood rushing through her veins. The cuts weep more freely.

I have to fight an overwhelming urge to lick at those bloody cuts. I fed from a human two weeks ago but still, I'm *hungry*. Now. And here's a feast of blood.

The vampire starts to rationalize. Why shouldn't I?

She's in my house, in my bed for god's sake. I won't kill her. Just take what I need. I can make it pleasurable for her. It would be so easy.

The human Anna inserts herself.

You're not going to feed from this woman. She's been dumped here. She's not a host. She's scared. Take fucking hold of yourself and untie her.

It's like a dash of ice water. The head clears, the lust recedes from raging need to dull ache. My features must lose the animal fierceness because the woman's body relaxes a little, her pulse slows. But the eyes still hold terror.

I approach the bed with hands outstretched. "Don't be afraid. I won't hurt you. This is my house."

She tries to wriggle away but one ankle is tied to the foot of the bed. She kicks toward me with her free leg. My words may be soothing now, but she has the memory of the vampire's face. It will take more than words to overcome that image.

I stand still and wait until she stops thrashing. "Will you let me take the gag out of your mouth?"

A moment's hesitation, then a jerky nod.

Slowly, carefully, I lean down and untie the ends of a scarf. When I pull it free, there's an instant when she looks up at me and I think she's going to be all right. I smile at her, reach to untie the ropes binding her hands.

She starts to scream. A loud, high-pitched, penetrating scream.

Startled, I jerk back.

My first thought is not for her welfare. It's for mine. I have neighbors on both sides.

I've got to quiet her.

Once more I reach out, making what I hope is a reassuring shushing noise, trying to calm her.

She screams louder.

Jesus.

I slam the slider shut behind me.

She's going to wake the entire block if I don't do something.

There's a crash of splintering wood. Somebody is breaking in my front door.

Too late.

At the sound, the woman turns up the volume.

Feet thunder up the stairs. Cops appear at the door, one shoves me away from the woman and one pushes me down onto the floor.

The instinct to fight is squelched because of a voice in my head.

*Anna, it's me. Relax. Don't say anything.*

It's Ortiz, back in uniform, with two of San Diego's finest.

Ortiz takes over. He gets the cop off my back and allows me to stand up. He tells him that he knows me.

The second cop is untying the woman. He throws a sheet over her and when she sits up, she starts to babble. She tells the cops how I appeared in the room from the deck and not the inside door and how I looked at her with an animal's face and yellow eyes.

They look at each other and at me. I put on as normal a face as I can and shrug.

Ortiz tells one of the cops to take me downstairs while he questions her. It's not until they've taken her away in an ambulance and the CSI team has come and gone (with a set of my best Egyptian cotton sheets) that he joins me at the kitchen table. He sends my cop custodian away, too.

"It was Burke," he says.

I hand him a cup of coffee. Dawn is breaking outside and it's obvious I'm not going to get any sleep. Neither is he.

"Burke." Not really surprising. Another part of her little game?

He takes a long pull at the coffee. "The woman says she was picked up leaving a downtown bar about midnight. Two men grabbed her. The last thing she remembers before getting stuck with a needle is a voice saying the name Belinda Burke."

"Not very subtle, is she? But what does dumping her here accomplish?"

"Maybe she thought you'd lose it when you smelled the blood. We got an anonymous call that someone saw you carrying a bound and gagged woman into your house. Came in ten minutes before we got here. Before *you* got here, evidently."

"How'd you catch the call? When I left you, you were still with Williams."

Ortiz smiles. "Police scanner. When your address was broadcast, I beat it over here. Changed in the car. The uniforms assumed I was on duty."

I sip at my coffee, processing what Burke could hope to accomplish with such a stunt. I let Ortiz accompany me as I sort possibilities. *Did she hope I'd land in jail to be off her trail? Give her a clear shot at Culebra? Was it simply a way to harass me? Let me know she can fuck with me whenever she wants?*

Ortiz shakes his head. "Any or all of the above. Maybe she hoped you'd kill that woman. That would be one way to get you off her trail."

Now I shield my thoughts. The woman was never in danger from me—not of being killed. She did come close to becoming a late night snack, though.

I need to feed.

I look at Ortiz. "How much trouble am I in?"

He shrugs. "She admits you weren't in on the abduction. She gave us good descriptions of the men who were and the van she was hauled off in. Unless we find hard evidence

that you arranged it, you'll be listed as a person of interest."
He laughs. "You didn't arrange it, did you?"

"Very funny."

He tips his cup toward me. "And you have the best alibi you could possibly have. At the time of her abduction you were hanging out with a cop and the former police chief."

I rub my eyes. The hunger is beginning to cloud my head. It shouldn't be this strong. Too much blood tonight. First the woman at the pier, then the woman in my bed. It has awakened the hunger. The vampire is close to the surface, demanding sustenance.

If Lance were here—

But he's not.

And I can't go to Culebra, either.

Ortiz is watching me. My thoughts are closed to him, but he's vampire, too. He may recognize the signs. He doesn't impose himself, though; he sits quietly and waits.

Maybe he can help. He's got a live-in girlfriend to provide nourishment. Maybe he knows of others? If I'm going to be of any use to Culebra, I've got to have a clear head.

"Ortiz?"

He looks at me over the rim of the coffee cup.

"I need to ask you a favor."

He nods at me to go on.

I still haven't opened my thoughts to him. It might be easier but for some reason, I don't want it to be.

"I need a host."

He puts the cup on the table, his eyebrows rising in surprise. "I thought you had this deal in Mexico."

"I did. I do." Obviously Williams hasn't filled him in on everything. I let him pick the story out of my head.

"Wow," he says. "I had no idea." He's quiet for a minute. Then he says, "I'll call my girlfriend. There's a friend of hers that I've used. Before I hooked up with Brooke, naturally. She might be available."

I feel embarrassed. I sit there while he calls his girlfriend and explains the situation. It's like asking your little brother to get you a date. Humiliating.

This is the uncool part.

# CHAPTER 20

IN AN HOUR, ORTIZ AND I ARE SITTING IN HIS LIV-
ing room. His girlfriend, Brooke, is a petite brunette
who is looking at me with open curiosity on her pert, co-
ed's face. I guess she's never met any female vamps.

She couldn't be more than twenty. She's barefoot,
dressed in a hoodie and a pair of sweats. Her hair is pulled
back in a ponytail. *Isn't she a little young?* I ask Ortiz.

He puts an arm across her shoulders and she snuggles
against his chest like a contented kitten. *Not for me.*

I'm seeing a side of Ortiz I wouldn't have believed an
hour ago. He's always displayed an air of chivalry toward
me. To see him on his home turf acting more macho than
gallant surprises me. I realize at this moment, though, that
I don't know anything about Ortiz—even how long he's
been a vampire or how old he was when he was turned.
Maybe he's younger than I think. Maybe Brooke is older.

And Brooke certainly seems to be enjoying the attention.

I look around the room. I followed Ortiz in my own car from the cottage so I could take off right after—doing what I need to do. He and Brooke live in a new housing development in Chula Vista. The homes are upper middle class, two story, fifteen hundred square feet of yuppie suburban delight. This room is decorated in Pottery Barn essentials. I expect a dog and a couple of kids to materialize out of the woodwork.

Hard to imagine why Ortiz, who will never be able to produce those kids, would choose to live here.

The moment I think that, the hypocrisy rises up to thump me on the head. Look at my lifestyle. Aren't I trying to do the same thing? Live a "normal" life?

Brooke is still rubbing her cheek against Ortiz' chest like she can't get close enough. He takes her chin in his hand, turns her face up and kisses her. There's no self-consciousness in the act, no embarrassment that I'm sitting right here with them.

Sharing intimate moments with strangers may be the norm for these two.

I'm relieved when the doorbell rings.

Ortiz extricates himself from Brooke's grasp and goes to answer it. The way Brooke is staring at me sparks the uneasy feeling that I may have asked the wrong vampire for a favor. It intensifies when Ortiz returns with a blonde in a raincoat.

"Anna," Ortiz says, "This is Edie."

Edie looks at me, head tilted, eyes shining with curious intensity. "Hi, Anna," she says. She unbuttons the raincoat and lets it slide off her shoulders.

She's naked.

Ortiz and Brooke are both standing beside her now. Ortiz cups her left breast while Brooke cups the right.

Edie crooks a finger at me. "Let the games begin."

I'm stunned into speechlessness. I know a lot of vamps

go for the group thing. I never expected Ortiz was one of them. Just as I never expected his girlfriend to be willing to share him. Color floods my face. I should have been more explicit in what I wanted.

I'm not a prude. I've had my share of one-night stands both before and after becoming a vamp. This, however, is too much.

Sitting in Ortiz' catalog-perfect living room and realizing what the three strangers staring at me expect puts me over the edge.

I swallow back humiliation and embarrassment and spear Ortiz with a look. *Not going to happen, Ortiz.*

Ortiz responds with a puzzled look. *What's wrong? You said you wanted a host.* He smiles at Edie. *I got you a host.*

*For me. Alone. Not this—*

He snorts. *Come on, Anna. Williams told me about you. You're no innocent. You've had plenty of human lovers.*

Embarrassment gives way to anger. *One at a time. In private.*

Ortiz is staring at me, as if he can't believe the direction this is going. The worst part is I do need to feed. The hunger is eating away at me. I refuse, though, to do it with an audience. I take a mental step back, breathe out a long sigh.

*Look, Ortiz. I'm sorry if I made you think I wanted more than blood. I can't do this. If Edie is willing to let me feed from her, I'll pay her. Do you want to ask her or shall I?*

Ortiz frowns. He looks seriously put out that I won't. *You offered me sex once.* His tone hums with protest.

*And you turned me down. Because of your girlfriend, if I remember correctly. I thought you didn't want to be unfaithful. I didn't realize it was because she wasn't there to participate.*

He starts to say something and Brooke interrupts.

"What's going on?" she asks. "Mario, you told me she wanted to play. You promised."

Mario? I didn't even know Ortiz' first name. We both turn to look at Brooke.

She's frowning at us like a petulant child. Suddenly, I get the feeling this kitten has claws. I look at Ortiz. *What did you promise?*

His mind snaps closed and anger tightens his jaw. He takes Brooke's arm. "Anna has changed her mind. She wants to be alone with Edie."

I changed my mind? I open my mouth to snarl a reply but Edie distracts me. She's picked up the raincoat and drapes it over an arm. "No problem. Let's go." She pulls a small penknife from the pocket of the coat and runs the blade over her tongue. She runs her tongue over her lips, smearing them with blood. "I'm ready."

When she smiles, my insides start to quake.

I'm ready, too.

Brooke stomps off to another part of the house. A slamming door makes me think if Ortiz expects to get anything from Brooke in the near future, sex or blood, he's going to have to do some serious groveling.

Ortiz recovers enough to offer Edie and me the use of a guest room. He escorts us down a hallway, opens the door, and leaves us to, I assume, begin the groveling.

As soon as the bedroom door closes behind us, Edie tosses the raincoat onto a chair and lays down. She stretches her hands over her head and grabs onto the headboard. Her body is long and lush. She licks her lips again, the blood is bright red and shines like liquid rubies.

I find myself licking my own lips.

I take off my jacket and lay it over her coat on the chair.

It's all I take off.

I perch myself on the side of the bed, suddenly feeling foolish and uncertain what to do next.

My throat tightens when I try to speak. I make a ridiculous croaking sound.

Edie laughs. "Are you nervous? I can't believe it. You don't have to be, you know. I've done this before—with men and women."

She waits for me to say something. I don't know what to say. I've fed from women before at Beso de la Muerte, but there it's a controlled situation and neither of us is naked.

She props herself up, leaning back on her elbows, and studies my face. "You've never had sex with a woman, have you?"

And I don't intend to now. I swallow a few times to make sure what comes out of my mouth won't be another undignified croak and say, "Edie, I don't think this is going to work. I can't give you what you want."

She tilts her head. The bloody tip of her tongue flicks toward me like an invitation. "But I can give you what you want. Why don't we give it a try?"

She turns on her side and lifts her hair, offering me her neck. The smell of her, pheromones, blood, a hint of lavender, melts my resolve. I lay down and fit my body against hers.

The vampire in me is ready, responding with a snarl and a sharp intake of breath. I hold her, one hand at her neck, one around her waist. She pushes back against me, rubbing her body against mine. I feel her shudder, feel her excitement through my clothes.

I nuzzle her neck, find her pulse point with my tongue. All my senses throb with anticipation. When I open her neck and begin to drink, she moans. She takes my hand and pushes it down, between her legs, holding it there with her own. I'm lost in my own passion; I don't fight her. A kaleidoscope of exploding sensations turns my world bloodred with heat and pleasure.

I drink.

It's all there is in the world. Hunger to be sated. The blood, her blood, warms me, fills me, completes me.

I'm sorry when it's time to stop.

Reluctantly, though, I drag myself back, withdraw my teeth from her neck, use my tongue to close the wounds.

All the while, she's writhing against me, moaning, her hands manipulating mine. When my fingers slip inside her, she cries out. She's hot and wet and feels like silk. Her orgasm builds, powerful, pulsing. I feel it. A new sensation for me. Not entirely unpleasant. I finger her until she comes. I'm no longer reluctant and no longer afraid. It seems the least I can do—give her sex.

Didn't she just give me life?

# CHAPTER 21

WHEN I WAS HUMAN, I'D FALL ASLEEP AFTER SEX. It's what Edie does now. She has a half smile on her face, a look of contentment. I cover her with a quilt from the foot of the bed and watch for a moment. The vampire is content; the human Anna wonders what the hell just happened.

I close the bedroom door behind me.

Ortiz and Brooke are nowhere to be found. The house is quiet. I let myself out.

What a bizarre way to start the morning. I don't think I'll ever be able to look at Ortiz the same way again. But the anxiety that had been building with the hunger is gone. I'm clearheaded, refreshed.

Horny.

Too bad Lance is in New York.

Too bad I have a witch to kill.

I call Frey's cell phone to check in.

Sandra picks up.

Her voice on his phone causes a ripple of alarm. "Where's Frey?"

"Don't worry," she says. "He's sleeping."

"And Culebra?"

She sighs. "The same. Any news?"

"I'm heading back to the warehouse now. I'll get that receptionist to talk if I have to scare the shit out of her to do it."

After I've finished, Sandra waits a beat to say, "Hurry, Anna."

It's all there in her voice—concern, uneasiness, fear. What isn't there is the antipathy she displayed toward me when I showed up two days ago. I ring off without bringing it up. When Burke is dead, when Culebra and Frey are safe, there will be time for us to talk.

It's not yet seven. Too early to head for the warehouse. I doubt the office staff reports before eight. I still have those two women Williams' identified as the blood-hungry pair who attacked their dates. The pictures are on the seat beside me. One has an address not far from Ortiz' house. I'll head there first.

I'm doing the thing I hate seeing others do, holding the pic up against the steering wheel while I drive so I can read the notes printed on the back. The first woman's name is Valerie Storm. The before picture shows a heavyset forty-six-year-old with dishwater blond hair. The woman in the after picture looks twenty-six with a good bleach job and glamour-shot makeup.

Maybe that's Burke's secret. Diet and a dynamite makeup artist.

Valerie Storm lives on Hilltop Drive. It's a nice neighborhood. I'm halfway down the block when police cars scream up behind me. Shit. Did Ortiz send these guys after me? Is he so pissed that I ruined his playdate he's having me arrested for that woman Burke dumped in my bed? I pull over, shoulders tight with aggravation. If he did this—

But the cars don't stop. They keep going. After a second, I do, too, still looking for Valerie's address.

I should have simply followed the police cars. We all end up at the same place.

There are three police cars at Valerie's, one in the driveway, one in the street, one on the front lawn. The cops in the two that passed me are racing toward the front door. I pull up across the street and watch. Neighbors are beginning to venture out to see what all the commotion is about. I join them.

The chatter among the neighbors tells me that the Storms are nice people, that no one can imagine trouble in the family, that if there was trouble, it probably had something to do with Valerie's remarkable transformation from suburban duckling to bombshell swan.

One of the men makes a comment about the transformation that earns him an elbow in the ribs from another of those suburban ducklings. She must be his wife.

It gets quiet when the coroner's wagon pulls up. The attendants go inside, followed a minute later by a man in a suit. I recognize him. San Diego's medical examiner. Either Valerie or someone in her family is dead.

My money is on Valerie.

The second of Burke's test subjects to turn up dead.

My stomach is queasy with the speculation that I may be responsible. Didn't Burke say she wanted to play a game with me? See how clever I was? I know she's capable of murder—she killed an innocent out of spite when Frey and I stopped her demon-raising last Halloween. But why is she killing the very women who are living proof of the effectiveness of her wonder cream? If her plan is to implicate me in their murders, I can't see how she'll do it. They have no connection to me. Even with her power, I doubt she could conjure up the kind of evidence necessary to make it look like they did.

After all, it didn't work last night.

What game is she playing?

I return to my car and flip open my cell. I call Ortiz. His voice mail picks up so I tell him where I am now and where I'm headed next—to El Cajon. To the home of the third of Burke's test subjects. I ask him to call me when he finds out what happened at the Storm residence.

That's two of three women connected to Burke to wind up dead. I hope I get to the third in time.

# CHAPTER 22

MADDIE COLEMAN LIVES ON EMERALD HEIGHTS Road. I've never heard of it and it takes my trusty GPS to get me there. It turns out to be a winding street off the end of Magnolia Avenue. It's a surprisingly nice neighborhood above an old and run-down area with views that stretch out over the El Cajon Valley. Maddie's is a low-slung ranch house with a tile roof and high chain-link fence that appears to circle a good-sized piece of property. When I stop in front of it, it becomes clear the reason for the fence. The biggest damned German shepherd I've ever seen appears out of nowhere and charges the fence before I get the car door open.

I stay put.

I can see the driveway and partway into the backyard. There's a swing set and slide. The garage door is closed. Except for the incessant barking of that damned dog, it's quiet.

What to do?

Dogs don't like me. It has nothing to do with being a vampire. I know this because dogs didn't like me before I became vampire. I have no doubt I could break the neck of the snarling beast, but that means getting close, and getting close means putting myself in range of those teeth. I may be a kick-ass vampire, but I still have an aversion to pain.

I hunker down. Surely, somebody will come to the door to see why the beast is raising such a racket. While I wait, I take another look at Maddie. In her before photo, she's standing beside a tall, pimply-faced teenager in a cap and gown. She looks midfifties, plump, mousey. She's dressed in a flower-print cotton skirt and pale blazer with a hand-bag on the arm that isn't clutching the graduate. Her shoes look like the kind nurses stereotypically wear—squared-toed, functional, ugly.

The transformation in her after photo is more remark-able than Valerie's. Again, it's a glamour shot. Maddie is almost wearing a black, tight, low-cut cocktail dress. It's slit up the side to reveal long legs and four-inch stilettos. She has a Veronica Lake haircut, long, shiny dark hair that falls over one eye. She's smiling at the camera with what can only be described as a "come fuck me" expression.

She looks about twenty-six.

Whew.

The dog is still going crazy in the yard. Maybe I should shoot it. Do the neighbors a favor. Except I haven't seen a neighbor peek out to see what's going on, either. Where in the hell is everybody?

Just when I decide I'm going to have to tackle the dog after all, a long black limousine whispers up to the gate. The driver honks the horn and the front door opens. A man appears in the doorway, calls the dog inside, disappears for a minute, then returns without the beast.

So, that's the trick? All I had to do was honk the horn?

The man walks down to the gate. He's dressed in a black

suit with a white shirt and dark tie. He walks with shoulders slumped. The lines of his face droop. When he opens the gate, he does it slowly, as if this simple task requires all his energy. When the limo pulls past him, his gaze falls on me. His expression doesn't change. It reflects neither curiosity nor concern.

The only thing those eyes reflect is pain.

He turns without acknowledging my presence and walks back to the house with the same slow, shuffling tread.

The scene is sickeningly familiar.

I know what he's feeling. See it in a face drawn in lines of sorrow. Sense it in the heaviness of his spirit. Recognize the unbearable sadness that weighs him down and makes the pain of loss the only sensation he's capable of experiencing.

I know it because I've been through it all myself. When my brother died.

I don't wait to see anything else. I don't have to. Maddie is dead and this is the beginning of her funeral procession.

What the hell is Burke doing?

This time I put a call into Williams.

He picks up on the second ring.

"What'd you find out from the receptionist?" he asks in way of greeting.

"Haven't been there yet," I reply. I tell him what I did find. Then I say, "Wouldn't three dead bodies elevate this in a judge's eye from coincidence to probable cause?"

"You don't know yet if Storm or Coleman are dead."

"Come on. What are the odds they aren't?"

There's a moment of silence. "I'll do some checking. In the meantime, maybe you'd better track that receptionist down."

We ring off and I put the Jag in drive and head back for the freeway—just in time for Tuesday morning commuter traffic.

Shit.

I'm stuck in stop-and-go traffic and I can't get the picture of that man as he came down the driveway out of my head.

Rage burns like acid. Burke is behind this. Why? And what's the connection between what she's doing to these women and that miraculous antiaging cream she's about to launch on the world?

Launch on the world.

Jesus.

I want to bang my forehead against the steering wheel. What an idiot I am.

There is one other person I can go to for answers. I don't want to do it. But I have to.

Gloria. Spokesmodel for Eternal Youth. She's certainly one person I know I can shake information out of.

Only idly do I wonder—has she used the stuff?

# CHAPTER 23

WHEN GLORIA IS IN TOWN, SHE STAYS IN A PENT-house at the Four Seasons. The clerk who takes my call refuses to put it through. His tone implies that the queen does not like to be disturbed.

I swallow back the impulse to say something rude and put a hopeful smile in my voice when I reply, "Look. I understand. If you've been around at all, you'll remember a few months ago Gloria got in trouble with the law. My name is Anna Strong. I helped her get out of that trouble. If you just call up to her room and ask, I'm sure she'll take the call."

And if she doesn't, I'll come over there, climb the fucking building and yank Gloria by the short hairs until she begs me to stop.

The clerk finally agrees to try. He puts me on hold. I'm on hold two minutes. I know because I'm timing it, plotting how to exact revenge if the bitch refuses my call.

The Kenny G elevator music I'm forced to endure dur-

ing this interminable hold cycle suddenly cuts off to be replaced by a ring.

Thank you.

The phone is picked up.

"Hello?"

It's a man's voice. Or rather a male voice—a sleepy,
sexy, incredibly young-sounding male voice.

"This is Anna Strong. I need to speak with Gloria."

No reponse.

"Hello? I'm calling for Gloria. Is she there?"

This time, the voice purrs, "Ms. Estrella is still asleep.
I'm not sure I should disturb her. If you tell me the nature
of your call . . ."

I get it now. Gloria is directing the conversation from
somewhere in the background. From the sound of this
guy's voice, they're most likely in bed.

"Look, dickhead, I don't care if Ms. Estrella is asleep.
Put her on now or I'll come up there and make it difficult
for you to fuck anything else for a long time. Ask Gloria.
She'll tell you I'll do it."

I hear a sharp intake of breath, a muffled conversation
as he relays my message and finally, "Jesus, Anna, you
never change, do you?"

"I could say the same for you, Gloria. The kid sounds
like he's about sixteen. His voice is still changing. Should
I send the police?"

Her laugh is short, brittle. "Did you have a reason to
call? Or do you get off badgering me?"

I did have a reason to call. An important reason. It galls
me that just the sound of her voice makes me lose mine.

"Yes. This Eternal Youth thing you're involved with. I
have some questions."

"Then contact my lawyer." Her tone morphs from aggravation to boredom. "Unless you're asking me to slip

you a few jars. Are you suddenly feeing old? See a few wrinkles when you look in the mirror?"

Laughter bubbles up. If she only knew—

"No, you idiot. I think there's something wrong with the stuff. Have you tried it?"

Now it's Gloria who laughs. "Are you kidding? Why would I put that crap on my face? I don't need it. And when I get to the point that I do, I'll have my own formula made up. This is purely a moneymaking thing. Tremaine seems to have stumbled on a unique product. She asked me to be the spokesmodel. I agreed. Period."

Part of me is relieved; part of me wants to howl in disappointment.

"How do you know Tremaine?"

"Why are you asking?"

My hands clutch into fists on the steering wheel. "Jesus, Gloria, will you just answer the fucking question?"

"Not the way to encourage cooperation, Anna. Okay, I'll answer your questions if you agree to answer mine. Quid pro quo."

I feel the blood rush to my face. If I had the time, I'd find her and snatch every hair from her head. Instead, I speak with slow deliberation. "Fine. Ask."

"How's David?"

My first impulse to deny her any information about her ex is quickly swallowed up by a better idea. "He's just great. He's in the Bahamas with his fiancée."

It provokes the desired result. A sharp intake of breath followed by an equally sharp, "Fiancée? When did that happen? Who is she? Do I know her?"

"That's three questions, Gloria. Now answer mine. How did you meet Simone Tremaine?"

At first, I think she's hung up on me, the silence stretches so long. Finally, though, she says, "Through my agent.

She contacted him, he contacted me. We did a deal." Tiny voice, "What's her name?"

"You don't know her, Gloria. David met her after you broke up. Do you have an address for Tremaine? A telephone number?"

"Not here. The contract's in my office in L.A."

Another dead end. At least if I can't track her down any other way, I'll follow up with Gloria. A surprisingly subdued Gloria. She's not snapping back with another question, so I take the initiative.

"The cream, has the stuff been tested?" I ask. "Approved by the FDA?"

That revives her. She snorts. "Your ignorance is showing. Cosmetics are not subject to FDA approval. It's left up to each company to substantiate the safety and effectiveness of their products."

Too formal.

She's been asked that before? "How do you know that?"

"I'm not stupid, Anna. I looked into it. I'm not going to jump into something I might get sued for later."

Ah. Meaning, her *lawyer* looked into it. Still, no human lawyer could have known or suspected that Tremaine was not what she appeared.

"Look, Gloria, I can't believe I'm about to say this." True enough, I'd like nothing better than to see her go down in flames. "But something is not right with Tremaine. I'm warning you. Get out now while you can. Disassociate yourself from Eternal Youth before it's too late."

There's a moment of silence and I think Gloria might be considering what I've told her. I brace myself for the barrage of questions sure to follow.

"Oh, Anna," she says finally. "You're still jealous of me. It's so childish."

The line goes dead and I'm left gaping openmouthed

at the phone. How like Gloria to interpret concern for jealousy.

I toss the phone onto the seat beside me.

Then I smile.

I tried to warn you, Gloria. Don't blame me when this Eternal Youth thing bites you in the ass.

# CHAPTER 24

THAT GLORIA REFUSES MY ADVICE DOES NOT SUR-
prise me. I'm only glad I was able to take the wind out
of her sales about David. Sure, it was lie; he's not engaged.
And she'll likely find that out on her own, but it shut her up
for a minute at least.

It's a tiny victory, even though I learned nothing new
about Tremaine.

What is surprising is arriving at the warehouse, my next
destination, and finding the parking lot empty.

I pull up to the door, park and look around.

Apprehension replaces the brief feeling of satisfaction.
This cannot be a good sign.

I get out of the car, shut the door quietly and approach
the front door.

The office is dark. I walk around the building. There is
one car parked beside the loading dock, a late-model Ford
sedan. On the sides and trunk of the car are those magnetic

signs with "Nelson Security Services" and a telephone number superimposed over a logo.

Did Burke hire security after I broke in? Surely, though, she wouldn't have suspended operations because of a missing file.

I walk back around to the office door and knock.

After about thirty seconds, two armed security guards appear from the back. One has a dog, another German shepherd naturally, on a short leash.

The guard with the dog comes to the door. He mouths through the glass, "Closed."

He's short and heavy-lidded and looks mean. So does the dog, eyeing me with a sneer and a trail of drool.

"Where is everybody?" I ask.

He shrugs. "Not a clue. Come back tomorrow. The place is supposed to reopen then."

He turns and walks back to his partner. They both watch me through squinty eyes.

Shit.

Guards now.

With a dog, no less.

I get into my car. I've got to find that receptionist. I don't want to bust my way in and subdue those guards (and dog), but I might have to.

Until I remember.

The receptionist uses Eternal Youth. Is she one of the test subjects? If so, she'll be in that file I gave Ortiz. All had contact information on the forms. When I try to call Ortiz, his phone goes again to voice mail.

I have no choice but to drive back to Chula Vista. Even if he's already left for work, it's likely Ortiz would have left the file at home. Burke is not yet an official suspect in the death of those two women. I'll just have to charm sweet Brooke into letting me see it.

This time, when I pull up, Ortiz' garage door is open. There are two cars parked inside. One is his—I recognize the Navigator—the other is a candy-apple red Miata with a San Diego State bumper sticker. Brooke is probably a college student. Ortiz, you are a dog.

At least my timing is good. I'd rather deal with Ortiz than his petulant girlfriend.

And there are no other cars around. I'm assuming Edie has left, which is a relief.

I don't know if vampires are capable of blushing, but I get the uncomfortable feeling I might if I was to see her again.

Brooke answers my ring. She must have just gotten out of the shower because her hair is wet and she's dressed in sweats. She doesn't say hello when she sees me, just turns on her bare feet and pads away with a curt, "He's not here."

I've accepted less cordial invitations. I let myself in and follow.

She's trounced off to the dining room table. That she's a student is reinforced by the open college chemistry text perched on a notebook next to a bowl of Cocoa Puffs.

She sits, thumbs a page of the text, takes a spoonful of cereal, ignores me.

I wait.

Another page, another mouthful of cereal.

Finally, I break the stalemate. "Where's Ortiz?"

She doesn't look up. "I told you he's not here."

"So. Where did he go?"

"He left for work. Ten minutes ago."

"Who picked him up?"

Finally, a question that gets more than a bored monosyllabic reply. She turns and stares at me. "Why would anyone pick him up?"

I jerk a thumb toward the front. "Because the garage door is open and his car is inside—"

She jumps up and takes off for the door. Her reaction triggers my own alarm. When we get outside, she clasps both hands over her mouth and gasps.

"Oh god—I heard a noise, but I thought—"

I pull her hands down. "What noise?"

She's crying. "A loud pop. Right after Mario left the house. I didn't go look. I was still mad . . ."

She takes a step into the garage, but I'm there first. The car doors are closed but unlocked. I open the passenger side door and look in.

Ortiz' folder, the one he had last night, is on the seat. It's unzipped and open.

It's also empty.

I get Brooke back inside and call Williams. He comes right over. We get Brooke calmed down and convince her that this is just some silly misunderstanding and one of Ortiz' cop buddies did pick him up for work. When she tries his cell, it goes right to voice mail. Not necessarily a bad thing, since she says he often turns off his phone when he checks in for duty.

The tears are dried, her fears at least momentarily alleviated. We ask if she has classes today. She says yes. We convince her to go, that we'll let her know as soon as we get through to Ortiz. She heads back to the bedroom to get ready.

Williams releases a long, pent-up breath. "Jesus. She got Ortiz."

I feel like knocking my head against the wall. "I never should have taken that file. I should have made a copy. I've let Burke know we can connect her to Eternal Youth. Is she going to kill every one of those test subjects? Why? It can't be simply to get even with me."

Williams shakes his head. "Maybe we'll know when we get an analysis of the product. I dropped it off on my way here. I put a rush in. We should hear in three hours or so."

"I can't wait that long. I'm going to the warehouse. There were personnel files that should tell me where the receptionist lives."

If she hasn't gotten rid of those, too. I rub my eyes as if to rub away the thought and look up at Williams. "Where will you be? I'll call as soon as I get to that receptionist."

"I'll be at the park. I'll get the witches started on another locator spell." He looks toward the house. "I'll give Brooke my cell phone number, to let her know as soon as we reach Ortiz."

His tone is lower, huskier than I've ever heard. His concern for Ortiz is genuine.

Maybe there's hope for Williams yet.

# CHAPTER 25

THIS SEEMS TO BE A MORNING FOR SURPRISES.

This time, I'm looking down at the warehouse from my perch on the frontage road and even the security car is gone.

Now, that doesn't mean one of the guards didn't drop the other off or go for coffee, but it does give me a window of opportunity.

One guard, with or without the mutt, is better than two.

I head for the back. It's still deserted. Eerily different from my first visit yesterday when the parking lot was full and trucks came and went like ants at a picnic.

I launch myself upward. The windows on the first floor allow me a peek into the factory. I'm looking for the security guard. No one in sight. It isn't until I've allowed myself a scan of the area that I'm aware of what else I'm not seeing.

I'm not seeing anything on the conveyor belt.

The conveyor belt is completely empty.

About the same time that registers, the hair on the back of my neck rustles as if touched by the hand of god.

It's the last thing I feel before I'm blown off the building and slammed into the ground.

# CHAPTER 26

THE FORCE OF THE EXPLOSION BLOWS OUT EVERY window and covers me with shards of glass.

I lay on the ground a minute, taking mental and physical inventory. My skin burns, my ears ring. Don't see any blood. I'm lying on my side, twenty feet from the building. I try to roll on my back, straighten out. My left arm aches and I realize it's twisted above the elbow in an unnatural angle. Probably broken, though no bone protrudes.

I sit up.

My back protests, but follows my mental command to move. That left arm is what's really protesting. I pass fingers gingerly up the arm until I find the point at which bone pushes against the skin. Grasping the arm with my right hand, I give it a sharp tug.

Pain causes my vision to go black. There's a popping sound and the bone shifts into place. It's all I need to do. Accelerated vampire healing will take care of the rest.

Except for the pain.

It hurts like a son of a bitch.

The ringing in my ears subsides to a dull roar, and I shake my head to clear it.

At first, I think what I hear next is a result of the blast. Some shift in decibel or tone that sounds less like percussion-induced noise and more like—

Screaming.

Screaming?

I'm on my feet and racing back toward the flames.

It's not my imagination. It's in my head.

*In* my head.

Vampires. Inside. Trapped.

The building is fully engulfed. Flames shoot out of the windows. Smoke and heat don't scare me. Flames do. Burning is one of the ways a vampire can be killed.

I race to the front. Maybe I can get in through the door. It hangs open on an explosion-warped frame. No flames here, not yet. But there's no *one* here, either. Not in the reception area, not in the office area in back.

I send out a mental probe. *Where are you?*

An answer comes back from a chorus of frantic voices. *The basement. We're in the basement.*

Basement?

The corridor at the end of where I'm standing leads only to the factory floor. I know. I traveled it last night.

*I don't know where that is. Tell me.*

An anguished cry, from a female voice: *We don't know. We were drugged when we were brought here. Please. Help us.*

Frustration and panic claw at my heart. I can't go back down those stairs into the factory. The flames are too intense. I feel the heat through the soles of my shoes.

Maybe there's another way.

Outside, I race around the building, circling, looking for

anything that might be another entrance. I tell the female vamp to keep talking, hoping her voice can guide me.

She babbles, crying, begging me to find her.

I can't.

There is no other way in that I can find.

Nothing. I find nothing.

The vamp's voice becomes shrill with fear.

I beat my fists against the loading dock. *Why can't you free yourselves?* Exasperation fuels my feeling of helplessness and it comes out in an angry wail.

*We can't. The collars.*

There is such despair in her reply, it floods me with remorse and determination. I start again. At the front, circling, searching, running my fingers along the base of the bays in the loading dock, ignoring the white-hot metal that singes my fingers.

Until I find it.

A seam in the metal of the middle bay.

There is no latch, no hinge, no keyhole. I pound at the metal with my fist.

*Yes!* A chorus of frenzied voices. *We hear you!*

I beat at the metal until it caves. Then I tear a great rip in the metal and bend it back. It's dark inside and smoke pours out like a genie released from a bottle. When I step inside, and my eyes have adjusted to the smoke and light, I follow the screaming voices filling my head.

Follow them to a scene straight from hell.

# CHAPTER 27

THERE ARE TWELVE OF THEM. YOUNG, FEMALE. They are naked, hanging upside down, hands bound behind their backs with silver chains. When I break into the room, I'm hit with their relief. It's so tangible, it fills me with panic.

Panic because they think I can save them. Their expectation and gratitude swamp my senses.

But I don't know if I can save them.

I don't know how.

I shut down my thoughts while I move from one to the other. My own senses are recoiling so violently, it takes all my strength to shield them. I force the revulsion down. Look at them, Anna. Figure out how to set them free.

Each vampire has a metal collar around her neck. Each collar is a small trough with a spiked spigot. The spike has been driven into the vampire's jugular, piercing it. From the spigot hangs a tube. Blood drips from the tube into collection bags. Or, in the case of the two vampires on the end, a stain where the last drops fell onto the floor. For those two, there's no help. They have been drained lifeless.

I squeeze my eyes shut. For a moment, I've forgotten the reason I'm here. Forgotten the heat that grows more intense, ignore the cries of the vampires that the flames grow closer. All I can think is, *Why would Belinda Burke do this?*

Does she hate vampires so much, she came up with this elaborate, horrifying way to kill them? Did she plan to bring me here after she finished her revenge against Culebra and Frey? The thought fills me with horror.

So what changed her mind? Why did she decide to destroy her demonic torture chamber now and let the vamps trapped here either bleed to death or be destroyed by the flames?

*The flames.*

The anguished voice of one of the vampire's brings me back. I push the fear and hatred to the back of my mind. How can I save these women?

I do the only thing I can think of. With shaking hands, I go from one to the other, turn the spigots until the blood flow stops. I avoid looking in their eyes. I'm afraid of what I'll see.

I unhook the tubes and chains and lower each gently and carefully to the floor. I don't touch the collars. I have no idea what might happen if I try to take them off, but the fact that just touching them brings shudders of agony numbs me. I unbind their hands. The four nearest the front get to their feet on their own. The ones behind are shakier and I help them to stand. Slowly, clumsily, we start to make our way outside. The stronger of the injured help the weaker.

We step outside under an apocalyptic sky. Smoke and ash turn day into evening. We cling to each other as we make our way to the shelter of some trees at the edge of the parking lot.

Only when we are away from the building does one of the women grasp my arm.

"There is another," she says.

I look back toward the building. Smoke is thicker now, pouring out the entrance to the underground torture chamber. The draft caused by my breaking in draws the flames downward.

"Another?"

"Brought in just before the explosion. Unconscious."

"I don't think I can go back."

She nods sadly. "I doubt he'll know what happens."

My heart jumps. "He?"

"A young male vampire. In a policeman's uniform."

Time stops. I dig my cell phone out of my pocket, hit speed dial, and thrust it at her. "When a man named Williams answers, tell him where we are and what happened. Tell him Ortiz is here at Burke's warehouse."

I don't wait for a response or to see if Williams picks up. I'm running full speed back to the warehouse.

The smoke can't hurt Ortiz, the heat, either.

But the flames licking at the back of the chamber can.

"Ortiz!" I'm screaming it at the top of my lungs. He's got to hear me, got to let me know where he is.

There's no response—no verbal or mental path for me to follow.

He must still be unconscious. I push back beyond the two dead vampires still hanging like broken dolls from the ceiling. I didn't look any farther into the chamber than this before. I didn't think I needed to.

Vampires don't breathe. The smoke and heat are an annoyance, they blur my vision, dull my senses. I have to keep wiping my streaming eyes, focusing on the dark beyond the corpses.

Where could he be?

There's a flash and a roar. The draft from the broken

loading bay door finally succeeds in drawing the flame to its source. Fire races down the back stairs and across the floor as if following an invisible trail.

I can't stay here much longer.

"Ortiz, where are you?" I scream it until my throat is raw.

Over and over. Then, I stop, listen.

*Tell me where you are. Please.*

The only sound that fills my ears is the crackle of the flame. The only thing I see is the hell of fire bearing down.

Then—

A muffled cry.

*Tell me where you are.* I scream it again like a crazy person.

There's no answer. In the corner, near the stairs, a figure suddenly rises.

Ortiz pulls himself up, shaking his head, confused, immobile. He looks across the room.

*Here,* I'm yelling. *Over here.*

I take a step toward him but there's a wall of flame between us. I can't jump it and I can't go through it.

*Ortiz—can you find a way around?*

He is looking right at me now. He sees me. He understands.

His eyes sweep the room. He's surrounded by flame.

I don't know what to do.

Ortiz' eyes seek mine. There's a rush of conflicting emotion—fear, regret, acceptance. He holds up a hand. *Be sure Brooke is all right. Tell her I loved her.*

*No. You can't give up. Look around.*

His gaze remains on me. *Help Williams. He'll need you now.*

*No. Find a way out. Look.*

But as I speak the words, the flames erupt around him

in a tornado of wind and noise. In one moment, he's there, watching me, smiling. In the next, his body bursts into flame. It ignites in a single, sparkling burst and is suspended a moment in the air, like an exploding star.

I don't want to watch.

I can't look away.

Ortiz dissolves into flickering embers and pinpricks of white light that rain down like the tears of an avenging angel.

And Ortiz is gone.

# CHAPTER 28

"*N*O*—"* I'M STILL YELLING EVEN THOUGH IT'S USE-
less. Ortiz is gone.

I'm powerless to move. I can't drag my eyes off the spot
where a moment ago, Ortiz stood looking at me. All that's
left is a wisp of vapor and a quick, bright discharge of light.
Like a dying sparkler.

No.

*Anna, are you in there?*

A voice from outside. A voice that keeps calling my
name. Urgently. Unrelentingly.

*Anna, where are you?*

It breaks through the miasma of my despair and brings
me back.

The heat on my skin, the roar of the flames, the acrid
smell of—what? My shoes. I look down and realize what
I'm smelling is the soles of my shoes. If I don't get out, I'll
be joining Ortiz in whatever afterlife awaits the vampire.

I'm not ready to find out what that is.

The flames have traveled on a straight path from the stairs to the gaping hole I tore in the bay.

Have I waited too long?

Panic raises bile in my throat.

A sound.

To the left.

Someone is pounding against the metal of the adjoining bay. Doing what I did just a little while ago to get inside this one.

I race over. Use my fists to pound, too, until the metal gives way. There's no seam here, I gouge into the metal with my fingers, using nails and finally teeth to tear a hole. With my hands, I yank at the hole, enlarge it, make it big enough to gain purchase with my hands. At last, I can rip back the steel fabric. It's not easy. Blood from lacerated palms makes my grip slip. I ignore it and the pain. Keep working until strong hands grab mine and pull me outside.

The hands drag me away from the building, across the parking lot.

I don't realize my eyes are squeezed shut until they open and I'm staring up at sky.

A face peers down.

*Are you all right?*

My savior is a woman with a kindly middle-aged face.

I attempt to sit up. When my palms press against the asphalt, pain in lightning sharp daggers races up my arms. I look down to see great jagged cuts like macabre lifelines scoring the flesh. My nails are torn to the quick.

My back hurts from being dragged, my left arm throbs, my eyes still stream from the smoke.

I glance back at the building, fully engulfed, smoke blocks the sun, staining the sky like angry storm clouds.

I see Ortiz—standing in front of me one moment, gone the next. His face, calm, accepting, will haunt me for a long time.

The cool night air on my skin, the smell of asphalt and burned rubber, the roar of the flames.

I'm alive.

Suddenly, I've never felt better.

# CHAPTER 29

T HE WOMAN WHO DRAGGED ME OUT IS KNEEL-
ing beside me, her face level with mine. She has long
hair, drawn back from her face, light brown dusted with
gray. Her eyes are deep blue and sparkle with an inner radi-
ance. She projects great kindness.

She's a vampire.

I've never met a vampire before who wasn't young—or
at least young-looking.

Before I can block that thought, she laughs.

*Not all of us are made at a young age. I was, as you see,
in my fifties. In reality, not a bad age to become vampire.
There's a certain wisdom that comes with middle age.*

*Wisdom is not something Anna knows much about.*

Williams' voice interjects itself in our conversation. He
walks up from behind and when I turn, I see several men
helping the injured vampires. They're covering them with
blankets and leading them to vans parked in a semicircle in
the back of the parking lot. They're all human.

*You were quick,* I say. *How did you arrange it?*

*There is a safe house nearby. I called, they mobilized.*

*Will the women be all right?*

Williams nods. *The humans will see to their needs. We can't remove the collars until they're stronger.*

I shake my head, shuddering. *What are those things? I've never seen anything like it.* Just the thought of how I found them makes me tremble. *She was* bleeding *them.*

*I've seen it before,* Williams replies. *In pictures. The collars were used by us, by ancient vampires, to bleed humans. Someone has a long memory and a great hate to use them now against us.*

*Not someone. Belinda Burke. The witch.*

Williams is looking around. *You said Ortiz was here. Where is he?*

His question unleashes a rush of alarm. He doesn't know. I don't know how to tell him.

I force myself to my feet, heart hammering, head swimming in anxiety.

Williams feels it. He takes a step closer. "Where is Ortiz?"

The woman with us senses my agitation. She puts a hand on my shoulder. "Maybe you should go with the others. You need to rest."

I push her gently away. "No. You go see to them. I have to speak with Williams."

She looks reluctant to leave us.

"It's all right," I say. "We'll be all right."

She moves off, looking back once, then takes the elbow of a young female who is stumbling toward the van. I watch as they walk away.

"Ortiz is gone."

I don't know how else to say it.

Williams expression stills, freezes into blankness.

"Gone? You mean he's left already?"

I shake my head. "He was inside."

Awareness blooms in Williams' eyes. A muscle quivers at the corner of his jaw. His thoughts draw inward, shutting me out.

Then I feel it. Feel the rage.

It hits with the intensity of a blast furnace.

I accept it. I understand it.

He and Ortiz were close. I expect Williams to lash out and since I'm the likely target, I brace myself.

Williams doesn't look at me. He turns away, head bowed. I feel his conflicted emotions as powerfully as if they were my own. Misery, like physical pain—a knife twisting and turning inside. The first swell of anger giving way to raw grief, a sense of deep loss, a terrible bitterness.

I was prepared for him to strike out but he's turned it inward. Somehow, that makes it worse. If he screamed or attacked me or slammed his fist into a wall, I'd know how to react. This way he's unreachable. There's nothing I can do or say. His desolation and despair wrap him in a cocoon of anguish.

I reach out a hand but stop short of touching him. "I'm sorry."

He barks a short, desperate laugh. "Sorry? You could have saved him."

"I couldn't. The flames were everywhere. I didn't know he was inside until it was too late."

His expression shifts, turns his eyes cold, his mouth into a thin, hard line. "You are such an ignorant bitch. You don't know your power. You could have saved him. If you had taken one minute from your precious, insignificant human life to *learn*, Ortiz would be alive."

His anger hits me like a punch to the stomach. I take a step away from him. "What are you talking about?"

He flings his hand in the direction of the warehouse.

"Flames can't hurt you. Nothing can hurt you. You are immortal. Truly immortal. You are the one."

The words lash at me. His face is contorted, twisted in anger. He comes closer. "You are a terrible disappointment to me, Anna Strong." A whisper, deadly, intense. "It's the last time you will fail me. I swear by Ortiz, I will make you pay."

His eyes burn with hatred. I can't move, can't look away, don't know how to respond. I don't understand. Questions flood my mind, but Williams has shut me out. His last words hang in the air between us. He blames me for Ortiz' death. I have no idea why.

"We have to leave."

A female voice. I turn to see who is speaking, but even the effort of this simple physical movement engulfs me in tides of weariness and despair. I feel drained. Hollow. Lifeless.

When I look up, I see Williams watching. Smiling.

I realize he is doing it—somehow he is not only in my head, but controlling my physical responses. I feel weighted down, sluggish, incapable of forming a coherent thought or breaking the bond that holds me.

Why is he doing this?

*Because I can.*

Simple. Without pretense. Because he can.

The other voice comes again. "The fire trucks. We have to leave before they get here."

I focus on that voice, center my thoughts on it, muster all my strength. I could not break Burke's hold on me, I'll be damned if I let Williams have that same kind of power.

Williams feels my resolve. He tries to fight it, but I won't let him. I turn his anger back on him. The channel between us breaks with an almost physical release of energy. When it does, my head clears, my body is free.

Williams jerks back. He tries to reestablish his hold.

This time, I'm in control. I grab hold of *his* mind in a grip as tight as the one he used on me. I twist the psychic connection until I feel him surrender to my will. *I understand your grief. You were close to Ortiz.*

*Close? You have no idea.* His fury blazes forth. *But you will understand. I will make you understand.*

My arm is throbbing, the wounds on my hands burn from being clutched into fists. Too much has happened today and in the past. I don't want to be a part of this anymore. I lean toward Williams.

*You have manipulated me for the last time. We will see this through. I need your resources to help Culebra. But then, you will answer my questions and it will be done between us.*

He looks at me with dispassionate indifference. *You've said the same thing a dozen times. It will be done when I say it is done.*

I don't fight. I release him. I have said it before. This time is different. I'm sick of the game. Culebra comes first. When he's safe, when Burke is dead, when I get from Williams what I need to understand what I am, then it will be done.

In the distance, sirens blare. The vans are pulling out of the parking lot. Only one remains. The woman takes Williams' arm and pulls him over to it.

I'm left alone. I run up the hill to my car. The sirens are louder, and when I look back, I see the flashing lights approach. The last van pulls away seconds before screaming fire trucks make the turn into the warehouse parking lot. Smoke and flame pour out of ruined windows and doors. The roof collapses with a tremendous roar. Flames leap to the sky like a bird from a cage.

What will the firemen find in the ruined building? Ortiz' badge? His gun? Will anything survive?

I hope so. He deserves to be remembered as a cop.

More cars appear on the frontage road. Curiosity seekers, I imagine, attracted by the smoke and sirens. For the first time, I give a thought to what I must look like. Wearily, I glance down at torn jeans, bloody hands and smoke-stained skin. I'd better get out of here before someone notices.

# CHAPTER 30

I'M BONE WEARY.

Scalding hot water cascades over me, soap and shampoo wash away the smell and soot of the fire. But the image remains.

Ortiz.

His face before he was consumed. His face as we spoke in my kitchen last night.

Barely twelve hours ago. Now he's gone.

I get out of the shower and slip into clean clothes. The cuts on my hands have already closed, the pain in my left arm has receded to a dull ache. My body hums with healing energy.

I wish my mind were so easily healed. *Could* I have saved Ortiz?

I refuse to believe it. Williams is playing games with me. If I had the abilities he says I do, I'd know it.

Wouldn't I?

Everything I had on this morning I bag for the trash.

Even if I could get rid of the bloodstains the smell would remain. And the memories.

In the bedroom, my glance falls on the bed. It's still stripped, I haven't had a chance to remake it after the cops took the bedclothes. I want nothing more than to lie down on the bare mattress, close my eyes. It's been two days since I've had any sleep.

Another image chases the thought of sleep out of my head.

Culebra—near death.

When I call Frey, he picks up. Nothing has changed. Culebra's spirit is being kept alive by Frey's efforts, his body by an intravenous feeding tube. He has not regained consciousness.

What has changed is the sound of Frey's voice. It betrays the burden of working such potent magic. He sounds like a palsied old man, his voice slow in cadence, tremulous.

He asks only that I find Burke, finish it.

I ring off with a promise. I hope I've succeeded at hiding what I'm feeling—a sense of futility.

So far, nothing I've done to save Culebra has worked.

Before I do anything else, though, I need to see Brooke—give her Ortiz' last message. Maybe if I'd told Williams' that his last thoughts had been with him, it would have eased the situation at the warehouse.

It's too late now for what-if.

Besides, what happened between Williams and me was a long time coming.

WILLIAMS' CAR IS PARKED IN FRONT OF ORTIZ' HOUSE when I pull up.

I should have known he'd be here.

Still, it doesn't shake my resolve to see Brooke. I have a message for her and it needs to be delivered in person.

When I ring the doorbell, Williams answers it.

I prepare myself for a psychic attack. He does nothing but hold open the door and stand aside, an invitation to come in. No challenge. No threat. When I probe, he is not questioning my presence. His mind reflects only sadness.

Brooke looks up when I enter the dining room. Her eyes are red-rimmed, her cheeks flushed. If Williams told her it was my fault Ortiz was dead, her expression doesn't suggest it. All I see on her young face is regret.

"I'm sorry," I say.

Her lower lip quivers. "I was mad at him," she says. "I let him leave without telling him that I loved him. Now, he won't know."

"He knew. He gave me a message for you."

She looks up. Tears well again, but there's also a spark of anticipation and hope. "A message?"

I touch her arm, wishing I had more to offer. "He said to tell you that he loved you. He wanted you to know. He wanted you to be all right."

Brooke starts to cry. A woman comes out of the kitchen, a glass of water in her hand. She looks like Brooke, same general build, same brunette coloring, same heart-shaped face.

Williams takes the glass from her hand and takes it to Brooke. "This is Catherine," he says to me. "Brooke's sister."

Catherine acknowledges the introduction with a nod. "Were you a friend of Mario's?"

"Yes."

"I heard what you told Brooke. Were you there when—"

For the first time since I came in, I feel antagonism stir in Williams' thoughts. "Yes," I reply simply. I look over her head to Williams. *How much do they know?*

He answers with an arm around Brooke's shoulders. He speaks aloud for their benefit. "They know Mario was there at that warehouse because he received a call about a fire. He went in to make sure the building was empty. He died a hero."

It's a good story. "Has anyone from the department been in touch yet?" I ask.

He nods. "The acting chief has already called. He's on his way over."

I can't think of any reason to stay. Catherine has taken a seat beside her sister, slipping her arms under Williams' so she's holding her sister as she cries.

Williams defers to Catherine, stands back and away. He does it reluctantly as if sharing in her sorrow lessens his own.

"I should go."

Williams walks me to the door. He hands me a piece of paper. "The address of the safe house," he says.

It's where I'll go next. The girls are my last link.

Williams is carefully guarded, his thoughts impenetrable. I'm on my way down the sidewalk to my car when he sends a message.

*I want Burke. Let me know what you find out.*

I pause and turn around. He's still in the doorway. There's a shift in what I see reflected in his eyes. Grief is eclipsed by a more powerful emotion. Here, with no one but me to see, his eyes shine with purpose. He grieves for Ortiz but that grief fuels a greater need.

It's clear now, the change in his attitude toward me. It may be temporary but he'll work with me. He wants Burke as much as I do. And for the same reason.

He wants revenge.

# CHAPTER 31

WILLIAMS SAID WHEN HE FIRST ARRIVED AT the fire that the safe house was close. It is. The address is less than a mile from the warehouse. Smoke and ash still cast an early twilight to the neighborhood and an eerie orange glow.

There are two of the white vans from the warehouse parked outside the rambling, shabby clapboard house. It's set back from the road by a wide expanse of withered grass and surrounded by a three-foot-tall wooden split-rail fence. Wild roses spill over the length of the fence. Bushes so dense, they have grown into the fence, becoming part of it. Bloodred roses saturate the air with the reek of their perfume.

My knock at the front door is answered by the same woman who pulled me out of the fire. She smiles. "Glad to see you looking so well," she says.

She holds out her hand and I take it. "Anna Strong."

"Oh, I know who you are." She turns and heads into the

interior of the house, beckoning me to follow and adding over her shoulder, "My name's Rose Beechum."

Rose? With the flowers outside, it seems appropriate.

She reads my thought. *Yes, it is, isn't it? I've lived in this house all my life. My parents planted those bushes sixty years ago.*

When we enter a back room, small talk ceases. Five of the vampires from the warehouse are seated on cushions on the floor. Curtains are drawn across small, high windows, plunging the room further into an eerie red-hued dusk. There is a peculiar stillness to the room, too, that is unnatural and disturbing. The sight and the feel of it sinks my spirits lower.

Rose is watching for my reaction. *You feel it, don't you?*

I'm not sure if she means the stillness these vamps are throwing off or my reaction to it. I let my gaze sweep the room without replying. Each young woman is now covered by a blanket. Each is feeding, eyes closed, faces burrowed into the neck of a human host. Each is still wearing that terrible collar. The spike cuts into the jugular, making it difficult to drink. Blood seeps from the wound with each swallow. None are experiencing the exquisite joy of feeding. This is a slow, painful act of necessity and survival. It sickens me to see it.

There's something else. The young vampires aren't projecting any emotion or response. No thoughts reach out to me, no greetings are returned. Is this what Rose meant?

*Maybe it's trauma. Maybe when the collars are removed . . .*

Rose looks doubtful. *We can't attempt to remove the collars until they are stronger. If we do, they will bleed out the same way a human would with a similar wound.*

I watch the interaction between host and vampire. There is no pleasure being offered or taken. For the human as for the vampire, it is an act of sacrifice.

"Who are they?" I ask Rose. "Where did you find hosts willing to do this?"

"There are some in the human community who think vampires hold the key to human survival. The ones who believe in the apocalypse. They align themselves to us because they think we alone will be saved. At the end of the world, they will turn to us for help as we have turned to them."

These humans want vampires to turn them when doomsday comes? I stare at Rose, to see if she's serious.

She is.

The idea turns my stomach. Still, what is important is what they are doing now to save the girls.

*Why can't we help?* I ask. *Why can't you and I use our saliva to staunch the flow? It works on vampires as well as humans. I know. I've done it.*

*They are too weak. They need human blood first. To start the healing.* She beckons me once again to follow and starts down a hall. *Come. The four strongest are back here. In the bedroom. We have been able to remove their collars. You can speak with them if you wish.*

She leads me into a back bedroom. It's set up like a dormitory, three sets of bunk beds along the walls. No windows. They have been covered over with sheets of plywood. No other furniture. It's an odd setup until I remember that Williams called this a safe house. But a safe house for what purpose?

Rose answers without prompting. *Sometimes it is necessary for our kind to go underground. You have not been vampire long enough to have experienced such a time. The last was ten years ago when the Revengers renewed their efforts to wipe us out. For now, my house and others like it are used for situations like the one you found at the warehouse. Safe haven for wounded vampires.*

My gaze sweeps the room. The four female vamps in

here are feeding. The collars have been removed. As I watch, the throat wounds on two are closing. The jagged holes are rough edged, as if the spikes were serrated. There are bruises where the collars bit into the flesh.

The other two are not so far along in the process. Their throats still bear gaping wounds, seeping blood and a clear liquid. There is desperation and pain in the way they grip their hosts. The humans are quiet and bear it well.

Better than me. The urge to turn away is strong.

But suddenly I realize what it has taken some minutes to register. Shaken, I turn to Rose. *There are only nine.*

She releases a breath. *One didn't make it. She was too far gone.*

One of the vamps whose wounds are almost closed sees me at the door and gently pushes her host away so that she can stand up. She is the first woman I saw when I entered the basement. Someone has given her a sweat suit, and she tugs at the hem of the top as she approaches. She's very young, can't be more than a few years older than Trish. Her blond hair is tucked behind her ears and she smiles at me shyly.

My mind recoils from the horror that this girl has experienced—first being made vampire at such a young age, then finding herself a victim of torture.

In spite of it all, she's smiling at me. "I'm glad you're here," she says. "I never got a chance to thank you."

She's small-boned and waifish. *How long have you been vampire?*

She looks at me expectantly as if waiting for a response to her greeting.

I try again. *How long have you been vampire?*

The expression on her face remains the same—eager, a little puzzled now at my silence. When I probe her thoughts, I realize with a start that she isn't hearing me telepathically.

*You see,* Rose says. *Something's wrong. She is much stronger than the others, much farther along in the healing process. She should be able to understand us.*

The girl is frowning now, picking up on negative energy without understanding the cause for it. "What's wrong?" she asks, her voice trembling.

Rose and I look at each other. Neither of us knows how to respond.

The girl is becoming agitated. Her hands fly to her throat, her body begins to shake.

I step to her, put an arm around her, hug her close. She doesn't deserve more terror. "I'm sorry," I say. "Nothing is wrong. You're safe." I feel her ribs through the fabric of her top. I turn her back to her bunk. "Sit, please."

She lowers herself onto the bed, clings to my hand.

The other three vamps are watching. The same sense of silence pervades this room that I felt in the other. I project my thoughts into their minds. I get flashes of emotion, but nothing else. No recognition, no response to indicate they are aware of my probe.

Rose echoes the question in my own head when she says, *They are not like us. They are vampire, but different.*

I look from one of the girls to the other. They are all staring at Rose and me, feeling our anxiety, projecting their own.

Anxiety is the only thing they project. I don't understand it. I know I heard them in the warehouse. Heard their screams. It's how I was able to find them.

But now?

The girl beside me on the bunk gives my hand a squeeze. When I look at her, she says, "My name's Rebecca."

I push my concerns away for the moment. "Hi, Rebecca. I'm Anna. Do you think you could answer some questions for me?"

She nods.

"How did this happen to you?"

Rebecca closes her eyes. "I don't know," she whispers.

"Can you tell me how long you were there?"

A voice on my left answers. "She was the newest. She was brought in three days ago."

I turn. The speaker is a woman in her early twenties, dark hair, huge eyes. The marks on her neck are almost gone. "They only brought in a new one when one of the others—"

Her voice breaks off. She pauses, gathers herself, continues. "It happened the same for all of us. We are newly made. We were to meet our sires for the first hunt. We were directed to an abandoned building. When we got there, we were drugged. We woke up in hell."

She speaks in a measured voice, calm, detached. She projects an inner strength, perhaps because of all who made it out, she, in spite of her youth, may be the oldest.

"What happened then?" I ask gently.

"We were given something to wake us up. There was a man, a human. He bound us and strung us up. Then he—" A sharp intake of breath, a hand to her throat. "He forced the collars on. The pain was terrible but we couldn't move, couldn't scream. To try only made it worse. When he was sure it was on properly, he attached the bags. We watched our blood—our life—drain into those little bags a drop at a time."

Rebecca is crying beside me. I put an arm around her shoulders. "I'm sorry." It's directed at all of them but it echoes like an empty sentiment even in my own head. Saying I'm sorry means nothing.

Killing the witch who is responsible will mean something.

Rose raises an eyebrow at me. *Find out what you can.*

She ushers the human hosts out of the room and leaves me alone with the girls. They all have the same expression on their faces. Expectant. They're looking at me as if I have answers, when in reality, I have nothing to offer. Not yet.

"I know this will be hard for you, but I need your help. I need you to tell me everything you remember about the people who did this. Can you do that?"

The brunette is the first to speak. "What do you want to know?"

"The man who collected the blood, did he ever talk to you? Mention what he was doing with it?"

They look at one another, heads shake slowly from side to side.

"Can you describe him?"

"Sadistic."

"Cruel."

"Enjoyed his work."

Rebecca wipes at her eyes. "He was big," she says, finally giving me something I can use.

"How big?"

"Like a sumo wrestler. But he had soft hands. I remember thinking how odd it was. He didn't talk to us. He just went about his work with a grim smile on his face."

Sumo wrestler—Burke's bodyguard?

"Was there ever a woman with him?"

Rebecca shakes her head. "No. He was always alone."

"What about the vamp who sired you? What was his name?"

"He called himself Loren," Rebecca replies.

"He sired all of you?"

The others nod. Rebecca adds, "But that wasn't his real name."

"It wasn't?"

"No. I overheard him on the phone once. When he answered he said, 'Jason Shelton.' Like he was answering a business phone."

"That's very good, Rebecca. Did you hear anything else?"

She shakes her head.

"What did he look like?"

"He was short. Maybe five feet five. Stubby. Had cold eyes."

"How did he find you?"

She looks down and away. "On the street." She points to the blonde. "He found her in a shelter. And her. He was a talker. When he first brought a girl in, he'd talk to her like she was awake and make fun of how easy it had been to fool her."

Runaways. Easy pickings for a predator. "How many died before I found you?"

"Six."

The bodies that Williams told me about in Beso de la Muerte. He was right. Someone had been killing vampires.

Rebecca rubs her eyes with the palms of her hands as if rubbing away the nightmare. "I thought I was so lucky when Loren—when Jason—found me. He promised me freedom and money and eternal life. I should have listened to my instincts. I knew it was too good to be true. And I was right. First he made me have sex with him, then he bit me. I didn't feel any different. He said that would change after I fed from a human. He sent me to a vacant building that stunk of piss and shit and was overrun with rats." She shudders. "I hate rats. I think he expected me to eat them."

Rose is back, listening from the doorway. She reaches out. *Have they given you anything you can use to track these monsters down?*

I can't answer. Rebecca's words have sparked a flash of—what? My brain wrestles with an image. It's blurred, like a picture through an unfocused camera lens. I concentrate harder.

An abandoned building.

Rats.

A man with something in his hand.

"Rebecca, how did Jason drug you?"

She shakes her head. "He shot me with something. It looked like a crossbow but it was smaller."

My heart begins to race.

I saw it.

I saw it all.

In a dream.

# CHAPTER 32

A DREAM. HOW IS SUCH A THING POSSIBLE?
Rose is watching me. *What's wrong?*

I can't answer. I don't know what to say. It's crazy. How could I have dreamed what Rebecca just described? I try to dredge up images from the dream but all that's left are impressions. Fear. Confusion.

I bury what I'm thinking deep in my subconscious.

To Rose, *I think I'd better go. I'll start a search for this Jason character. He's the only real connection I have right now to the one who did this.*

I face the girls. "You're safe here. Rose will take care of you. I'll be back when I have news."

Rebecca's eyes burn with questions I can't answer. Yet. I hurry out before she can give voice to them. There are four new human hosts standing just outside the bedroom and Rose calls them in. At least I can leave knowing the girls are in good hands.

Williams is still at Brooke's when I call. I tell him I may

have a lead. He agrees to meet me at the cottage in two hours. I head straight there.

A shower. Cold this time, to clear away the cobwebs and try to make sense of a senseless notion. I saw what happened to Rebecca in a dream? Crazy. There's another explanation. There has to be.

I can't think of any. I'm as confused when I step out of the shower as when I stepped in. The only thing that's changed is that my skin is puckered and blue-tinged from the cold. I wrap myself in a robe.

Coffee. I head downstairs. I'm filling the pot when I realize what I really want is a good stiff drink.

Fortified with a tumbler of good scotch and my laptop, I begin the search for Loren aka Jason Shelton. I google his name. The only thing that comes up is a reference to a company. Nelson Security Services.

That name was on the logo on the car in the warehouse parking lot. I click my way to their website.

Company policies, guidelines, testimonials from satisfied customers.

Pictures. A group shot in front of the company office. One of the guards in particular catches my eye.

A flash of recognition.

Clear now. But disturbing in its implication.

The guard with the dog at the warehouse was the man in my dream.

And that man was Jason.

But a vampire?

I got no such vibe from him. I got nothing except an impression of hostility and ugliness—that he was a mean son of a bitch. But a human one.

When Williams arrives, my head is swimming with confusion and fuzzy from the scotch. I keep both to myself, preferring to adopt a matter-of-fact attitude as I fill him in on the condition of the vampires at the safe house and what they told me. That Burke's bodyguard was the one who tortured them. That I have no doubt that the security guard, Jason, was the one who set the explosives that blew the place up. Since he's an employee of a company listed in the Yellow Pages, I figure that would be the logical place to start looking for him.

I don't mention that he's a vampire or that he was the one who found the girls and turned them.

Or the dream.

I don't know why I don't tell him. Maybe the thought of another lecture on my ignorance is more than I can stand tonight.

I take another gulp of scotch. It burns in a good way, and a comforting burst of warmth radiates from the pit of my stomach. I cradle the glass against my cheek. Scotch was a much better choice than coffee. I'm not feeling nearly as anxious.

Williams reaches over and takes the glass out of my hand.

"Hey. I need that."

"Tomorrow," he says in reply.

"Tomorrow?"

"You'll start looking for Jason tomorrow." He takes the glass to the sink and empties it. "You look beat. Making love to a bottle of scotch isn't going to help. Sleep is going to help. Go to bed. I'll work on finding Jason. And in the morning, we should have the analysis of that face cream."

He lets his voice drop off, but I pick up a feeling that he's guarding something from me much the same way I'm guarding my uncertainty from him. What comes through is Ortiz, his sorrow at his loss. The sensation is gone in a heartbeat but it sobers me.

"What do you think Burke was doing with the blood she was collecting from the vampires?" I ask after a minute.

"If I was to guess? The blood is an ingredient in her cream."

I close my eyes for a minute, processing the idea, repulsed by it. "How? For what purpose?"

"It's an antiaging cream." His tone is abrupt, accusatory. "Women will go to any lengths to recapture youth. Burke found a way to capitalize on that compulsion."

His indictment of all females should spark an argument. Tonight it only sparks a weary sigh.

"How would it work? Have you ever heard of vampire blood being used to enhance a human product?"

"No. I've never heard of a topical application of vampire blood having any power. That's not to say it doesn't." He stands up. "We'll know tomorrow. Now get some sleep. I've arranged for one of our security patrols to—"

"Security patrol? What for?"

He casts a glance toward the bottle. "To make sure you have a tomorrow. Burke may be having you watched. If she is, she'll know how you spent your afternoon. She's bound to be pissed you got those girls out of that warehouse. I would have suggested you sleep somewhere else tonight, but you're never inclined to take my suggestions. I did the next best thing."

For once, I don't argue, object or balk at what he's saying. Truth is, I never gave a thought that Burke might come after me directly. She seemed to be having too much fun watching me dance. But saving those girls may have ratcheted the stakes up a notch.

"Culebra."

It's all I say. Williams shakes his head. "I'll check in with Sandra. If there's any change, I'll let you know."

I walk him to the door, close it, lock it and trudge upstairs.

Now drinking all that scotch doesn't seem like the good idea it was earlier. My brain is fuzzy, my limbs heavy. I eye the bed, still unmade. The scotch and lack of sleep make that detail as unimportant as the fear I should be feeling that any minute Burke might strike.

For once I hope Williams was telling the truth about assigning a security patrol. Idly, I wonder if will be composed of vampires or some other supernatural member of the Watchers. The one thing I am sure of is it will be no ordinary security patrol.

I shed my clothes, grab up a blanket and pillow and fall across the bare mattress. My last thought before I drift off is how my conversation with Williams tonight is the only one in a long time that hasn't ended with our threatening to kill each other.

# CHAPTER 33

I T'S RAINING WHEN I WAKE UP WEDNESDAY MORN-
ing. I'm in bed listening to it beat against the windows
and the deck and wishing I could pull the covers up over
my head and go back to sleep.

Then I think about Culebra and those girls and I roll out
of my blanket cocoon and propel myself up.

The newspaper is on the front porch next to its plastic
sleeve. The exposed half of the paper is soggy and drips all
over the floor when I carry it in.

Shit.

I get it over to the kitchen counter and spread it out. Page
one headlines blare "Police Officer Killed. Fire at Cosmetics Company Warehouse Claims Life." Piecing together the
story from rain-soaked newsprint, there isn't much to learn
that I don't already know. The article says the warehouse
was destroyed along with all the product being prepared
for next week's gala launch of Eternal Youth, the heralded
new antiaging cream. An unidentified spokesperson for the

company issued a statement saying how devastated they are about the fate of policeman Mario Ortiz, who died a hero when he entered the building to make sure no one was inside. Their condolences go to his family. Second Chance management plans to have the factory back up and running in the next few months.

Not happening.

Simone Tremaine, president and CEO of Second Chance, was not available for comment.

I'll bet. Burke has gone to ground.

I tap a fingernail against the paper. The article claims all the product was destroyed in the fire. I saw *something* being loaded into trucks when I arrived at the warehouse on Monday. And there was nothing at all on the conveyor belts just before the fire broke out. Burke stockpiled her precious cream before she had the place torched.

Not that she's going to have a chance to sell it. I'll make sure of that.

Williams calls just as I'm about to step into the shower.

"I got the product analysis back," he says.

"And?"

"A lot of stuff with chemical names I can't pronounce along with one I can. Animal glycoprotein."

"Animal glycoprotein? What the hell is that?"

"Vampire blood."

"*Animal* glycoprotein? How can that be *vampire* blood?"

Williams pauses a long moment before he says, "You seem unable or unwilling to accept the fact that we are no longer human, Anna."

His words send a tremor through me. "I am not an animal."

He waits even longer this time to respond. "And you are not human, either," he says at last. "But this is not the time for debate. The point is, she was using vampire blood in her cream."

"Where would she get an idea like that? Didn't you say you'd never heard of vampire blood having any topical application?"

"I also remember saying just because I hadn't heard of it didn't mean it might not be possible. We now know it is. The extraordinary results she was getting must have been due to the infusion of vampire blood. It has to be. The remaining ingredients in the cream are found in every commercial product on the market."

I get another shiver of disgust. Explains the smell I detected—raw meat.

Williams continues, "I also found out from an associate that Burke seems to have disappeared. He said *Simone Tremaine* has disappeared and I didn't correct him. The PR rep for Second Chance has no idea where she is. The fire is being investigated as suspicious, possibly an insurance scam, though the same rep swears the cream is legit. They claim they lost everything in the fire, including formulas and the names of test subjects."

Not everything. I saw those trucks. To Williams, I reply, "Convenient, that. What about the security guard?"

"No record. He's an employee of Nelson, has been for several years."

"Then I'll be paying them a visit."

Williams releases a breath. "I wish I could go with you, but my place is with Brooke."

Certainly out of character for Williams, placing concern for a human over his own desires, but I'm not going to argue the point. I don't want to spark more animosity between us.

A bit of the conversation I had with Gloria flashes into my head. "Is it true cosmetics are not regulated by the FDA?" I ask.

Williams launches into cop-speak. "The FDA's legal authority over cosmetics is different from other products regulated by the agency. There's no premarket approval process. The exception is color additives."

"Great. You can use blood but not red dye."

"Not really. Burke took a huge chance. Maybe she realized it."

"And had the place burned to the ground."

"Odd, considering the success she seemed to be having with the cream."

Maybe not. Something obviously went wrong. Like the fact that the test subjects were attacking people. Or maybe it was my involvement. Still, she's got a fleet of semis full of the stuff *somewhere*. Perhaps Jason can shed some light on that.

There doesn't seem to be anything else to say. I ring off, promising to call Williams as soon as I've had my talk with Jason Shelton.

BY THE TIME I HIT THE ROAD, THE RAIN HAS LET UP, but clouds still hang heavy over the beach, blurring the line between sea and sky. As usual, the commute is a bitch. Southern California drivers don't make exceptions for road conditions. They forge ahead at well over the legal speed limit, figuring if they ignore the standing water on the freeway, it can't hurt them. Unfortunately, I'm forced to slow to a crawl twice on my way to the Nelson Security office because some jackass in an SUV hydroplaned himself into an accident.

It's always an SUV.

By the time I get to the address listed for Nelson Security, I'm a coiled spring of aggravation. I've experienced enough shock, horror and frustration the last couple of days to be wound so tight, I can't wait to come face to face with Jason Shelton.

I'm ready to kick some vampire ass.

# CHAPTER 34

NELSON SECURITY HAS ITS MAIN OFFICE LO-
cated in a strip mall in Chula Vista. Not a particularly nice office in a not-so-nice neighborhood. Two Hispanic teens in baggy jeans and dizzyingly white T-shirts
lounge in front of the 7-Eleven next door. They eye me first,
but it's my car that holds their attention. And not in the car-
enthusiast kind of way, but the wondering-what-they-can-
get-for-it-from-the-neighborhood-chop-shop kind of way.
I've seen the look before.

I make a point of sounding the beep on the Jag's remote. I have a state-of-the-art alarm system. Not that it did
me any good when a pack of werewolves attacked it a few
months ago. These guys don't look like werewolves. And I
can keep an eye out through the window while I'm inside.

There's no one behind the reception counter when I
walk in. There is a two-way mirror behind it.

Shit. Let's hope I can keep the attention of whoever

comes out to greet me before he or she notices I'm casting no reflection.

And wouldn't it be nice if that someone was Jason Shelton.

No such luck.

A woman pushes through a door to the right of the desk. She's about thirty, a little thick through the middle but with the biggest breasts I've ever seen. They strain at the buttons of a pink cotton blouse like two overripe melons. It's hard to keep my eyes off them, but I force myself to look up, noting that she has beautiful green eyes and a great smile. I doubt many men have ever noticed, either.

"Good morning," she says. "How can I help you?"

"I'm looking for an employee of yours. Jason Shelton."

She sniffs. "Welcome to the club."

The reply raises my eyebrows. "He doesn't work here anymore?"

"Good question. He never quit, just hasn't shown up for work for the last two weeks."

"Great." I let a whine of irritation creep in. "And his phone has been disconnected. He's my cousin. He invited me to stay with him for a few days but this is the only address he gave me. Shit. My place is being fumigated. I can't believe he forgot."

She raises a shoulder. "Sorry, I can't help."

I blow out a breath. "How about giving me his home address? Maybe he hasn't left town, just got a new job. It really isn't like him to walk out without giving notice. I could tell him he needs to get in touch with you."

She eyes me. "We *are* a security company. We don't give out employee's personal information."

Okay, lie number one didn't work. I blow out an exasperated breath and reach into my jacket. I pull out a small leather wallet and flash a badge—quickly.

"Okay, I'll be honest with you. My name is Cordelia Case. I'm an undercover cop working a robbery detail."

I repocket the badge before she gets a good look at it. Otherwise, she'd see it was a tin sheriff's badge I'd picked up in Deadwood on vacation three years ago. David and I have used it in our work. No one yet has looked at it closely enough to realize it's a fake.

Green eyes, here, is no different. However, her expression does change from suspicion to concern. "You think Jason—?"

"We *suspect* Shelton is involved in a series of burglaries. Most of the houses involved belong to your clients. The robberies started two weeks ago. About the time you say he stopped showing up for work. The address we have for him belongs to his dead mother. We're hoping you'll be willing to cooperate. Save your company the embarrassment of being implicated."

She raises an eyebrow. "We haven't had any reports of burglaries."

Smart cookie. "We've encouraged the victims to keep it quiet. When our investigation is over, you'll be given full credit for cooperation. And exonerated from any hint of complicity." A pause. "Of course, you have to swear you won't mention this to anyone until we have Jason in custody."

She fixes me with a steely gaze that makes me think she may ask to see the badge again "Not even my boss?"

"Especially not your boss." I lean over the counter and lower my voice. "He's not out of the woods yet himself."

Her eyes widen. Then abruptly, she turns away from me and heads for the desk.

I barely have time to dive below counter level, out of mirror range. I fumble with my shoelaces until I hear her once more at the counter. When I straighten up, she's walking her fingers through a Rolodex. She pulls out a card and hands it to me.

"This is the address we have for Jason. You're sure we'll get exonerated when Jason is arrested? My boss will kill me if I keep this from him and something goes wrong."

I raise my right hand. "You have my word."

Now to get out of here before she thinks too long about my story or turns around and glances in that mirror.

I'm almost at the door when she calls out for me to stop. I freeze.

Shit.

I swivel to face her, prepared to bolt.

But she's looking at me, not at the mirror. "When you arrest Jason," she says, "think you can get him to return the magnetic car signs? Those things cost us fifty bucks a piece."

"Absolutely."

Back in the car, I release a long breath and take a look at the card. The address is here in Chula Vista, but at the other end of town. Since the streets are still slick with rain, I forgo the freeway and take surface roads. Might take me a little longer to get there, but I don't need any more frustration.

Jason's address is an apartment complex on H Street right on the boundary between Chula Vista and unincorporated San Diego County. It's close to the freeway and there's the constant drone of fast-moving traffic in the background. With the rain, the sound is muted and rhythmic, almost like the sound of the ocean at my place.

That's the only romantic illusion. The place is a dump. Reminds me of the apartment Trish lived in with her mother. Could have been built by the same developer. The building is squat, two-storied, flat-roofed. The place is in bad need of a paint job. Asphalt tiles curl like withered leaves exposing the tar paper roof underneath. I wouldn't be surprised if residents in that top floor aren't scurrying around to find pots to catch the leaks.

Jason's apartment is on the ground floor. I pick my way through a courtyard littered with broken bottles and fast-food containers. His door sports an unpainted patch, as if someone kicked it in and nailing up a square of rough plywood was the extent of the repair work. Fits though. Anything else might have spoiled the trashy ambience of the place.

I stop outside the door and listen. First I hear music, both the volume and type of which surprises me. It's soft jazz, played at a softer level. I would have expected something along the lines of heavy metal played at an ear-splitting decibel.

Then I hear voices—two. Male and female. The man is being gently persuasive. It takes me a second to realize what he's being persuasive about.

When I do, I put my shoulder to the door and burst through.

# CHAPTER 35

JASON SHELTON'S VAMPIRE FACE IS UNLIKE ANY I'VE seen. The pupils of his eyes haven't turned catlike the way mine do, but cornea and sclera blend together so there's no white at all. It's like looking into black marbles. He has two needlelike fangs that descend past his lower lip. He's clutching something in his right hand. His face looks normal except for the fangs and strange eyes.

We stare at each other for a moment, he looks as shocked by my appearance as I am by his.

The only light in the room is streaming in from the broken door. Heavy black-out drapes cover the window. We appear to be in a living room, though the only pieces of furniture are a bed and a dresser. The music comes from a radio perched on that dresser. Next to a half dozen condoms.

Condoms? Since when do vampires use condoms?

The smell of sex is strong.

"Jason Shelton?" I ask.

That galvanizes him into action. He lets something drop to the floor and scuttles over the bed like a crab.

"What are you?" he rasps by way of answer.

What am *I*?

I reach down and pick up the thing he'd dropped. It's a capped syringe filled with a pale gold liquid.

Is this the way he'd subdued the girls after he turned them? Am I too late to save this one?

The girl I'd heard through the door has backed herself into a corner. She's naked and her small, emaciated body looks frail in the dim light of the room.

I face Jason, send out a probe. *Let the girl go.*

There's no response. Just a wild-eyed, creepy stare out of those onyx eyes.

*If you let the girl go, I won't hurt you.*

Not exactly a lie. I'm not sure what kind of monster he is, but I don't intend to hurt him. Exactly. I intend to kill him when I get the information I need.

Still, no response. Nothing. Just like with the girls at the safe house, there's no psychic connection.

"Let the girl go."

That provokes a reaction. Jason reaches out and the girl rushes to him. He grabs her arm. She yelps as he pulls her close. "I asked you what you are."

The girl finds her own voice. "Kill it, Jason," she screams. "You're a vampire. Kill it."

Kill *it*? If I wasn't so angry, I might find the situation funny. I take two steps. Jason pulls the girl closer, shielding his own body with hers.

"Nice move, Jason. Very brave." I grab his fingers and bend them back until he releases the girl. I spin her away from him. "Get your clothes on and get out."

She plants herself in front of me. "No. I want to be a vampire. Jason said—"

I smack her across the face with the palm of my hand. "It's not life he's offering you," I snarl. "Now get out."

She backs away, rubbing her cheek but still not making a move toward the pile of clothes at the foot of the bed. Maybe if I scare her enough, she'll get the idea.

I reach out and grab Jason by the neck, lifting him off his feet. I bite his cheek, tearing a piece of flesh from the bone and spitting it back at him.

Jason is screaming and clutching at my hands with his own. I turn toward the girl, show her the beast, let her see and feel the full fury of my anger.

That gets her moving. She grabs her clothes and runs out.

I would have let her get dressed.

Now that she's gone, I turn my attention to Jason.

"Where is Simone Tremaine?"

He gasps and continues to snatch at my hands, finally croaking, "I don't know who you're talking about."

I put my face close to his, lap at the blood on his ruined cheek. Whisper, "Think about it, Jason. The woman you've been turning girls for. The woman who bleeds them to death. Where is she?"

I release my grip on his neck enough to allow him to speak.

"Where is she?"

"I don't know."

"Wrong answer. Guess I have to use a little more persuasion. You like to fuck?" I tighten my hold on his neck with one hand and grab his balls with the other. They're slick with sweat and sticky with the girl's sex. I can barely restrain a gag reflex.

But I manage. My fingers tighten and squeeze. "Better think fast, Jason."

Jason flies into a full-blown panic. His legs flail, his face reddens and his breath comes in short, rasping gasps.

And I'm not even squeezing hard yet.

"Please. Stop."

The hammering of his heart thunders in my ears. I'm afraid he's going to have a heart attack. Reluctantly, I relent.

I release him and he falls to the floor, curling into a fetal position, using one hand to cover his head and the other his genitals. I give him a second to catch his breath, then haul his ass up and throw him on the bed.

"I'm not going to waste any more time with you. Get your pants on. We're going to see a friend of mine. Between us, I'm sure we'll find a way to loosen your tongue."

Jason looks up at me but makes no move to get up.

"Did you hear me? I said get dressed."

His eyes have morphed back into a human's and his fangs retracted until they no longer peek through his lips. The expression on his face is pure terror. "I can't go outside."

"You can and will." I grab his arm, give it a shake. "Unless you want me to carry you out naked and throw you into the trunk of my car, you'll get moving now."

"I can't." He pulls away and scoots himself back until he's huddled against the headboard. "I'm a vampire."

"I don't know what you are," I say. "But if it's vampire, you can and will go outside. One way or the other."

His eyes dart to the door. "The sun. I can't go outside from sunrise to sunset."

"Get with the program, moron. Vampires adapted to the sun centuries ago." I pull the curtains back. The rain has stopped and a weak sun peaks through storm-tossed clouds. I hold out my hand and expose it to the light. "See? No problem. Now quit stalling."

He makes no move to comply. I'm done fucking around. I reach across the bed and yank him to his feet. "Don't say I didn't give you the chance to ride in front."

He struggles against me, but his strength is no match for my own. I snatch up a pair of jeans from a nearby chair and thrust them at him. "You can put these on in the trunk."

He's yelling at me to stop, but I ignore him. I'll take him to the park and work on him there. I'll bring Williams the syringe. Maybe if he has that analyzed, it will be a clue to Burke's whereabouts.

At the doorway, I give Jason a shove that propels him through the door and into the daylight.

He stumbles once, and turns toward me. His hands fly to his face, letting the jeans fall. His eyes have turned again. It's the last thing I notice before his body explodes like a camera flash in a burst of white-hot light.

# CHAPTER 36

THE SMELL OF SULFUR DRIFTS ON A GUST OF WIND. A smell and a pile of ash. It's all that's left of Jason Shelton.

Reflexively, I jump back. Even seeing what happened, I can't wrap my head around it. I stare at the crumpled pair of jeans that a moment ago was clutched in Jason's hands.

Jason *said* he was a vampire. Yet I had no connection with him psychically. He was certainly not as strong as any other vampire I've come in contact with. The girls he turned for Burke seem to have no powers, either. Now this. Will the same thing happen to them if they step into the sun?

God. I'd better warn Rose.

I step gingerly around the spot where Jason stood. I'd have killed him in a heartbeat once I got Burke's whereabouts from him. But this is the second vampire immolation I've seen in two days. Ortiz' death was horrible enough but I understood it. This is completely beyond my comprehension.

My hand shakes when I try to fit the key in the Jag's ignition. I don't know whether to call Rose or Williams first. I do decide to wait until I'm away from the apartment to do it. I pull over on a side street a mile away.

The sight of Jason spontaneously combusting the moment he stepped into daylight has my heart pounding.

What was he? A vampire subspecies?

I pull the paper Williams gave me yesterday with Rose's address on it. He'd also jotted a phone number and I punch it into my cell phone. Rose picks up on the second ring. Her "hello" resonates with worry and ratchets my own anxiety up a notch.

"Rose, this is Anna. What's wrong?"

Her voice is shaking. "I don't know what's happening. They're dying, Anna. Three this morning. I thought they were all getting stronger."

"Which three?" I'm thinking of Rebecca and how she clutched at my hand.

"Three of the weaker. We had a steady supply of hosts for them. They were feeding. But something happened. They grew weaker instead of stronger. Then, this morning, they started dying."

A picture of Jason bursting into flame flashes through my head. "How, Rose? How did they die?"

Rose's breath catches. "I don't know. They were feeding. Then they just stopped. It was as if their hearts gave out. They were alive one minute and dead the next. I've never seen anything like it."

Different from Jason. Because they weren't exposed directly to sunlight? I remember the room and the large windows.

"I'll come over. But I have to talk to Williams first. Rose, don't let them go outside. And keep the curtains pulled. Better yet, take them all to the back room."

"Why?"

"They're not like us. I don't know why, but they can't be exposed to daylight."

"That makes no sense." But her tone is halting.

"Trust me. None of this makes sense. Just please, keep it dark."

She draws a quick, sharp breath. "God, Anna. The curtains are open now. The ones who died were in the living room—closest to the windows."

She clicks off without saying good-bye.

I don't have to guess why.


WILLIAMS IS UNCHARACTERISTICALLY QUIET WHEN I call him next to fill him in on the events of the morning. He has no explanation for what happened to Jason or how daylight could have affected the girls who died. I tell him about the syringe I found in Jason's apartment.

Maybe whatever Jason used to sedate the girls after he changed them is the reason for their weaknesses. Williams agrees to meet me at the park. He's with Brooke now but says he can be there within fifteen minutes. I ask him to have the witches try another locator spell, and he says that he will. With Ortiz' death, he never got around to asking them yesterday. His voice is heavy with guilt.

I should care that he forgot. Should rail at him for forgetting Culebra. But he had other things on his mind.

Ortiz.

A rare moment of compassion stills my tongue and I hang up without rancor.

I've never felt so helpless. It's been three days since Culebra fell under Burke's curse. I'm afraid to call Frey for an update. He's put his life on hold and his own health at risk. If I don't come up with something fast, I may lose two friends.

Williams is at the elevator when I step out. The bank of

telephone operators that occupies the center of the supernatural command center is bustling with activity. The tele-
phones are manned by an army of psychics, real psychics,
extraordinary men and women possessing heightened sen-
sitivity to things outside the sphere of scientific knowledge.
Their clients include the power brokers of the world.

Today, however, I detect a different timbre to the buzz
of conversation. *What's going on?*

He steers me away from center. *I have our people working to locate Burke. If the witches can't find her, maybe
someone else can.*

He's set the psychics on Burke? His guilt that another
night may have brought Culebra that much closer to death
is showing. No matter. I'll take all the help I can get.

He pushes open a door to a side room. The same three
witches I met two days ago are assembled around the same
pentagram. A map is laid out and one of the women, Min
Liu, dangles that diamond on the end of the silken string.
As I watch, the diamond jumps and skitters across the map
but it fails to light on any particular location. Frustration is
painted on Min's face. The other two watch, each holding
a candle and chanting in low voices.

Susan Powers looks up when we enter. She touches the
young Hispanic woman's arm. Ariela Acosta motions us
in.

"It's not working, is it?" I ask.

Min lets the charm drop. "I'm sorry. The witch is pro-
tecting herself."

"She's put up a powerful blocking spell," Susan says.
"There is nothing we can do."

I sink into a chair and cover my face with my hands.

Culebra is fighting for his life.

Ortiz is dead.

It's my fault.

I should never have confronted the witch at the restaurant. It only alerted her to the fact that I was on to her. Now she's gone into hiding and I've exhausted any lead I might have had to find her.

There's a knock on the door. Williams answers it and a man hands him a slip of paper. He opens it, looks over at me and shakes his head.

Even his army of psychics has drawn a blank.

Weariness washes over me. I feel the anxiety and unhappiness of the three women standing nearby. Their empathy only heightens my own sense of futility.

I can't think of anything else to say. I pull the charm from inside my blouse. "You may as well have this back."

Min stays my hand with a touch of her own. "No. Keep it." Her eyes flash with determination. "Don't give up, Anna. We don't intend to."

Williams is watching, too, strangely silent.

These women don't know me, but he does. He understands how foreign this is to me.

For the first time in a long time I don't know what to do. No idea. No plan. No way to save Culebra.

Williams leaves me alone in the room while he escorts the witches out. Jason is gone. The file is gone. Burke is gone.

I wish once again that I had done things differently—made a copy of the test subjects' information instead of stealing the original file. That act set in motion all that followed, including Ortiz' death.

I have one last hope. Maybe Gloria has a contact number for Simone Tremaine.

But that hope is dashed when the operator at the Four Seasons tells me that Gloria has checked out—on her way to Europe for Fashion Week.

Gloria wasted no time coming up with alternative photo opportunities now that the launch party for Eternal Youth has been canceled.

Either that or she wants to distance herself, literally, from the fallout of an arson investigation.

Shit. Arson will be the least of Gloria's concerns if the cream is linked to the murder of those test subjects.

Williams comes back. His black mood matches my own, partly because of the helplessness we feel and partly because of the guilt. It puts us both on guard.

"How is Brooke doing?" I ask finally.

"Barely making it. I wish I could do more. Ortiz will be buried with full honors on Friday."

*Buried* is a euphemism. We both know there is nothing left of Ortiz to bury. I feel cold, suddenly, remembering.

"It's a good gesture. Ortiz deserves it."

My mind drifts back to Jason. I remember the syringe. I pull it out of a jacket pocket. "I don't know what this is. I think Jason was about to use it on the girl he had in his apartment. The girls at Rose's all said they'd been sedated. Maybe this stuff is the reason they're different."

Williams takes it from my outstretched hand. "I'll send it to the lab." He steps aside when I stand and start for the door. "What are you going to do now?"

The only thing left for me to do.

"I'm going to see Culebra. And Frey."

"What will you tell them?"

I close my eyes and turn away. I don't know what I'll tell them. I'm afraid it might be good-bye.

# CHAPTER 37

THE LINE AT THE BORDER CROSSING IS LONG. I'M stalled behind twenty cars waiting to be waved through.

I don't mind. I'm in no hurry.

I drum my fingertips against the steering wheel, replaying everything that's happened since Sandra's call Sunday night.

Every mistake. Every blunder. Every miscalculation.

Following Burke to that restaurant. Revealing myself to her.

Stupid mistake number one.

Breaking into the warehouse the first time. I could have copied every fucking file in the place. Why didn't I? Instead, I memorized useless information. Burke knew that I'd be looking for her. How could I have thought she'd hang around that house in Coronado waiting for me? Learning the names of her employees and those test subjects would have been far more valuable.

Stupid mistake number two.

A driver behind me honks. I restrain the urge to flip him off and roll a foot or so forward.

My head aches.

One hundred test subjects. Three dead. In all the confusion, I'd forgotten to ask Williams if he'd seen the coroner's reports. Maybe when I get back, I'll call him.

Maybe.

If Culebra dies, I won't really care what killed them.

The before-and-after shots of the three dead women flash through my brain like a slide show. The transformation was incredible. Vampire blood had that effect? I wonder if they'd have been as happy with the results if they'd known the price those young girls paid for their vanity. Twelve vampires dead. Would they have cared?

I mentally sift through everything I found in Burke's file—insurance forms, utility bills—there was something else, wasn't there?

I slam into reverse, forcing the guy behind me to back up. He's yelling and waving a fist at me, but I keep at him, pushing him back until I have room to make the U-turn.

When I pull out of line, I give him my sweetest smile and wave farewell.

I remember what else was in Burke's file. There was a telephone number. No name. No address. Just a number.

I'm driving with one hand on the wheel, the other rummaging through my purse.

Where is that damned cell phone?

My fingers finally close around it. I let the number float to the surface of my consciousness and punch it in. It rings once, twice, ten times. No answer. No machine.

Shit.

The next call I make is to Williams. I catch him on his way back to Brooke's.

"I just remembered something that was in Burke's personal file. Can you do a reverse search on a telephone number?" I ask. "Get me a name and an address?"

He doesn't question the request, just says, "What is it?"

I recite the number. "Will you call me as soon as you have the information?"

"Hang on." The line goes silent as he puts me on hold for nearly a minute. I'm starting to get angry when he clicks back on.

"It's a Denver number. Meet me at the airport."

"The airport? Why? Is it listed to Burke?"

"Just meet me there." Williams rings off.

A Denver number?

If it's a Denver number, maybe I'm wrong about its significance. Maybe it doesn't belong to Burke.

Maybe I'm wrong again.

I get back on the freeway and head west. Why would Williams want to meet me at the airport? He must have a reason. What isn't he telling me?

I call Frey's cell next.

The sound of his voice sends a tremor through me.

"My God, you sound terrible."

He manages a laugh. "You should see the way I look. Anna, where are you?"

I tell him, putting as much hopefulness as I can into a new development that may prove worthless.

He listens. Then he says, "Better make it fast. I've got maybe twenty-four hours."

"Twenty-four hours? Until what?"

Frey coughs once. Clears his throat. "Until I end up like Culebra. Or worse."

# CHAPTER 38

THE SAN DIEGO AIRPORT IS SMALL BY COMPARISON to other international airports. It does, however, have three terminals. I realize when I pull into the first that I didn't ask Williams where he would be.

When he picks up the call, I hear the whine of jet engines in stereo.

"Which terminal?"

"Where are you now?" he counters.

"In front of the commuter terminal."

"You'll have to get back to Pacific Coast Highway. I'm sorry I didn't make it clear in our last conversation. I'll meet you at Jimsair. The private terminal. Do you know where it is?"

I tell him that I do and ring off.

The private terminal? What is he doing there?

I park the Jag in the lot off Pacific Coast Highway and head for the terminal in back. Williams is waiting for me in the lounge. Unlike commercial terminals, there are no ticket counters or security checkpoints here. Just some comfortable chairs spaced around low tables. There is one person behind an information counter. He looks up and smiles when I come in, but turns away when Williams steps up to meet me. Through big plate-glass windows, I see a dozen private planes of various sizes and descriptions parked on the tarmac.

"What are we doing here?"

Williams leads me over to the corner, glancing back to the guy behind the desk. He has a folded piece of paper in his hand. "Before I give you this, I want you to agree to something. If Belinda Burke is at this address, you are to call me immediately. Don't go after her yourself."

He's whispering. Afraid of being overheard? The logical question then is, *Why are you speaking to me out loud?*

"Not important. Just promise me."

I can't get anything out of him psychically, either. "Okay. I promise. Where is she?"

He holds out the paper. "The number was traced to this address. It's listed to a Sophie Deveraux in Denver."

"Deveraux?" My insides churn with the sick feeling I'm chasing another dead end. "Not Burke? What makes you think there's any connection?"

"There might not be," he admits. "But I checked with one of the witches at headquarters. She says Burke has a sister. One who was active in the community until she dropped out of sight a few months ago. Her first name was Sophie. I've been calling the number for the last hour and there's still no answer. I hope this isn't a wild-goose chase."

For the first time in three days, though, I feel a flutter of optimism. If this Sophie isn't Burke's sister, why would her number be in her personal file? It's a place to start. Shit. It's the only new lead I've got.

Impatiently, I wave a hand. "What are we doing here? I should be on the other side, arranging a flight."

Williams raises a hand of his own. "That's being taken care of."

He looks toward the tarmac outside where a ground crew is bustling around one of the jets. His expression is conflicted. He's trying to hide it, but the truth is there in the frown, the set of his jaw, the feelings he thinks he's suppressed. He wants to come with me. Brooke is the reason he's not.

"How is Brooke?"

He shrugs. "She's coping. She's very young. I think things will be better after the funeral."

His voice drops off. He's not looking at me but watching what's going on outside.

I follow his gaze. The crew seems to have finished their preflight preparation. One of them signals to Williams. He nods and gestures me toward the door. "Go. I'll have someone waiting for you when you land. He's one of us and he's lived in Denver for a hundred years. He'll get you where you need to go."

I glance out of the window. "In that? How did you arrange it?"

His answer is to walk me out onto the tarmac, toward a jet whose engines have roared into life. He acts like the noise is preventing him from answering, like we have only one mode of communication.

He's avoiding the question.

The plane we approach is a Learjet. Not so small now that I'm standing beside it. The cabin door opens and a man at the top of a short flight of stairs beckons me on board.

Williams makes a "go along" gesture and mouths, "Safe trip."

But just as I start to walk away, he lays a hand on my arm. Not a tight grip, just a restraining one. *Remember, I want Burke. Don't cross me on this, Anna. I have a score to settle now, too.*

His eyes are hard, threatening.

That's the Williams I'm used to. I shrug out of his grasp and climb up the stairs. When I turn around at the door, Williams is already gone.

The guy who greeted me introduces himself as the pilot. He's about fifty, tall, well built, gray-haired. He's wearing a typical pilot's uniform—but his coat and cap each carry an emblem I don't recognize. Maybe a coat of arms. His name badge reads "Tom Lawson." He has an air of quiet competence and he's human. He instructs me in a few safety measures and disappears into the cockpit. The whine of engines gets louder. I settle into my seat, buckle in and look around.

I've never been in a private jet. Six big, oversized seats in beige leather occupy the main cabin with a bar stretching along the back. Thick carpeting underfoot. Luxurious. To the right of the bar is a closed door. Bathroom maybe?

The jet crouches on the runway, waiting for our turn to take off. After a few minutes, another guy appears in the doorway, wearing the same uniform. He looks to be midthirties, shorter than Tom, with dark hair and eyes. He holds out a hand.

"Sorry for the delay, Ms. Strong. I'm Jeff Shelby, the co-pilot. The captain sent me back to let you know we should be on our way in ten minutes."

We shake hands and he turns to go.

"Wait a minute. I'm curious, does this plane belong to Mr. Williams?"

He turns back, a puzzled frown on his face. "I don't understand. This used to be Dr. Avery's plane. Mr. Williams said it belongs to you now."

A snicker. "Of course it does."

But Shelby is not smiling.

The jet belongs to me? Why am I surprised? Just another of Avery's toys. No wonder Williams disappeared so quickly. He wanted to be out of meltdown range when I found out.

"Is there anything else?"

I shake my head and he withdraws into the cockpit. I settle my head back on the seat.

Since becoming vampire, Avery has been a constant intrusion in my life. Every time I think I've divested myself of his damned legacy, something else turns up. But the truth is, at this moment, I'm happy to have the plane. The sooner I get to Denver and track down this—I dig the paper out of my jacket and look for the name—this Sophie Deveraux—the sooner I can come back and help Culebra and Frey.

A voice crackles over the intercom. "We're up next, Ms. Strong. We'll be in the air in about five minutes. Flight time to Denver is estimated two hours and thirty minutes. Sit back, buckle up and enjoy the ride."

The plane rolls into takeoff position. I watch through the window, dread churning my stomach.

Enjoy the ride?

Not with only twenty-four hours to save my friends.

# CHAPTER 39

A SMALL JET LEAPS RATHER THAN LUMBERS INTO the sky. It's a strange feeling. I watch the earth and sea fade away through a break in the clouds as the plane banks to the east. Then we're swallowed up once more and all I see is a blanket of white. In another few minutes we're above the clouds and the sky is flawless and brilliant.

The intercom buzzes to life. "We're at cruising altitude, Ms. Strong. Feel free to move about the cabin. There is water and liquor in the bar. If you need anything else, press the button on your armrest and we'll be back to assist you. We'll let you know when we're fifteen minutes out of Denver."

A click and I'm left to my own devices.

May as well explore. I head for the bar. It's fully stocked all right, with high-end liquor and several good imported beers. There's also a wine rack. I pull out a bottle. The label bears the same coat of arms as the patch on "my" crew's uniforms. It's Avery's coat of arms. Here, too, on the label of the bottles from the winery my family "inherited."

I push the bottle back onto the rack. I'm not ready to let that genie out of its elegant cabernet decanter.

It's interesting that the pilot mentioned water and liquor in the bar but nothing about food. And there isn't any. Not even a bag of peanuts. I guess any pilot of Avery's would know his boss wasn't human. After all, his housekeeper at the mansion had been a host. Maybe the two at the control are, too. Makes me wonder if I buzz, how much assistance they're willing to give.

I open the door at the back of the cabin. There's a bathroom, with shower, along with a small bedroom with queen-sized bed, built-in credenza and closet. There's even a vanity, although instead of a mirror, an oil painting hangs in a recessed alcove. Like the bar, everything is made out of a fine-grained, honey-hued wood. Teak? It reminds me of something you'd find in a luxury yacht.

Maybe I own one of those, too.

I eye the bed, thinking perhaps I should stretch out on that silk damask spread and close my eyes.

How many women did Avery have in that bed?

Does Avery's smell still cling to the bedclothes?

The thought propels me back into the main cabin. I close the door behind me.

I've just settled into my seat when Shelby reappears. He points to a telephone on the console. "Mr. Williams is calling."

He waits for me to pick up before returning to the cockpit.

"Hello?"

Williams doesn't speak right away. Waiting for me to yell at him, I suppose.

Like it would do any good.

When I remain silent and don't launch into a tirade, he jumps in. "Got some more information on the cream. Further analysis showed the blood in the cream is breaking down rapidly. It's doubtful that the cream could remain potent long enough to achieve those remarkable results for more than a couple of weeks."

Perfect to assure repeat customers. And to necessitate a steady stream of vampire donors.

Williams continues, "No official COD yet for Burke's three test subjects. The wounds they sustained were critical but not necessarily fatal. It might take up to two weeks to get complete tox screens back."

"Any other attacks reported?"

Another brief hesitation. I can imagine the relief he must be feeling that I'm sticking to business. I glance around the plane. There'll be time later to pursue this flying palace.

"No," he says. "It may be that with the declining potency of the cream, the other effects wear off as well. If the two are related."

"What are the odds that they aren't? What about that syringe?"

"Nothing. Preliminary results ruled out most common narcotics. Identifying the compound is going to take time."

There's a pause, then he adds, "There will be a car waiting for you at the airport in Denver. The person meeting you will be of assistance if you come up against Burke or any of her followers. Locate Burke as soon as you can and get back to me. I have a plane of my own standing by. I can be there in two hours. We will do this together. Remember—I intend to be in on the kill."

I mouth the right words, tell him I understand and will wait.

It gets him off the phone.

I replace the receiver and cross to the bar. I choose a thirty-year-old scotch, pour two fingers into a glass, add a couple of ice cubes. The liquor burns my throat and hardens my resolve.

I take the little .38 I'd clipped to my belt this morning and lay it on the bar. Williams can remind me that he and I are in this together, that he has as compelling a reason to want Burke dead as I do, that Ortiz was his friend, not mine.

And he'd be right.

It doesn't matter.

The simple truth is if I get Burke in my sights, there's no fucking way I'm going to wait.

The drink both relaxes and settles me. Since Culebra's black-magic illness, I've had little time to think through a course of action. Explains the blunders. This time I plan to be ready for any contingency.

Best-case scenario? I arrive at the address and spy Burke through a window. One shot through the forehead should do it.

Wonderful fantasy. Probably won't happen. I have no reason to believe she'd go into hiding with, or running to, her sister. What would she be running from? Up to this point, I've proven to be nothing more than an inconvenience.

What if Burke has donned a new persona? What if she and this Sophie are the same person? My fingers touch the charm nestled between my breasts. I'm glad my witch friends insisted I keep it. This little beauty will identify the bitch no matter how she's cloaked herself.

I let my head rest against the back of the seat and close my eyes. How did Burke come up with the idea of using vamp blood in a cosmetic? However it happened, that such a bizarre notion would appeal to her is not surprising. She's sadistic and cruel. Where did she find Jason? What exactly was he? He was still attempting to turn others when I found him yesterday at his apartment. Had he been in contact with Burke? Had she set up another factory from hell somewhere? Or is it in his nature to turn others, a biological imperative of his species—whatever the hell it is.

Questions I may never get answered. Questions I *hope* I don't get answered. I don't want to have a discussion with Burke. I want to kill her.

I glance at my watch. The pilot said flying time would be two and a half hours. We've been in the air for forty-five minutes.

The sky outside my window is cloudless. When I glance down, I see the beginnings of a mountain range, white-capped and rugged. The Rocky Mountains? They look cold.

Give me the beach anytime.

My thoughts turn inward once more—to Burke's test subjects. What's going to happen to them? Williams said the effectiveness of the stuff breaks down with the blood. According to the file on the test subjects, most of the women had been using the cream for two months. Will the women return to their former middle-aged dowdy selves when the effects wear off? Are there more sinister side effects? Could the three who developed a taste for blood be reacting to a withdrawal symptom? Maybe the craving is brought on by the cream losing its potency. Is that why they were killed? Will more bodies show up?

Christ, Burke, what have you done?

The intercom crackles on, alerting me that we are beginning our descent into Denver's Centennial Airport. I'd been through Denver once before on a job with David. We'd landed at Denver International, not Centennial. Maybe this is closer to where I'm headed. I seem to remember DIA being forty minutes or so from the city.

If it gets me to Burke quicker, I don't care where we land.

# CHAPTER 40

THE JET CRUISES TO A STOP IN FRONT OF A LARGE hangar with the logo XJet. There's a limo parked to the side of the hangar, and a man stands beside it watching our approach. I assume this is Williams' friend.

When the engines have shut down, Shelby comes back to open the airstair door. "I see you have a car waiting."

I precede him down the short set of steps. We're being buffeted by a cold wind blowing, I presume, off the white-capped mountains to the west.

To the west. Even the mountains are in the wrong place here.

At the bottom, an XJet employee in jeans, a long-sleeved blue shirt and a Windbreaker welcomes me to Denver. He addresses me by name and with a defer-ence I'm not used to. Avery must have paid well for that obsequiousness.

Shelby hands me a card. "Tom and I have rooms at the Clarion right down the street. Here is my cell number.

When you're ready to leave, call. We'll make sure the jet is ready whenever you are."

At the same time he's telling me this, I hear the limo engine crank up.

A private jet and a limo waiting at the airstrip—maybe I've been too hasty in refusing every perk of Avery's inheritance.

The limo pulls alongside the jet. The back door opens and the guy I saw watching a moment before steps out. He's handsome, young and, as Williams mentioned, vampire. Which means although he looks twenty-five, he could be hundreds of years old. Lawson has joined Shelby at the foot of the stairs and the guy greets them in a way that makes it obvious he's met them before. It also puts me on alert that if he was a friend of Avery's he may not be a friend of mine.

When the social niceties have been observed, he turns his attention to me. "Pleased to meet you, Ms. Strong. I'm Joshua Turnbull."

With his slight southern accent, the name fits. He is making no attempt to probe my thoughts, allowing me to be frank in my appraisal. He is just under six feet, a little thicker through the middle than most vampires I've met. He has blond hair and blue eyes. He's dressed in jeans, a long-sleeved cotton shirt and a denim jacket. He's wearing well-worn boots with a stacked heel and a leather belt with a silver belt buckle. He looks like a cowboy. All that's missing is a pair of six-shooters on his hip.

Since I figure he's sizing me up, too, I let a moment go by before motioning to the car. "Shall we go?"

His smile is neither overly friendly nor solicitous. Still don't know if he's friend or foe. Doesn't matter. I need him for only one thing.

We get into the car. On the backseat there's a tan Stetson. Turnbull picks it up and places it on the seat opposite us, sliding in beside me. The hat adds to the impression that he's a cowboy, though I've never spent any time in Denver. Maybe everybody here wears cowboy hats.

We don't speak until the car has left the airport. "The driver has the address?" I ask then, itchy to get on with it.

"Yes. The address is in Cherry Hills. Very upscale. We might have trouble getting past security."

I look away, suppress a smile. *We* might have trouble getting past security? *I* don't intend to have any trouble at all.

Turnbull snatches the thought out of the air. He smiles, too. *Williams said you were a bit of a hothead.*

I turn back to Turnbull and frown. Good old Williams. Instead of the Williams-can-blow-himself reply I'd like to make, I say instead, *I'm not a hothead. What I am is determined. You'd know that if he told you why I'm here.*

He nods. *I understand you have a personal stake in finding this woman.*

*Not as personal as my friend who is near death because of her. And she's not a woman. She's a witch. It's important you don't forget that.*

He's projecting a smug cockiness that feels a lot like male chauvinism. He's making a big mistake if he thinks he can control the situation. I have only one reason for being here. Find out everything I can from Sophie Deveraux. As far as I'm concerned, Turnbull's only function is as a vampire GPS system. That's it.

Turnbull is watching me, sifting through the thoughts I've purposefully left unguarded. After a moment, he looks away. He's not happy to be here.

So why is he?

To repay a debt to Williams? Or to keep an eye on me?


TURNBULL WAS NOT EXAGGERATING WHEN HE SAID Cherry Hills was upscale. There is a ten-foot stone wall stretching as far as I can see with a guardhouse at the entrance. Over the top of the fence peek the rooflines of two huge homes.

Turnbull raises an eyebrow. *I hope you have a plan B.*

We pull up to the gate. Before the driver can answer the guard's "May I help you," I've launched into the story—the story about just having arrived in town with my uncle Bull here from Georgia and how we're meeting a Realtor for a look at a property. Only we're late and she's going to be waiting for us at—I look at Uncle Bull—what was that address again?

Turnbull stammers Sophie Deveraux's address.

The guard smiles and makes small talk while he jots down the driver's name and license number and the limo's license plate. Then he waves us through.

"You've done this before," Turnbull comments dryly when the gate swings open. His tone is more grudging than laudatory. "What would you have done if he decided to call the Deveraux house for confirmation?"

David and I have used the ruse more than once to get into high-security communities. Usually I'm the Realtor and David is the client. Left my supply of bogus realty cards at home, though, so I had to improvise.

To Turnbull, I reply, "Place like this isn't going to post for sale signs on the lawns. Most deals are made quietly. He'd have no reason to question us."

Turnbull is eyeing me. He thinks, *Tricky bitch*, then slips into silence, dropping the curtain on his thoughts.

Why do I get the impression he was hoping we would be denied admittance? Once again, I remind myself to be on the alert. He may owe Williams, but he's no friend of mine.

The exact address turns out to be a rambling, brick mansion surrounded by an iron fence. Behind the house are paddocks and a stable. There's no guardhouse here but a buzzer and a security camera located to the left of the gate.

When the driver rings, there is a moment's delay before a female voice with a Hispanic accent asks, "Yes?"

I lean forward to be able to answer. "I'm looking for Sophie Deveraux."

"May I tell her who's calling?"

"Anna Strong."

"And your business with Ms. Deveraux?"

"Private."

The intercom clicks off. I settle back in the seat. The camera rotates to get a clear view of the car. The tinted windows will prevent whoever is watching from seeing in the back.

The disembodied voice returns with the message, "I'm sorry, Ms. Deveraux is not at home. Would you like to leave a message?"

"No. I'll try again later."

Turnbull looks relieved. He instructs the driver to turn around. Once we're back on the road, I tell the driver to pull over.

"Why are you telling him to stop?" Turnbull asks, voice tense with irritation.

I ignore him and instruct the driver. "Find the access road that runs behind the property."

Turnbull raises a hand. "Wait a minute. What makes you think there's an access road?"

"There's a stable in back. I didn't see anyway to get to it from the driveway so there's bound to be another way in. A delivery entrance."

The driver looks to Turnbull, unsure how to proceed.

Frustration burns through me. "Look, one way or the other, I'm getting into that house. I'll get out right here and walk if I have to."

He glares at me a minute before waving the driver on.

"What the hell is it with you? I thought you were supposed to help me."

Turnbull's jaw is set, his shoulders bunched. "I have lived here since the beginning of the nineteenth century. I have roots that go deep in this community. I don't need trouble. I wasn't happy when Williams called, but I owed him a favor. I'm telling you now, I won't be a party to killing."

So Williams told him the purpose of my "visit." I understand Turnbull's reluctance to get involved. This is his home turf and we're dragging him into a fight that could easily turn nasty.

"Look, I'll try to keep you out of it. You've gotten me this far. If you want to drop me off and leave, I'm sure I can find my way back to the airport."

His shoulders relax a little, but not his apprehension. I can taste it in the air. "We're here now," he says. "Let's get it over with."

Not a ringing endorsement of cooperation, but better than nothing. "This Sophie Deveraux, do you know anything about her?"

He shakes his head. "Not much. She's the last living relative of Jonathan Deveraux—a cousin five generations removed. Sole heir to his fortune, so the story goes. Deveraux was a vampire. A nasty bastard according to the stories. He was killed at his one hundred fiftieth birthday party. By his wife. She disappeared not long after. Rumor has it this Sophie had something to do with it, but there was never any proof. I think it's safe to assume she's dangerous."

"Is she a vampire?"

"Not that I know. There's been some talk that she may be a witch. One of her cousins was."

"A cousin?" My fingers touch the charm. "What was her name?"

"Sophie Burke. Best damned caterer in Denver. She died not too long ago."

Shit. If Sophie Burke is dead, what connection does Belinda have to Sophie Deveraux? There must be some reason she kept that telephone number.

Turnbull is rambling on, "Sophie's said to be a strange bird. Keeps to herself. Doesn't get involved in the human or supernatural community. For inheriting such vast wealth, she's kept a remarkably low profile." His eyes hold mine, then slide away. "Gives you and Sophie something in common."

The usual rush to deny claiming any part of Avery's fortune is tempered by the reality that I just arrived in Avery's private jet. I focus on the scenery.

We're winding through tree-lined streets, past properties that must cost tens of millions of dollars. The silence in the car is oppressive. Makes me think of how much I have to lose if this turns out to be another wild-goose chase. I turn to Turnbull. Even small talk is better than what I'm thinking.

"What about you? Williams said you've lived in Denver for over a hundred years. How have you managed it?"

He looks surprised by the question, but then he smiles and shrugs. "I 'kill' myself off in various ways every forty or fifty years and introduce a new heir. A few makeup tricks, a change in hair color and styles, colored contacts." He pats his chest. "Padding to change body shape. It's not so hard really."

"And no one notices?"

"I have an entire gallery of 'family portraits' showing the remarkable Turnbull family resemblance."

"And do you also keep a low profile?"

"I'm a philanthropist. Made my fortune in mining. I manage a foundation, attend a few charity functions, but mostly I keep to myself. I have a ranch outside of Durango. My house here in Denver is closed most of the year."

"Sounds like you've made a good life for yourself."

My voice must have a wistful ring to it, because Turnbull raises an eyebrow. *No reason why you can't do the same thing.* A laugh bubbles up. *Or not. Williams seems to think you have a death wish. Is that true? You really choose to live as a human?*

"I think this is it, Mr. Turnbull."

The driver's voice saves me from either confirming or denying Williams' charge. Death wish? Seems to me I've had to defend my life more since becoming vampire than I ever did as a human.

The driver has pulled to a stop at the junction to an unpaved road that skirts the back of several of the larger properties. Sophie Deveraux's is one of them. I get out to take a look around.

The Deveraux property sits on about ten acres of rolling pastureland. I can just see the back of the stable from our vantage point. The same iron fence that surrounds the front of the house extends back this way.

Turnbull has gotten out, too, and comes to stand beside me.

"I'm going in," I tell him. "Give me fifteen minutes. If I'm not back, call Williams and tell him there was trouble."

Turnbull's expression darkens. "Are you sure this is what you want to do?"

No. I'm not. If this Sophie turns out to be another dead end, I've squandered more than time. I've squandered the remaining hours of Culebra's life.

"Fifteen minutes," I repeat. "Then call Williams."

If I don't come back by then, I'm most likely dead. Culebra and Frey are, too, if Williams can't find a way to prevent it. The only consolation is that Ortiz' death has given Williams a personal stake in finding Burke. If I can't save them, I know he'll try.

It's a small comfort.

"We'll be right here," Turnbull adds, reading my thoughts but not commenting on them. "Be careful." His voice suddenly has an edge, an urgency, as if he *understands*.

I wonder if he now questions why I choose to live as a human.

# CHAPTER 41

IT TAKES LITTLE EFFORT TO JUMP THE FENCE. I RUN past a half dozen horses grazing in the pasture. They shy away from me, ears back, eyes wild. I can't tell if it's the human Anna or the vampire that's spooking them.

When I get close to the stables, I keep out of sight of the open barn door. I can't hear or sense anyone inside, but I don't want to take a chance. A hundred yards from the stables is a patio area. There's a pool, a cabana and what looks like a guesthouse.

Nice digs.

I crouch behind a hedge and scan the roofline. I don't see a security camera back here. Curious, although I suppose if the house belonged to a vampire, he may not have felt he needed one.

The ground floor of the house is a long rambling affair. The only entrance seems to be a pair of French doors opening from the house onto the patio. There are two huge ceramic pots, one on each side of the doors, planted with five-foot-tall evergreens. Perfect cover to check out the inside.

At first glance, all I see is furniture. It's a living room, formal, with two oversized couches and a heavy, dark wood coffee table occupying the middle of the room. To the right is a fireplace. To the left, a credenza. Sunlight flashes off a silver tea set displayed on a lower shelf.

I move in to try the door.

That's when I realize there's someone in the room. I duck back but the woman is unaware of my presence. She's standing in the shadows under an archway in the back of the room, facing away from me. She's agitated, hands waving, shoulders stiff, weight evenly distributed on both feet as if ready to fend off an attack. I can't hear what she's saying and I can't see anyone else in the room.

Is she on a telephone?

My fingers once again find their way to the charm around my neck. Nothing. No warning blast of heat.

Whoever the woman is, she's not Burke, nor does Burke seem to be in the vicinity.

I'm not sure if I'm disappointed or thankful.

But it does spur me into action. I have about ten minutes before Turnbull calls Williams. I move to the door and knock.

Startled, the woman jumps and whirls around. She steps into the light.

I find myself staring at one of the most beautiful girls I've ever seen. Not in the traditional sense. Her hair looks windblown, like she may have just come inside, and her features are far from perfect. But she has a glow about her. A natural beauty that radiates from within. It's captivating. It's magnetic. It's mesmerizing.

Turnbull said she might be a witch.

It's probably magic.

I shake away the wonder and take a more dispassionate

look. She's not particularly tall, maybe five feet four, but well built and slender. She's dressed in jeans, an open-neck shirt of pale yellow and leather riding boots. Her hair is shoulder length, dark and straight, framing thick-lashed blue eyes and a generous mouth.

Right now the mouth is turned down at the corners. She comes to the door and yanks it open. "Yes?"

"Are you Sophie Deveraux?"

She's staring at me. "Who are you? How did you get back here?"

Seeing her up close, I realize she couldn't be more than twenty, yet there's an old soul quality to her that comes through. A maturity of spirit that makes her seem older than her years.

It sends a tremor straight through me. Shit. Is she one of Burke's customers? Is that why her number was in the file?

"Do you know Simone Tremaine?"

The frown becomes deeper, sterner. "Why do you ask?"

"Look, Ms. Deveraux, I need you to talk to me. If you're one of Tremaine's customers, you are in danger. The product you've been using has some nasty side effects. I can help you, but you've got to tell me if you know where she is."

A subtle change comes over her. A stillness. She turns away from me and walks into the middle of the room.

I'm right on her heels. "Please. You are not the only one in danger. Tremaine's product has already resulted in three deaths, maybe more. She's a monster. If you know where she's hiding, you have to tell me."

"Only three?"

She says it so quietly, I lean close. "What?"

She turns to face me. "Only three deaths? You mean *human* deaths, right? But there have been others, haven't there?"

She asks the question as if already knowing the answer. "Yes. Twelve."

"Vampires? Like you?"

Her directness at first startles me, then I throw it back at her. "Yes. She tortured and killed them. She bled them. Do you know why?"

Now there's another shift. Nothing overt, but it's there in the slump of her shoulders, the softening lines of her mouth. Resignation? She looks away.

"For the cream." I touch her cheek. "For the magic that turned you from what—a middle-aged housewife—to this. Was it worth it?"

Then Sophie Deveraux does the last thing I expect. She sinks into a chair and begins to cry.

I park myself in front of her and take her chin in my hand.

"I know you're a witch. I know you've used the cream. I have to find Simone Tremaine. I'm desperate. Do you think you can help me do that? Maybe there's something you know about it that can help me locate her? Some supernatural marker we can use to track her?"

She nods, tentatively, tears still welling in her eyes.

"You are my last chance. If you want to grab a jacket or change clothes, this would be the time."

She turns those china blue eyes on me. "I don't need anything. I'll come with you."

My cell phone rings. Sophie and I both jump. I fish it out of my jacket. "Yes?"

"Turnbull just called me. What's going on?"

It's Williams. "I found Sophie Deveraux. I'm going to bring her back to San Diego. Burke isn't here, but Sophie has agreed to help us locate her. Call Turnbull and tell him to come to the front gate to pick us up."

I disconnect, then call the pilot at the hotel. I tell him to get the jet ready, that we're on our way to the airport. If he's surprised at the quick turnaround, his voice doesn't reflect it. I ring off and shove the phone into my pocket.

It should take about ten minutes for the car to make its way to the front gate.

Sophie sits up in the chair and squares her shoulders. "Have you stopped her from draining them?"

The way she asks it raises goose bumps on my arms. "Yes. We stopped what she was doing with the cream."

"I'm glad."

"How did you know about it?"

She stands up. "Because Simone Tremaine is my sister and the cream was my idea."

# CHAPTER 42

I PEER AT THE PERFECT FACE, THE INNOCENCE THAT shines from her eyes. This young girl came up with a plan to bleed vampires to death for the sake of a damned cosmetic? It doesn't seem possible. Is she telling the truth?

She releases a breath. "Simonè is my sister, but her real name is Belinda Burke. I think you knew that though, didn't you?"

Not all of it.

I'm immediately suspicious. "Your name is Sophie Deveraux. Not Burke. A friend told me you were a relative of the Jonathan Deveraux who used to live here. How could you be Belinda Burke's sister?"

A small, sad smile tips the corners of her mouth. "It's a long story. I'll—"

There's a buzz from somewhere in the back of the house. Sophie pauses. "I think your friends are here."

A Latino housekeeper appears in the doorway. She looks

surprised to see that her mistress is not alone. She says something to Sophie in Spanish and Sophie answers. I understand enough to know her housekeeper just announced Turnbull's arrival. Sophie tells her to open the gate.

Then she turns to me. "It's time to go."

She's not resisting the idea that I want her to come with me. It's surprising, if she's the mastermind behind the whole scheme. Still, it's better than having to drag her kicking and screaming. I keep my eyes on her as she leads the way through a maze of rooms to the front door. If she's cloaking great power, she's doing a good job of it.

The limo is right outside the front door. The housekeeper accompanies us, speaking to Sophie in rapid-fire Spanish. I pick up from her expression and the timbre of her voice that she's afraid for her mistress, mistrustful of the woman with "*ojos salvajes*" who appeared from nowhere and is now taking her away.

Sophie throws me a calculated glance, reads that I understood most of what the woman was saying and replies with a few reassuring words to her before walking down the steps to the car.

The remark about the "wild-eyed" woman, though, goes unchallenged.

Turnbull is standing outside the car, passenger door open. When Sophie slips in ahead of me, he gives me a raised-eyebrow look and asks, *That's Sophie Deveraux?*

*Any reason to doubt it?*

*She's a lot younger than I imagined. A spell?*

*Or another satisfied customer.*


IT'S A QUIET RIDE BACK TO CENTENNIAL AIRPORT. I have many questions to ask Sophie, but I don't want to ask them in front of Turnbull. I don't trust him.

Turnbull keeps to himself, too. He doesn't introduce

himself to Sophie. Afraid, maybe, that if he does and they meet at some charity function in the future, she'll remember. I'm sure he's relieved that he's not been asked to dispose of a body. The sooner he gets Sophie alive and on that plane, the better.

The silence gives me a chance to study Sophie. There's something—an unidentifiable quality—about her that's unusual. Every once in a while, she gets an expression on her face that makes me think she's listening to—what? Her focus turns inward. If she were vampire, I'd say she was reading Turnbull or me. She's not vampire. I'm certain of it. I'd have recognized it when I saw her for the first time. She was startled and had no chance to put up psychic defenses.

It's creepy. Could Sophie Deveraux be psychotic? Does she hear *those* kind of voices?

She knew Tremaine was Burke. She knew about the deaths from the cream. She says she came up with the idea. With her sister.

My hands curl into fists. They itch to get her alone on that plane, to find out what else she knows.

The jet is primed and ready when we pull onto the airstrip. I say good-bye to Turnbull. It doesn't take long. He's as glad to be rid of me as he is Sophie. I thank him for helping me find Sophie. I mean it, too. Saved me from hassling with a GPS system on a rental car.

He's gone before we take off.

He doesn't ask me back for a visit.

Once aboard, Sophie slips into a seat and belts herself in. She's neither curious nor impressed by the plane.

Probably has one just like it.

Lawson comes back to greet us. He gives us a weather update and tells us we'll be on our way in ten minutes.

I wait until we're airborne and he's given us the okay to move about the cabin. I tell him we won't be needing anything and don't want to be disturbed. Then I unbuckle my seat belt and swivel my seat to face the girl.

"Let's start at the beginning. Who are you?"

Sophie squares herself in the seat. Resolute blue eyes look into mine. "My name was Sophie Burke. Belinda is my sister."

"You call yourself Sophie Deveraux. Jonathan Deveraux was vampire. You assumed a new identity, set yourself up as heir to his estate. Why?"

If she really is the bitch Burke's sister, I expect her answer will have to do with distancing herself from the black-magic witch.

Instead, Sophie smiles. "Black-magic witch. She is that, yes. But that's not the reason I became Sophie Deveraux."

I jerk upright in the seat. There's no mistaking it this time. She does hear voices. She heard mine.

*What are you?*

*What do you think I am?*

The voice is masculine, touched with a hint of an accent, like Turnbull's, faintly southern. It's coming from *inside* Sophie but it's not Sophie speaking. Gooseflesh raises icy bumps on my arms.

The memory of another male voice addressing me from a female form plunges me into a nightmare.

Avery. That time it was Avery and the female was Sandra.

Dread roots me to the spot. I'm trapped at twenty thousand feet with something I can't identify and rising panic. Has Avery done it again? Did he manage to escape from Sandra? Is he here on his own plane to exact revenge?

*Who's Avery? I thought you were the Big Bad.*

The voice this time is diffused with curiosity and a hint of humor.

It's laughing at me.

Not a good idea. Anger replaces panic, cracking the

shell of fear paralyzing me and allowing the vampire to break free. The growl and hiss erupt from the dark place determined to protect itself.

*I'll ask you one more time. What are you?*

It's Sophie who answers after a moment's hesitation. "Sorry, Ms. Strong," she says with quiet resignation. "I should have told you." She makes a sweeping gesture with her hand, down the length of her body. "I'm not exactly alone in here. You've been talking with my alter ego, Jonathan Deveraux."

# CHAPTER 43

A VISCERAL RUSH OF ALARM SWALLOWS THE AN-ger. A hundred questions pop into my head. The most important, because of Sandra and Avery, raises the hair on the back of my neck. "Did he take you by force? Is he holding you against your will?"

A sad, slow smile touches her lips. "I wish I could answer yes." She sighs. "But I can't. I did this to myself.

"How?"

"Curiosity and vanity. A dangerous combination."

I don't understand. Is she lying to protect herself? Can this Jonathan Deveraux hurt her the way Avery did Sandra?

*Only if I want to hurt myself, too.*

I've experienced a lot of strange things since becoming vampire. Watching this young girl speak with two distinct voices ranks among the creepiest.

*She's not so young,* Deveraux says with a chuckle. *Go ahead, Sophie, tell Anna the story.*

Sophie stands, begins to pace, stops, turns back to me. "It started as an experiment," she says. "I'm a witch. To support myself I am—I was—a caterer. I worked the supernatural community. It was a good life. I should have been satisfied."

She comes back and sinks into her seat. "A few months ago, at a birthday party, at Jonathan's birthday party, there was an accident."

*Not an accident,* Deveraux interjects with a snarl.

Sophie nods. "He's right. It turned out not to be an accident. His wife killed him—set him on fire with his birthday cake. When I was called in to clean up the—what was left—I got the idea. I've always dabbled in cosmetics. Made my own, in fact. It was a dream to start my own business. Thinking about what happened to Jonathan, touching the ash, gave me an idea. Maybe if I used some of his ash, mixed it in a face cream, it might be the breakthrough I was looking for to start a new line."

"Did you know the ash had any power?"

"No. It was desperation. I was tired of my life. I wanted to be young. Beautiful. I wanted adventure, romance. Things I never had."

"So how old are you, really?"

She looks away. "Eighty," she says softly. "Not so old for a witch, but definitely past the midpoint of life."

"Eighty?" I flash on Burke. "What about your sister then? How old is she?"

"Belinda is ten years older. She's ninety."

I shake my head. "No way. You said this happened a few months ago. I saw Burke before that. She looked thirty. How is she doing it?"

Sophie shrugs. "Magic," she says. "You saw how she worked the glamour that transformed her into Simone Tremaine. She can be any age or look like anyone she wants to. She's very powerful."

"So why didn't you do the same thing?"

"It takes continuous and exhausting effort to maintain a change in physical appearance. I wish to direct my effort to more positive things." She catches herself. "Or at least I *used* to direct my efforts to positive things."

"Christ. So you came up with another idea. All this because you couldn't be content to age gracefully like the rest of the human race."

A snicker. *This from a vampire who will never age.*

*I wasn't speaking to you.*

*Tough.*

I brace for a smart-ass rejoinder. When none comes, I focus again on the girl. "Sophie, so what happened when you mixed the ash in your cream?"

"This." She glances down. "I awoke one morning to find I'd achieved my dream. A perfect, beautiful twenty-year-old face and body."

*And I found myself trapped in a nightmare—the body of an eighty-year-old virgin living in a hovel who cooked for a living. A teetotaling vegetarian. Could it get any worse?*

I can scarcely contain my rage. "But how is this possible? Is it permanent? Does Belinda know what you did?" I jerk around to face Sophie. "No. She can't. Otherwise, she'd have been setting vampires on fire instead of bleeding them, right?"

Sophie nods, but it's Deveraux who answers. *We thought it best to keep what happened to Sophie and me quiet. Sophie knew her sister had a dark side.*

"A dark side? Is that what you call turning and torturing young girls for their blood? Whose idea was that?"

"It was Jonathan's idea," Sophie says. Then she adds quickly, "Not the torturing part. Jonathan realized using ash resulted in absorbing the entire essence of a vampire. He thought if we used just the blood, we might be able to achieve only physical results. It's blood that makes a vampire immortal, that stops the aging process and achieves physical perfection."

*And it worked.*

At that, I do slam my fist against the back of Sophie's seat. *Shut the fuck up. As a result of it "working" Belinda set up a slaughterhouse.*

*That was never meant to happen,* Deveraux whines. *Our idea was a blood bank, where vampires would be paid for donations. The problem arose because the effects weren't permanent and the side effects—*

*I know all about the side effects. We have three dead women in San Diego because of side effects. I think Belinda is killing off her test subjects to cover her tracks.*

I stop, swallow back the anger. "Let's go back—why did you take the name Deveraux? How did you explain that to Belinda if she didn't know you were"—I search for the right word—"*harboring* this thing inside you?"

*Thing?* Deveraux's outrage squeals through.

*Shut up. Let Sophie talk.*

Sophie doesn't seem privy to all my conversations with Deveraux. My guess is that she and he communicate, but since she doesn't have a vampire's ability to communicate psychically, Deveraux can block what passes between him and me. A mute button he can push when he wants to. Just as well. I can tell Deveraux what an asshole I think he is without fear of offending her.

Deveraux snorts but urges Sophie to answer.

"Deveraux's wife was gone."

"Gone?"

Sophie's eyes slide away. Deveraux doesn't comment. I imagine "gone" doesn't mean she ran away or got a divorce. I shake my head and wave a hand at her to get on with the story.

"There was no other heir to his fortune. With the help of a vampire lawyer he'd had on retainer for a hundred years, a name change was arranged and I was presented as Jonathan's niece, the last of the family line. That way Jonathan could continue to live in the manner to which he was accustomed."

The last is said with a hint of sarcasm. It makes me smile and Deveraux grunt.

"Belinda didn't wonder about your newfound wealth?"

"Belinda didn't care. She was busy trying to figure out how she could get a piece of it."

"Is that how she got involved in the cream thing?"

When Sophie looks at me, her eyes reflect sadness and regret. "Jonathan and I came up with the idea for the cream. I shared the idea with Belinda. I thought it was something we could do together. She was excited, of course. Especially seeing how it had 'worked' on me. She was eager to pursue it. We tested it here in Denver. Just a bit of vampire blood produced remarkable results. The test subjects wanted more. Belinda increased the potency and the results were even more astounding."

"And tell me again, how did you obtain the blood?"

"Donors," she says. "We paid vampires to use their blood. We set up a blood bank. And it was working. The cream turned middle-aged women young again. We never intended to hurt anyone. Two weeks after the tests started, some of the women began to exhibit side effects. A craving for blood. It only occurred in the ones who got the stronger formula. I cut off their supply, replaced it with a placebo. The women lost the craving. Unfortunately, the physical effects reverted, too. That's when I realized that long term, the cream would never work."

*She warned Belinda,* Deveraux says. *How could she know what her sister was planning when she left Denver?*

Sophie continues, "I thought once she saw what happened here, she'd let it go. But she didn't. She stole the formula. Maybe she thought she could find a way to ameliorate the side effects. After all, I wasn't suffering any side effects. I tried to tell her it was because of the witchcraft, but she wouldn't let it go. I wasn't aware of how far she'd gone until I saw an article in a magazine about Simone Tremaine and her amazing new antiaging cream. I recognized Belinda through the glamour. She wouldn't return my calls or emails. Yesterday, I decided to go to San Diego. Then I saw it on the news. Her factory burned. The cream destroyed. I thought it was finally over."

Over? Images flash in my head. Culebra and Frey. Ortiz and the young vampires hanging in that basement. Three mortal women dead.

I don't know how to begin to respond without unleashing the beast. It's here, close to the surface. I pause until I get myself under control. Even then, I can't keep my voice from shaking. "Over? Burke is killing a friend of mine. She has him under a spell. You are going to help me find her. Or you will die, too."

*Wait a minute,* Deveraux counters with an angry hiss. *Sophie can't be held responsible for what her sister does.*

*Maybe I'm not holding Sophie responsible. Maybe I'm holding you responsible. Wasn't it your idea to use vampire blood in the cream? How irresponsible can you be? Didn't you think about the consequences of exposing innocent people to vampire blood?*

*What consequences? It's never been done before. And it wasn't as if they would be drinking it—they would be applying it. Topically. Who could have predicted there would be a problem?*

I feel his anger escalating. It's apparent in his arrogance that before he and Sophie were merged, he was a powerful vampire. Now?

Sophie sits quietly during the exchange. Once again, she projects an air of resignation. Perhaps she's prepared to accept whatever happens because she's grown tired of this dual existence. It must be draining to have a war waging constantly inside. And I sense there *is* conflict waging. Jonathan's old-soul vampire egotism against what I suspect is a well-meaning, sweet-tempered witch.

It doesn't change the situation. Nor does it soften my resolve.

"What has my sister done to your friend?" Sophie asks when Deveraux's voice has grown silent.

I tell her about Culebra. And our history with Burke. I don't leave anything out. I start with the first time I saw her at Beso de la Muerte, how she shot Frey when we stopped her demon raising, how she sold me out to a renegade FBI agent who had kidnapped my lover. I told her about the innocent she killed and Culebra's vow to avenge the girl's death. How he tracked her down three days ago and returned home near death. How I discovered her new identity as Simone Tremaine and found the slaughterhouse she set up to harvest vampire blood. How I lost a friend in the fire she set to cover her tracks when she realized she couldn't make the cream work. How Culebra and Frey are now both battling her spell to stay alive.

How we have only a few hours left to save them.

How if we fail, if my friends die, I will hold both her and her sister responsible. Sophie is the only leverage I have to force Burke's hand. Reasonable or not, I'll use it.

I have to. I don't have that many friends left.

# CHAPTER 44

$S$ OPHIE IS QUIET FOR A LONG MOMENT WHEN I finish. If she's shocked that I am holding her as responsible as her sister, she's not showing it. Rather, there is understanding and sympathy in her expression. And a tacit agreement to help. Deveraux is quiet, too. I'm glad. I'm not sure how I would have reacted if he'd thrown out another smart-ass comment.

The intercom buzzes and Tom's voice comes on. "We're beginning our descent into San Diego. Please make sure your seat belts are fastened. Ms. Strong, Mr. Williams radioed to say that he'll meet your party in the terminal."

My eyes seek Sophie's. "I hope the connection between you and your sister is powerful."

She understands what I'm saying. I see it in the depths of her eyes. If sacrificing Sophie is the only way to break Burke's spell or to bring her out of hiding, I won't hesitate.

Williams is waiting for us when we deplane. There is no warmth in his greeting when I introduce Sophie. I tell Williams that Sophie is Belinda's sister and that she's going to help us stop the bitch. Williams is grim. He blames Burke for Ortiz' death and now finding the witch is as important to him as it is to me. He only wants to exact revenge, however, which means I'll have to make sure Burke's hold on Culebra and Frey is broken before he strikes.

All this goes through my head as we start toward the car Williams has waiting for us. It's a big Lincoln Navigator. I take the front passenger seat and Sophie climbs in back. Deveraux is silent. I don't know whether he's made his presence known to Williams or not, but I don't mention it and Williams is guarding his thoughts, letting nothing through.

Sophie finally speaks once we're all in the car and Williams has started the engine.

"I understand what you want me to do. But to reach Belinda, I'll need a few things."

Not *Where are we going?* or *What are you planning to do to me?*

I put a "hold it" hand on Williams' arm and turn to face her.

"What do you need?"

"Black beeswax candles. Herbs. Horehound. Goldenseal. Angelica. Foxglove. I'd prefer fresh, but dried will do. A crystal goblet and holy water." She lists the items as calmly as a grocery list.

"What? No fatted calf for sacrifice?" Aggravation spikes my voice up a few notches. "Where are we supposed to get fresh horehound? Christ. Are you kidding me?"

It's Williams' turn to do the "hold it" thing. "I know."

He steers the car out of the parking lot and heads up PCH to Laurel. From there we jump on 5 South. He takes Imperial Avenue to 15 South and exits on National.

No one has spoken since we left the airport. I break the silence. "Where are we going?"

Williams is heading into a residential area in a shabby part of town. He navigates the maze of streets with an ease borne of familiarity. He doesn't answer until we pull up to a tiny, weather-beaten cottage off Thirty-fourth. "Here," he says.

The cottage sits on a lot under the freeway. The pollution and dust from the thousands of cars that pass by each day coat the shingles with a gray haze. I couldn't begin to guess what the original color was. What we can see from the curb is a ramshackle fence and an overgrown yard. Vegetation is so thick, it's difficult to distinguish one plant from another. The tangle of growth extends around the sides of the house, giving the impression that the cottage is an afterthought planted in the middle of a jungle.

"This will do nicely."

Sophie's voice from the backseat.

I turn toward her. The question, "For what?" dies on my lips. Her eyes are shining, fixed on the yard. She has a hand on the door.

I take another look at the yard. Obviously she sees something I do not.

Sophie climbs out and goes through the gate, scanning right and left. She stoops and plucks a few leaves from one of the plants, moves to the next, repeats the process.

"What is this place?" I ask Williams, following him as he trails behind Sophie.

Before he can answer, the front door opens. An old woman walks onto the porch. She doesn't look at Sophie poking through her yard like a bloodhound on the scent. Instead, she looks directly at Williams and me.

"Your kind are not welcome here," she says, pointing a skeletal finger. "Get out of my yard."

The woman looks a hundred years old, with a wizened, lined face, silver-and-gold-streaked hair drawn up in a bun. She's stooped-shouldered, supporting her weight on a shiny aluminum walker. But her voice is commanding and her tone sends a chill up my spine.

Williams bows his head. "Sorry, Mother. We will wait for our friend outside your fence."

I don't know what surprises me more: his gesture of deference to the old woman or the reverence in his tone. My spidey sense is telling me not to argue. I follow him quietly out of the yard.

When we're standing beside the car, the old woman limps down the steps, her long black skirt dragging in the dust. She goes to Sophie. The young girl and the old woman look at each other for a moment, not speaking, not communicating in any way I can tell. Then, abruptly, the two embrace, move apart and, arms entwined, stoop together over a patch of weeds.

"What the hell was that?" I ask. "And what did she mean by our kind not being welcome?"

Williams leans against the car. "Vampires. Vampires are not welcome here. She's a crone. Do you know what that is?"

I rack my brain. I know I've heard the term. "Earth mother? Divine feminine? Am I close?"

"Close."

He doesn't elaborate. When I prod, he adds, "Her name is Eldora. She's well known in the magical community."

Not much in the way of useful information but by the set of his jaw and the curtain drawn around his thoughts, I know it's all I'm going to get. I try a different tack. "What does she have against vampires?"

"Immortality. Humans are born, they live, they die. Vampires threaten the cycle, subvert the natural order."

Immortality? "Living forever offends her, but blood-sucking does not?"

His shoulders lift, fall. "Didn't say it made sense. It's just the way it is."

"What powers does she possess?"

"None that I know of."

That gets a double take from me. "Then why the reverence? You did everything but grovel at her feet."

He shoots me a pitying look. "Respect. But I don't suppose you're familiar with the concept."

The all-too-recognizable deprecating Williams is back. Naturally, my hackles rise. I bite back an angry retort and turn away, focusing on Sophie. She's still rummaging around the yard, the old woman following behind her. Sophie points to this and that, plucks leaves, crushes them between her fingers. The old woman watches the beautiful young girl with rapt attention.

An interesting reversal of roles. Wonder if she recognizes the eighty-year-old spirit of Sophie the witch trapped in that young body? Does she sense they are kindred spirits? Wonder what she'd think if Deveraux put in an appearance.

The attention Williams is paying to Sophie, though, is not as positive. "Do you think we can trust her?" he asks finally.

"Do we have a choice?"

His hands ball into fists. "I will avenge Ortiz. Belinda Burke or her sister, makes no difference to me."

I don't say it, but for once, we're in agreement.

Impatience nips at my heels. I want to get on with it. Each passing hour brings my friends closer to death. Just when I'm ready to call out to her, Sophie and the crone disappear into the house.

I lunge at the gate, ready to follow them. I don't want to let Sophie out of my sight.

Williams grabs my arm, yanks me to a stop. "She'll be back. Wait here."

I glare at him and pull free. I'll give her ten minutes.

She's out in eight, holding a large grocery bag. She

walks toward us, her face wreathed in a smile of satisfaction and pleasure. She climbs into the backseat and waits for us to join her in the car before saying, "What a wonderful place."

Deveraux's sharp voice cuts like a razor. *Are you kidding me? Jesus. The place smelled like dinner in a morgue— boiled cabbage and decaying flesh. I couldn't wait to get out of there.*

I glance over at Williams, waiting for his reaction to Deveraux's remark.

He isn't reacting. He's got the car started and half turns to look at Sophie. "Did you get what you needed?"

Sophie says, "Yes. I have everything."

Williams acknowledges her reply by straightening in the seat and steering the car away from the curb.

*You didn't hear that?* I ask him.

*Hear what? What Sophie said? Yes, I heard her.*

I pause, wondering how or if I should tell him about Sophie's dual personality.

*Why tell him?* Deveraux says. *He can't hear me. He may not even believe you. He doesn't like you. Telling him you're hearing a vampire's voice from the body of a witch will just make him distrust you more.*

*Hear what?* Williams repeats.

I sit back in the seat. "Nothing."

# CHAPTER 45

A HALF DOZEN CARS ARE PARKED IN FRONT OF THE bar when we arrive at Beso de la Muerte. I take it as a good sign. If the bar is open, maybe things aren't as bad as I suspect.

I direct Williams to continue along to the back. To the caves.

When we pull up there, my heart starts to pound. This time it's not from any residual effects of the spell on Culebra, but because I'm afraid. I couldn't bring myself to call ahead to let Frey know we were coming. If he answered and Culebra was gone, or worse, if he didn't answer at all, I'm not sure I could have controlled my wrath.

Or Williams' rage.

Sophie steps out of the car, grocery bag in hand. She follows Williams and me into the cave.

The quiet wraps around us like a thick blanket. It's eerie and gooseflesh rises on my arms. The only sound is three distinct footfalls—Sophie's rubber-soled riding boots, Williams' hard-soled loafers and my soft-soled tennis shoes. We could be alone in the universe, the feeling of isolation is so complete.

I'm hoping that's all it is—a feeling—and that we're not alone.

By the time we approach the area where I last saw Frey and Culebra, I've worked myself into a state of high anxiety. Chest tight, pulse racing, palms sweaty. I wipe my hands on my jeans and call out.

"Frey? It's me, Anna."

The words bounce off the cave walls.

"Frey? Are you here?"

We round the last corner and I break into a run. Why isn't he answering?

Williams and Sophie are right on my heels. I feel their panic and it fuels my own. "Frey? Answer me."

We sprint into the ward.

I skid to a stop.

The cot is there.

Empty.

No.

I whip around, eyes seeking a clue. They can't be gone.

Williams snarls and I whirl toward him. He has Sophie by the arm, the vampire unleashed. "Bring us Burke, witch." His eyes glow yellow in the dim light. "Or I will kill you right here."

Deveraux's voice reaches out to me. *Stop him. It's not her fault.*

But I won't intervene. I feel my blood quicken as the vampire lies in wait, ready to leap to the surface. Reason flees to be replaced by cold fury.

My friends are gone.

Someone has to pay.

"Do as he says, Sophie."

I barely recognize my own voice. It's hoarse with the

effort of fighting the beast. "Bring us Burke. You are her sister. I know you can do it."

Sophie does not struggle against Williams' grip. "I'm not sure I can."

Williams' shakes her until her teeth rattle. "Do it."

I let it go on for a moment, then stop him. I pry his fingers from her arms and step between them. Harder than keeping my anger at bay is keeping the depth of my fury out of my voice. "Sophie. This is not a game. We will hurt you. My friends are dead. Burke is out of control and needs to be stopped. You are our only connection to her. Use your power to summon her. Tell her we'll kill you if she doesn't come."

Sophie's eyes are wide, but her voice betrays no fear when she says, "If your friends are dead, the spell has already been broken. I have no way to reach her. She will have a powerful spell in place to protect herself."

Williams growls in anger, elbows me aside and slaps her with full force across the face.

Sophie's head cracks against the wall of the cave and she slumps to the ground. Her eyes close for a moment, blood trickles from the corner of her mouth. When she looks up at us again, tears of pain and sorrow shine from her eyes.

"I hold no ill will toward you. I'm sorry my sister has hurt your friends. I will not fight you, but I can't help."

Williams lunges, pulls her to her feet. His teeth are at her neck, all control relinquished to the beast. "You have lived this long only because of Anna's friends. If you cannot bring us the witch responsible, your life is forfeit. This is for my friend, Ortiz."

*Stop him,* Deveraux screams. *You can't let this happen.*

The panic in his voice is more than concern for Sophie. Once she is dead, he is, too.

But I won't stop it. I don't want to. If anything, I want to take her blood as badly as Williams. I want to tear her head from her body, a sacrifice, a tribute to Frey and Culebra. They didn't deserve to die, either. It's not punishment. It's justice.

The vampire needs no further coaxing. I grab Williams and pull him away, slamming him back against the wall. *She's mine.*

*No.*

He's on his feet, snarling, lunging back at me. His hands are extended, his mouth twisted. We circle each other, growling, like two dogs spoiling for a fight.

"Hello?"

A voice, a familiar voice from the entrance to the cave.

"Who's there?"

And like a dog, I shake myself to allow the blood thoughts of the vampire to recede.

*Who is that?*

Williams and I both turn, wary, eyes flashing yellow to watch as a figure emerges from the darkness.

Sandra approaches, hands on her hips, head tilted as she takes in the scene.

"What's going on here?"

I swallow hard, pushing the beast down so I can answer as a human. "Frey and Culebra are gone." I point a shaking finger at Sophie. "She will pay the price."

Sandra goes to Sophie, helps her to her feet, glares at Williams and me. "You two are crazy, you know that?" She puts a gentle hand on Sophie's arm, examines the bleeding wound on her neck from Williams' bite. "It's not too bad. Let's get you out of here."

Her eyes spark with anger as she pauses only long enough to throw caustic words back at us. "Culebra and Frey are in the bar. We moved them there to make them more comfortable. Why didn't you stop there first?"

Culebra and Frey are still alive. I watch Sandra take Sophie back along the trail.

Shame sends heat to flood my face.

We almost killed her.

How anxious will she be to help us now?

I probe to see what Williams is feeling. I get only the red tide of residual anger. His animal eyes still glow yellow as he follows the women out of the cave.

It puts me on alert.

I know now that whether or not we save Culebra or get Burke, as far as Williams is concerned, Sophie is a dead woman.

# CHAPTER 46

I WHIP PAST SANDRA AND SOPHIE AND LEAVE WIL-
liams behind to run down the path to the bar. The back
door stands open. As soon as I pass through it, I smell it.
The acrid stench of illness and impending death.

It intensifies the fear fluttering my stomach.

I follow the smell to one of the feeding rooms.

Frey sits with his back to me, slumped in a chair. Still,
unmoving. Only the sound of his labored breathing gives
hint of life.

I tiptoe around to face him. My stomach contracts. I'm
glad his eyes are closed. A violent jolt seizes me and if he
was watching, the shock that must be stamped on my face
could only add to his misery. The smell of decay comes
from him.

Frey's dark hair is streaked with white. His face is pock
marked and gouged with lines from the corner of his eyes
to his chin, as if someone had drawn a trowel down the
length of it. He looks emaciated, dehydrated . . . and old.

I squeeze my own eyes shut to stop the tears.

"Do I look that bad?"

Frey's voice, full of humor and, thankfully, life, brings me back. I fling my arms around him and hug until he gently pushes me back.

"Easy. I'm not in the best shape right now."

I release him and step away. "You're alive. That's all that matters." A tug at my conscience makes me turn around, look toward Culebra. If Frey looks this bad, what must Culebra look like?

When I approach the cot, I'm amazed to see Culebra looks no different than the last time I saw him. He might be sleeping peacefully in his own bed. His face is unmarked and his body unchanged. The shallow, rapid rise and fall of his chest and the intravenous tubes feeding him are the only indications that something is wrong.

I turn a questioning eye to Frey. "How is this possible?"

His smile is both sad and ironic. "My counterspell protects Culebra. Unfortunately, it drains me. Remember when I said magic always exacts a price?"

I turn my eyes away. "I put you in this position. I'm sorry."

"Don't be. I knew the risks before I came." He looks toward the door. "I hope you brought reinforcements."

"Sophie. Burke's sister. She should be able to break the spell."

"Burke's sister?" He frowns. "Can we trust her?"

"Oh, we can trust her all right." Williams pushes Sophie ahead of him into the room. "She knows if anything goes wrong, she's dead."

Frey looks around. Whatever he might have imagined a sister of Burke's to look like, it's obviously not the dark-haired, shiny-faced young woman Williams shoves toward him. He stares at her, his face betraying his surprise. "She's a girl. How can she help us?"

Sophie lays a hand on his shoulder. At her touch, Frey grows still, his muscles relax, his eyes close.

I'm on her in a heartbeat, slapping her hand away. "What are you doing to him?"

She turns gray-clouded eyes on me. For an instant, I see the older Sophie, the witch, and it sends a shudder down my back. There's strength and power and a strong will.

The next moment, Sophie, the girl, is back. "He is resting. He cannot be a part of the ritual."

She turns away and empties the contents of her bag onto the floor.

She picks through the herbs, separates them into piles. With a piece of chalk, she marks a pentagram on the floor. She picks up a small portion of one of the herbs and places it on a point of the pentagram.

"Horehound," she says. "Protection against spells and sorcery."

She moves on, scooping up more herbs and laying them on a second point. "Angelica. To ward off evil spirits."

On a third point, she places a different herb. "Goldenseal. Healing herb."

In the middle of the pentagram she places the fourth herb. "Foxglove. For the heart."

She moves away from the pentagram, back to the bag. She picks up a goblet. Its delicate, carved crystal winks in the light and throws off flashes of light like rainbow glitter. She places it in the middle of the pentagram, reverently, as if the thing was a religious relic. Into it she pours half the contents of a small vial. She places the vial on the cot beside Culebra's body.

Holy water? I recall it was one of the items Sophie requested. The crone's house must double as a witch's one-stop convenience store.

The only things left in the bag are a dozen black beeswax candles. Sophie places one at each of the pentagram's five points and the rest she arranges in a circle around Culebra's cot.

I watch her, fascinated by how calm and deliberate her movements are. She is in a room with two vampires who have sworn to kill her if she doesn't perform the miracle of breaking Burke's spell.

She exhibits no fear, no concern. Her features are composed, serene. Deveraux, too, seems to have removed himself from her consciousness.

She might be back in the garden with the crone.

I glance at Frey, the steady rise and fall of his chest the only indication that life exists in that ravaged body.

Can we trust Sophie? The question Williams asked, and Frey. The question I keep avoiding.

The answer is as ominous as a death knell.

We have to trust her. There's no one else.

# CHAPTER 47

SOPHIE STEPS BACK, HER GAZE SWEEPING THE room, the cot, the objects placed in front of her on the floor. She turns. "You three had better wait outside."

Williams and I answer as one. "No way."

Only Sandra moves to the door. "I'll be in the bar. I've reopened it and we have customers."

She hurries out, not looking back, obviously relieved to be allowed to go. She must have regretted agreeing to come here every day since Culebra came back from his "vacation."

Sophie frowns at Williams and me. "If you stay," she cautions, "you must not interfere. No matter what happens. Do not approach me or Culebra. I won't be responsible for what happens if you do. Understood?"

Williams and I both nod that we do. Williams' thoughts are concealed beneath a black layer of hatred toward both Burke and her sister. I suspect we'll be watching for different things. If I see further harm coming to Culebra, I'll interfere any way I can. He'll be watching for any indication that Sophie is betraying us to her sister. Either way, agreeing is meaningless.

Sophie must suspect our acceptance of her terms is a hollow gesture; still, she turns away from us and steps toward the cot.

She makes no other move that I can detect, and yet all the candles spontaneously light, the flames leaping toward the ceiling like Roman candles before retreating to burn in a steady glow.

The sight makes the hair stir on the back of my neck.

She lays a hand on Culebra's chest and begins to chant. She picks up the vial and dribbles a little of the holy water into Culebra's mouth. It bubbles up like peroxide on an open wound. A thin wisp of smoke rises. Culebra gasps and my hands curl into fists. I take a step toward him.

Sophie turns to me, her eyes clouded again. "Don't."

One word, spoken in a voice that resonates to the depths of hell. It freezes me to the spot.

Like her sister before her, Sophie has the power to immobilize.

Why didn't I see that coming? Why didn't she use it on Williams when he attacked her?

She watches me a moment, turns away when she's sure I can't break free. She returns to Culebra.

The chanting continues. I strain to break the bonds holding me, but it's no use. *Williams. Can you move?*

His voice comes back, rough, angry. *No.*

Shit.

Then the rumble begins. Like distant thunder. For a moment I'm conscious only of the sound until, suddenly, darkness descends as if from a fast-moving storm. The room is plunged into night. The flickering candles cast grotesque shadows on the walls. Sophie's shape distorts, her face turns ghostly, indistinct against the gloom. Only her voice is the same, strong, unwavering.

My skin crawls.

The room begins to shake. Gusts of cold air swirl around us, stinging my face like the gale of an arctic storm. The candles sway in the violent blasts of air. My guts heave. I feel as if I'm on the deck of a bucking ship, helpless in the face of a raging storm.

Sophie's voice carries over all. Only the tempo and volume increase. I don't understand the words. All that I see are her eyes—bright, fever-lit, consumed by an inner fire. It's frightening and compelling and I can't look away.

Sophie pauses in her incantations, pours another drop of holy water on Culebra's tongue. This time, he groans, his back arches as if pulling against invisible bonds.

He's in pain. I struggle to break free of Sophie's hold. I can't. Did I make a mistake bringing her?

What choice did I have?

Sophie continues the chant. The wind increases, whipping her hair around her face. A small cut appears on her cheek, followed by another and another until her face is streaming with blood. It drips onto her clothes, onto Culebra, a crimson stain that spreads until they're both covered with it.

Still, she persists. Her voice carries with it power and energy. Yet the opposition she's fighting is powerful, too. I'm watching a clash of titans. Two mighty forces in a battle of wills.

The howling wind shrieks, filling my head until I think my eardrums will burst. Head and heart pound with the pressure. I want to press my palms against my ears but my arms refuse to move.

The charm around my neck gives the first warning. A fiery blast of white-hot heat. I can't protect myself from it. All I can do is cry out.

Suddenly, there is another sound. A voice. Shrill, furious.

"You are my sister," Belinda Burke's scream rattles the walls and shakes the floor beneath our feet. "If you break this spell, you break the bond."

Her image floats in the air above Culebra's cot. Not the image of Simone Tremaine or the younger Burke Frey and I battled months ago. This is the true image. An old woman, face contorted in anger, body stooped and bent. Her eyes burn red and focus with mad intensity on her sister.

"Stop. Stop now. You can't win."

But Sophie doesn't stop. The chanting continues. Tears stream down her face, mixing with the blood. She picks up the vial and flings it into the apparition.

Hell breaks loose.

# CHAPTER 48

THUNDER IS IN THE ROOM WITH US. MORE THAN
sound. It takes shape, reverberates off the walls, beats
at our ears, shakes the ground. Hell rides with it, the face
of the witch hovering, waiting to draw us down into the
darkness. I'm so afraid, my teeth grind together, my flesh
puckers and draws tight. My hands rise in an instinctive
reflex to shield my face. The spell that bound me to the
spot must be broken, but it doesn't matter. I couldn't run if
I wanted to. It's all I can do to keep my balance on a floor
rearing and rolling beneath my feet.

Frey's chair skitters against the wall. He's flung out of it.
The chair breaks apart as if made of balsa wood.

Frey doesn't awaken.

He's lucky.

I glance at Williams. He's been pushed against a table
at the back of the room. I can't tell if he's broken free. His
thoughts are no longer on his hatred, they center now on
his fear. His eyes are on Burke.

She reaches out a skeletal hand to touch Sophie. "Sister."

One word.

But Sophie doesn't waiver. Her voice rises like the perfume of incense—thick, pervasive, somehow comforting. Her hand is again on Culebra's chest. Shielding him. She is not looking at Burke; her eyes are closed.

Burke shrieks and holds out both arms. She scoops them as if to draw Sophie up.

I can't let that happen. I look to Williams for help.

His eyes meet mine, but he refuses to move. He won't help. These are your friends, his expression says, not mine.

I move toward Sophie alone.

Burke turns burning eyes on me, full of fire and rage. She snarls and her right hand becomes a sword. The force of her fury is directed at me. She lashes out with the sword, breathes smoke and flame, blinding me.

I shield my face with my hands, feel the tip of the sword slash both forearms. Pain runs the length of my arms. The charm blazes inside my blouse, the smell of burnt flesh, my own, fills my nostrils. The floor beneath me is buckling, caving downward.

Still, Sophie's voice is there. She does not stop.

But something changes.

In the instant that Burke turns her attention to me, the timbre of Sophie's voice swells, grows more powerful. She raises her eyes and arms, and in her hands she holds the goblet. She holds it like a supplication, an offering. She draws her own power inward, summoning the force of the elements whipping around us.

Burke senses the shift. She turns her face away from me, howling.

The thunder no longer answers.

In its place, deathly quiet.

Burke realizes her mistake. I was a decoy.

Sophie's voice drops to a whisper. The goblet trembles in her hand.

Burke blinks, opens her mouth. "No."

Her face contorts. Her body shrinks into itself. She holds up her hands. "Don't."

But Sophie raises the goblet higher.

Burke releases a sigh, a death rattle. An acknowledgment. She has been tricked. She turns dead eyes on me.

Then she is drawn into the goblet.

Sophie holds it against her chest, shielding it.

It's then I know.

Sophie's eyes find mine. The message she sends is both admission and appeal.

I can't let it go. Too much has happened. Too many deaths.

I reach for the goblet.

She could fight me. She could render me immobile with a thought.

Her breath catches. Her eyes fill. Still, she refuses to move. Gently, softly, I place my fingers over hers. One by one, I remove them from the goblet until her hand falls away.

The goblet falls to the floor.

With a burst of light, it shatters, sending particles as fine as sand through the air.

The only sound now is the ghostly echo of Burke's scream.

# CHAPTER 49

T HE SILENCE IS MORE DEAFENING THAN THE thunder.

The candles sputter and extinguish as one.

The charm grows instantly cold.

When I look around, I see for the first time that not only Frey's chair but every bit of furniture in the room has been reduced to shards of broken wood. It's a wonder Williams and I weren't staked by flying debris.

Suddenly, Culebra sits up on the cot. He looks around, his eyes full of questions.

Then he frowns and looks at me.

"What in the hell have you done to my bar?"

# CHAPTER 50

IT TAKES A MOMENT TO REGISTER—CULEBRA SITting up, speaking.

I don't pay attention to what he said. I'm at his side in two seconds, searching his face for reassurance that he's all right and back with us.

He returns my stare with a bewildered frown. "What's going on?"

I touch his cheek. It's warm, color flooding up from his neck at whatever emotion he reads on my face.

"Do you remember?"

A flash in the depths of his eyes. It comes flooding back—a shared memory. The helplessness, the spell, dangling on the edge of death.

He remembers.

A sound from the corner.

Frey.

I'd almost forgotten Frey.

I turn around.

In the pile of rubble that was a chair, Frey struggles to his feet. When he straightens, a rush of relief loosens another knot in my stomach.

His hair and face are morphing back to normal. The white streaks fade, the deep claw marks fill in. He's shaking his head as if to clear it, but I can tell by the way he's moving that he hasn't suffered any permanent physical damage. He meets my eyes and smiles, and I know he's going to be fine.

Two down.

Williams hasn't moved from his place against the back wall. He's watching me, too, trying to figure out if I know the truth—that we were paralyzed by our own fear. It isn't until this moment that I understand Burke's power drew strength from that fear. She cast the spell, but it was our own weakness that forged the chains that bound us. It makes me ashamed. If I had stopped Burke in the restaurant, many lives would have been saved.

I turn away from him. I have my own guilt to deal with. Let him come to the realization on his own.

Now there's only Sophie.

She's slumped on the floor at the foot of Culebra's cot. Her face is drained of color, of emotion, a blank slate from which two dark eyes stare dully at nothing. She looks so young, so fragile. It would be easy to forget that there is a powerful witch concealed in that childlike body.

A witch who just allowed her sister to what—?

I realize that I don't know what happened to Burke. And I need to.

I kneel down beside her.

She raises her eyes to meet mine. Immense sorrow and deep regret are reflected there.

"Where is she?" I ask.

"Gone."

"What does that mean?"

*For Christ's sake,* Deveraux snarls. *Leave her alone, will you?*

I ignore him. Take one of Sophie's hands in both of my own. It's cold, colder than mine, and it raises gooseflesh on my arms. "Is she dead?"

"Is that what you want?"

Yes. "I want to know my friends are safe."

"They are."

"Then she's dead?"

This time, I see the shift in Sophie's eyes. Resolve replaces the dull ache of loss. "She can't hurt anyone."

It's not the answer I wanted to hear. "She's still alive."

That gets a reaction from Williams. Moving faster than I can stop him, he yanks Sophie to her feet. He looses the vampire with a snarl. "Where is she?"

This time I recover quickly enough to meet his beast with my own before he can do any real harm. With one hand, I grab the back of his neck and fling him away. *Don't touch her.*

He hits the wall, stumbles, loses his footing. He's back on his feet in an instant, hands twisted like claws, snarling. But when he looks at me, instead of attacking, he stops. For the first time since I've known him, Williams hesitates. He isn't flouting his contempt or screaming at me. His fists open, his body loses its rigidity, his vampire face disappears. He meets my eyes, a terrible calmness replacing the fury. The words he hurls at me are filled with hate. "The witch lives. You can't protect them. Both will pay."

Before I can respond, he turns and leaves through the door that leads to the bar.

A different chill crawls down my back. Williams' threat hangs in the air. It isn't finished.

I make sure the beast is contained before turning back to Sophie. She shrinks back from me anyway. "I'm sorry if he hurt you." I keep my voice low. "We both have concerns about Burke. We need to know what happened."

She peers into my face. I don't know what she sees. I don't know what she's looking for. I appeal to Deveraux. *What's wrong?*

He hesitates a heartbeat before answering. *I told her who you are,* he says.

*I don't know what that means.*

*She recognizes you now. She knows what you are. The chosen. The one.*

I'm too shocked to do more than gape at her. *What did she recognize? What did I do?*

Deveraux is chuckling. *You beat down that old-soul vampire like a dog. You met Burke head-on. You hide your power well. I wouldn't have suspected it if I hadn't seen it with my own eyes. You don't seem the type, really. Too— ordinary, I guess.*

I don't know whether that's a compliment or an insult. It's too ridiculous. I put steel in my voice. *Listen, in a minute Culebra is going to start asking questions. He's the one Burke almost killed. You're going to have to get Sophie to talk to us. He's going to be as pissed as Williams.*

*He's already as pissed as Williams.*

Culebra's voice at my elbow makes me jump. I'd forgotten he could get into my head as easily as Williams. Since Williams didn't seem to be able to hear Deveraux, I assumed Culebra wouldn't hear him, either.

I was wrong.

Culebra stands beside me, eyeing Sophie. *What's going on? I thought she was a witch.*

*You want to tell him,* I ask Deveraux, *or should I?*

# CHAPTER 51

"I'LL ANSWER YOUR QUESTIONS." SOPHIE FINALLY inserts herself into the conversation. Color is returning to her face.

Culebra extends a hand and helps her to her feet. I'm amazed at how quickly he's recovered. For someone who's been in a magic-induced coma for the last three days, he's showing remarkably few ill effects.

He puts a hand on the small of Sophie's back and steers her gently toward the door. "Let's go to the bar," he says. "I could use some food."

Frey and I follow. I shut the door behind us, casting one last look at the debris. I hope the rest of the bar fared better than this.

Sandra looks up when we appear in the doorway. She rushes to Culebra and Frey and hugs first one, then the other. I suspect her relief is as much the hope that she can go home now as it is her happiness to see them back among the living.

But looking around the bar, at the dozen or so assorted vamps and human hosts sharing drinks and either making or concluding their dining arrangements, it strikes me that no one here has a clue about what went on in that back room. We're just four more customers and the glances our way reflect only curiosity. There isn't anything to indicate we were just involved in a fight that might have killed us all. Even the blood that stained the clothing of Sophie and Culebra is gone. Dissipated by the magic of a broken spell.

There's no sign of Williams, either. Did he leave through the back door? Is he already on his way to San Diego?

Culebra stops at the bar, murmurs something to the human barkeep and ushers us to a table. When we're all seated, he leans forward, hands flat on the table. His eyes shine with something that looks a lot like tears, the gruffness I'm used to gone completely. He looks from one of us to the other.

"I owe you my life."

Even his voice is different, softer, more vulnerable. Has the nightmare left a mark?

He continues, "You risked everything to save me. I won't forget it. I'm in your debt. I give you my oath. We are family. No favor you ask will ever be denied."

Uneasy silence follows his declaration. Not caused by the gratitude evident in Culebra's words, but by the feeling we're now inexorably bound together. I don't know if it's what Culebra intended, but it's what I see on the faces of Frey, Sophie and Sandra.

It's Sandra who breaks the tension. "Well, then. I have the first favor."

We all look at her.

"I want to go home."

It's exactly the right thing to say. The bubble of anxiety bursts with an almost audible pop.

Culebra laughs. "You can go whenever you like."

The barkeep approaches the table. In his hands he has a tray filled with shredded beef, chicken, marinated vegetables, beans, a plate piled with steaming tortillas. He plunks the dishes down along with half a dozen bottles of Dos Equis.

"I hope you will eat first," Culebra says. He casts an eye my way. "Sorry, I have nothing to offer you, Anna. Unless you see something at one of the tables—"

I shake my head, but reach for one of the beers. "I'm fine, thanks."

I hide my impatience as Culebra, Frey and Sandra dig into the food. Only Sophie holds back.

Because of Deveraux?

He picks the question out of my head. *No. It's one of the things I like best about taking up residence in a human body. I can enjoy food again. No bloodlust.*

*Then why isn't Sophie eating?*

She looks over at me. "I'm not hungry. Maybe we can take a walk."

Culebra sends a thought, cloaked, so that only I hear it. *There are still questions. This may be your chance to get answers.*

He's busy eating, but his eyes are veiled and serious when they meet mine.

I push back the chair and stand. "Good idea, Sophie. I can use some air."

I hadn't realized night had fallen until we step out onto the boardwalk. A light breeze carries the pungent sharpness of mesquite and the subtle sweetness of night-blooming cactus. A crescent moon and a diamond-studded sky present a peaceful contrast to the hellish storm that threatened us inside just minutes before.

"It's surreal, isn't it?" Sophie asks.

I'm not sure what she's referring to, the still desert night or the tempest conjured up by Burke, but I nod anyway.

Her face is tilted up toward the sky. "I never see stars like this in Denver. The desert is so beautiful. A person can hear herself think."

I smile at the irony in that expression. "You always hear yourself think, don't you? Literally, I mean."

She chuckles. "You mean I always hear Deveraux think. It's hardly the same thing."

"Where is he? Right now, I mean."

She puts a hand to her chest. "He's here. He knows you and I have things to discuss. He won't interfere."

"Isn't it odd? Having another consciousness, a separate being as part of you?"

The look she throws me is half amused, half surprised that I'd ask the question. "No different than you living with the dual sides of your nature. You are in constant battle against the beast, are you not? In any case, Deveraux and I aren't so dissimilar as you might suspect. In fact, I imagine it's easier for me than it is for you. His beast is contained. All that's left are his thoughts." She laughs again. "Disturbing as they sometimes are."

Her simple, bittersweet awareness amazes me. How much of it is the witch and how much the vampire?

We walk on in silence for a few moments, enjoying the quiet and the calm. But I know I have to broach the subject at some point, it may as well be now.

"Where is she, Sophie?"

There's no faltering in Sophie's step or hesitation in her answer. "She's no longer a threat."

"That doesn't answer the question." It comes out sharper than I intend.

Sophie draws a deep breath. "When I broke her spell, the evil behind the magic had to go somewhere. I captured it in the goblet."

I remember the moment before the goblet shattered. Burke was drawn into it, too. "So the evil—?"

"Was directed back into her."

"Could she have survived?"

"What we saw inside was a reverse image of my sister. Not her physical being. She lives but the damage done to her physically, psychically and mentally will take a long time to heal. Years. Decades, maybe."

I watch her. Sorrow and guilt are in clear conflict with the simple truth: Burke's actions sealed her fate.

It's not enough. My gut aches with my own truth, there's no comfort in Sophie saying Burke is no longer a threat. The bottom line is that as long as she is alive, she is a threat. I want her dead. "Do you know where she is?" I ask quietly.

"No." She stops and turns to face me. "That is the truth. She may be on this earthly plane, she may be on another. She's gone away to heal. I can't reach her. I won't try. I promise you, she is no longer a threat. It's all I have to offer."

But I think of Williams and Ortiz and those girls tortured in that warehouse. "She has much to answer for. I'm not sure I can let it go."

Sophie's voice is just as determined. "You may not have a choice."

We continue walking along the boardwalk. The wind has picked up a little, dust whirls at our feet, clouds skitter across the sky. The silence stretches between us.

At last Sophie says, "What are you going to do?"

"I don't know. Burke hurt—"

"No. I don't mean about Burke. What are you going to do about *you*. Deveraux called you the chosen one. You seemed distressed by the idea."

Distressed doesn't begin to cover it. When I don't answer, Sophie turns to look at me. "We can't fight our destiny, Anna. We shouldn't try."

She's smiling softly, I see it in the darkness. It strikes me that if Williams had said that to me—shit, he has a million times—my back would be up, my defenses at the ready. Sophie, however, brings forth a startling burst of clarity.

"I'm afraid."

"Of what?"

"Of not knowing what it means to be the chosen."

She laughs. "That's easy enough to find out. Ask Williams."

I shake my head. "He'd be only too happy to tell me. But it would be his version. I don't trust him. He's too far removed from—" I struggle to find the right word.

"Humanity?"

"Yes. From humanity. He's forgotten what it means to be human. I can't let that happen to me."

We've reached the end of the boardwalk. The dirt road out of Beso de la Muerte stretches before us like a faint silver ribbon. I can smell a wolf prowling in the darkness, hear the rapid heartbeat of a rabbit, see the winding path left by a snake as it skims the desert floor. The animal side of my nature recognizes and is recognized by the life teeming just out of sight.

In the dark, my voice is an echo, haunted, wistful. "I didn't ask to become vampire. It's a battle every day. I'm determined to take care of my family, to take care of the people I love. I don't think I'm strong enough to do more."

Sophie sighs and touches my arm. "You are much stronger than you think, Anna. You need to let go, trust your instincts instead of fighting them."

She shivers suddenly.

*She's exhausted.* Deveraux's voice chides me. *We should go back.*

We turn and head back toward the bar. Golden shafts of light spill from the windows and doors. Laughter and the sound of music drift on the wind. The smells now are of grilling meat, the perfume of women, the musk of men and vampire.

Sophie is quiet. Just as we reach the door, she says, "I'd like to take care of the vampires my sister hurt."

The offer is as unanticipated as it is surprising. "They're being cared for."

"They're different, right? They're not the same as you and Deveraux."

"How did you know that?"

"I don't know. Maybe Deveraux picked up on something when you told us about them. I want to take them back to Denver."

I glance at my watch. Midnight. "It's too late to go to the safe house. Stay with me tonight and I'll take you in the morning."

She brushes a lock of hair out of her face and gazes into the bar. "I think I'd rather stay here," she says. "Enjoy the desert while I have a chance. Think Culebra can put me up?"

I laugh. "After what you did for him this afternoon? He'd not only put you up, he'd give you his firstborn."

But before we go inside, I put a hand on Sophie's arm. "I will be honest with you, Sophie. Williams isn't the only one concerned about Burke. I'm not sure I can rest until what we started today is finished. As long as Burke has breath in her body, she is a threat."

# CHAPTER 52

T HE PARTY IS STILL GOING STRONG WHEN WE step inside. Sophie leaves me to rejoin the group, my last words casting a pall that dims the spark of friendship that had been building between us. I'm sorry about that; I have few friends and I like Sophie. I'm not sorry for being honest, though. I don't just need for Burke to be out of commission, I need for Burke to be dead.

Weariness turns my thoughts to home and bed. I realize when we go back inside that I have no way to get home. Williams left with the car. Culebra arranges for one of his customers to drive Frey and me. She's a human, a host, and luckily for us, keeps up a steady stream of chatter that requires Frey and I to do nothing more than nod and grunt.

Fatigue settles on my shoulders like a coat of chain mail. I can't believe all that's happened in twenty-four hours. The fire and losing Ortiz. Tracking and losing Jason Shelton. Going after Sophie. The ritual to save Culebra.

I wonder where Williams went when he disappeared.

Did he go home? Did he go back to the park to set his witches on Burke? Try another locator spell? If she's as weak as Sophie implies, she may be easier to find.

What happens if he does? First thing tomorrow, I'll call and find out.

Frey gets dropped off first. He grabs the tote bag from the backseat and climbs out, a little more slowly than he climbed in. I realize if I'm feeling this tired, he must be exhausted. Look what he's been through.

I step out with him and touch his cheek in parting. "Thanks. Again."

He smiles a weary but wolfish grin and places his fingers over mine. "Let's not make this a habit."

"I hope you told Culebra that."

"Believe me, I did."

He punches his access code into the security panel on the gate and steps through. "I'm going to sleep for a week," he calls over his shoulder, lifting a hand in a halfhearted wave as he moves down the walk.

I get back into the car. Our driver, young, enthusiastic, bubbling with curiosity about Frey and me, launches into a dozen questions about what happened tonight in that back room. She says rumors started flying as soon as Culebra made his entrance with the three of us trailing behind. Was it true he had been kidnapped by a witch? That he had been held in an astral plane and that we transported ourselves by way of a supersonic spaceship to rescue him? That we were now part of a paranormal superhero squad that will be called upon to break demonic spells all over the world?

Wow.

The truth dulls by comparison.

I let her prattle on, neither confirming nor denying, all the time it takes us to get back to the airport and my car. When she drops me off, she rolls down the window.

"I could be a great help to you," she says, thrusting a

card at me. "I'll do anything." She pushes her hair away from her neck. "Anything."

At that moment, another young face flashes in my head: a girl in a seedy apartment being seduced by that asshole Jason. I turn angry eyes on her innocent face. "Go home," I snarl. "Before you get what you're asking for."

I SLEEP FOR TWELVE HOURS. IT'S ALMOST ONE IN THE afternoon when I'm finally able to pry open my eyes long enough to look at the clock. My first thought, how good a cup of coffee is going to taste, is chased out of my head by another.

Shit.

I sit straight up in bed and throw off the covers. I was supposed to take Sophie to the safe house this morning.

I grab up my cell and phone Culebra.

It's good to hear his brusque "Yes" when he picks up.

He isn't a fan of technology. If he's barking a curt greeting when interrupted by the cell phone, it's a good sign he's back to normal.

"Feeling better, are we?"

"Anna?" His voice softens. "Sorry, I should have checked the ID."

"I take it you're feeling well?"

"Remarkably well. It's amazing how rejuvenating three days in a coma can be."

I flash on Frey. Not so good for the person intercepting all that bad mojo.

Culebra instantly realizes the implication of his last statement. "That didn't come out right. How is Frey?"

"Haven't spoken with him since last night. He planned to sleep for a week. I thought I'd wait at least a day to call him."

"I'll do the same."

There's a pause until my as-yet-decaffeinated brain clicks into gear with the reason I called. "Is Sophie there? I was supposed to take her to the safe house this morning. Obviously I overslept."

"No problem. Williams came by this morning. He took her."

Why does that start alarm bells shrieking in my head? "Williams took her?"

In the background, I can hear someone—sounds like Sandra—calling Culebra's name. He shouts a reply and then says into the phone, "Sorry, Anna. I have to go. Sandra is taking off. I want to say good-bye."

"Wait."

There's a pause.

"I never got the chance to ask. Is it true that Sandra wanted me to stay away from Beso de la Muerte? That she didn't want to see me?"

Another pause, then Culebra says, "I think you should talk to her about it."

"She's leaving."

He draws a breath. "I can say only this—Tamara was more than a friend to Sandra. While Sandra knows Tamara betrayed her, she still finds it hard to see you. You killed her lover."

In the background, a Harley engine roars to life.

"I have to go, Anna. We'll talk later."

The phone clicks dead in my ear.

I'm stunned by Culebra's words. It seems to be escaping Sandra that Tamara planned to kill her so that she would be one with Avery. And she's angry with me? If I ever see Sandra again, I'll point that out.

Love makes people stupid, my own voice reminds me. Gloria and David were a perfect example. Forget it. Concentrate on Sophie.

I jump to my feet and head for the closet.

Why would Williams go back to Beso for Sophie? The question nags at me.

I can come up with only one logical answer. Burke is still alive. Williams' thirst for revenge won't be satisfied until he knows she's dead. He sees Sophie as the means to that end.

And that makes me afraid for Sophie.

# CHAPTER 53

ALL THE TIME I'M GETTING DRESSED, I'M ASKING myself, where would Williams take Sophie? He wants revenge. He wants Burke.

The logical part of my brain says don't jump to conclusions. Call Rose at the safe house first. Maybe he did take her to meet those vampires.

Rose picks up on the second ring, her cheery greeting a balm to my troubled spirit.

The joy isn't long-lived. "Williams? Here this morning?" she replies in answer to my question. "Nope. Haven't seen him since the fire."

Not the news I was hoping for. Before I ring off, I ask, "How are the girls?"

Her smile is evident in her tone. "They're doing great, Anna. The collars have all been removed. We saved six. It's odd, the differences between us. But we keep the curtains closed during the day, let them out at night. I'm not sure long term what will happen, where they'll go, but for now, they're welcome here."

I guess I should feel happy at the news. Six out of twelve—eighteen if you count the six bodies that showed up before the fire—isn't exactly heartening, but it's better than having lost them all.

Still, I wonder at how they're recovering mentally. Being tortured and bled for days has to leave a psychic scar. It's one thing to heal the body, it's quite another to heal the mind.

I promise Rose to stop by as soon as I can and disconnect.

Now what? Where is Williams?

I call his cell. It rings six times and goes to voice mail.

Would he have taken her to the park?

Probably not. I remember the fury in his voice and eyes when he pledged to make Sophie and her sister pay. He wouldn't want witnesses for what I fear he intends to do.

I move toward the front door, grabbing purse and keys as I go. Perhaps if I go to the park, consult the witches, they can locate Sophie.

The newspaper is on the porch. I trip over it in my haste to get to my car. It flops open as I toe it out of the way.

The headline story on page one answers my question.

Ortiz' death is still the top story. His funeral is tomorrow. Along with his picture is another.

Why didn't I think of that before?

The warehouse.

Williams will take Sophie back to the place where Ortiz died.

I SMELL SMOKE AS SOON AS I PULL UP TO THE FRONT of the warehouse. It hangs like an oily curtain over the building. Yellow crime scene tape stretches around the perimeter although there are no security guards or police personnel that I can see.

I listen.

It's ghostly quiet. There are no cars in the lot in front of the building. If Williams is here, did he go to the back?

I spot Williams' Navigator, backed up to the loading bay. Twisted metal, shrunk by heat and compressed by pressure, fills the area that was the basement. When I look inside, there isn't enough space for a person to stand. The second-floor ceiling collapsed, sending filing cabinets and bits of ruined office furniture to fill the void.

Where is he?

I stand back, listening, sniffing the air, probing for his telepathic signature.

It's not Williams' marker that I pick up.

It's Deveraux's.

He's sensed that I am here. But he's not sending words, he's sending feelings. Desperation. Fear. Pain.

I'm careful not to respond. Williams might intercept.

He's somewhere in the rear of the basement.

How did they get in?

I crouch down to peer in again. This time I see a pattern to the debris. Something strong pushed girders and beams aside, forging a squat tunnel that snakes back. I have to get on my hands and knees to wiggle through. It's wide enough, but only three feet high. The rough edges of torn metal soon eat through the fabric of my jacket and T-shirt and scour the skin on my back. No matter. The torment in Deveraux's cry for help still reverberates in my head.

The smell and feel of my own blood running in rivulets from the cuts awakens the beast. I keep it in check. Williams will recognize the presence of another vampire even before he picks up the scent of my blood.

I concentrate on moving forward, ignore the white-hot pain as my skin is being flayed. Think of something else.

Like how was Williams able to get Sophie to maneuver the narrow passageway? Did she allow herself to be taken? She has an air of resignation about her that sparks irritation in me. Is her guilt about her part in Burke's plan so great she is willing to give up to him without a fight?

Not so with Deveraux. He took the chance to reach out.

The tunnel ends about twenty feet in. I remain on hands and knees and peek out. Near where the foot of the staircase used to be, where I last saw Ortiz, someone waits. The ruins of the staircase form an alcove tall enough for a person to stand. Williams' scent comes to me first, saturated with hate so strong it blocks out everything else.

Then the smell of blood. Sophie's. Where is she?

Williams' back is to me. I can't tell what he's doing, only that his attention is held by whatever it is. Hate is giving way to pleasure—potent, sexual. I taste it in the air. He's excited.

Where is Sophie?

Deveraux has been waiting for me. As soon as he senses that I'm close, he says, *Stop him. Now. He's going to kill her.*

I spring from the tunnel and hit Williams low and hard.

He is taken by surprise. He falls back and away. He doesn't know it's me until he springs up, whirls around.

I expect to meet the vampire.

Instead, I meet the man.

What I see in his human eyes is more frightening than any beast.

# CHAPTER 54

"ANNA." HE SMILES AT ME. "I SHOULD HAVE KNOWN you would show up."

His expression is disingenuous, cold.

He holds up his hands. They're soaked in blood. Sophie's. His body hides her, but I know. I move to the side, wary, on guard, to see.

Sophie.

She's bound hands and feet to a girder. Her jeans and shirt have been sliced from neck to navel. Her blood soaks through fabric, puddles on the ground. Whatever weapon he used was sharp, a single downward thrust ripped through fabric and skin, leaving a bloody trail.

Her head droops. Her eyes are closed but her chest labors as she struggles to breathe. Is she drugged?

"Williams, what are you doing?"

He pulls a bloody knife from a scabbard at his waist. "Exacting justice."

"This isn't justice. It's not Sophie's fault Ortiz is dead."

"No. It isn't, is it? It's Burke's."

His eyes flick to Sophie. "She won't tell me how to find her. I tried the beast. I tried the human. She refuses to show me the way."

"The way?"

A nod. "The others at the park said there's a conduit between the earthly plane and the ethereal one. They couldn't locate Burke on earth. To traverse into the higher plane, they said it would take blood. Familial blood." He points downward with the knife. Near his feet is a small crystal bowl filled with blood. "I'm going to take the blood to them. Let them send me to the other world. First, I'll finish what you stopped me from doing yesterday."

The beast is contained. Williams isn't letting the vampire surface either mentally or physically. He wants to do this as a human. He wants not only to collect Sophie's blood for the spell but to watch her die.

It's a side of him I've never seen before.

"Williams, listen to me. Sophie is human. You've been a cop. You know it's wrong to kill her. You have what you need. Take it to the park. I'll go with you if you want. We'll go after Burke together."

Deveraux stirs in Sophie's consciousness. *What are you waiting for? Kill the bastard. He's crazy. Don't you see that?*

But it's not insanity I see in Williams' eyes. It's pain.

Pain I understand. Pain I felt every moment for the last three days. Pain that would have become unbearable had I lost Culebra and Frey the way Williams lost Ortiz.

I take a step toward him, hands outstretched. "I promise. Let Sophie go and we'll go after Burke. Together."

If I unleashed my own beast, force him to give me the knife, would he respond?

"Don't."

His eyes are penetrating. He seems able to read my intentions as easily as he can my thoughts.

"Do you want to know why her vampires were different?"

I don't know whether to be encouraged by or wary of the change of subject, but I nod.

"The serum in those syringes. The serum she had her lapdog Jason inject into those girls. It turned them into genetic freaks—made their blood simulate vampire blood but gave them nothing of vampire strength or power to protect them. They were vampire only for what they could provide for her business. And once they had been drained, their shells were tossed like garbage. Jason alone was different and even he was tricked in the end. He was a throwback to the beginning, created by magic, destroyed by sunlight. Weak. Pathetic. Stupid."

For the first time I see Williams as vulnerable. I am as outraged as he is by what Burke did. But it was Belinda Burke, not Sophie. As a vampire, I could rip his human throat out in ten seconds if he refused to meet beast with beast. But would I?

Yes, to save Sophie. I center myself.

Williams watches me.

"I can't you let hurt Sophie. You know that. You're grieving for Ortiz. I understand. I want revenge, too. But against Burke. Sophie fulfilled her part of the bargain. She broke Burke's curse. It's what I asked of her."

"It's not what I asked of her." Williams' voice thunders in the closed space. "I never agreed to let her go."

A low moan escapes Sophie's lips. The sound spurs Williams into action. He whirls around with a snarl, the bloody knife poised.

It's all it takes to loose the vampire. I don't try to hold it back; there isn't time. When I lunge at Williams, it's with full force. He flies back, twenty feet, to land in a pile of scrap.

I brace myself, ready to intercept the charge, every

nerve in my body poised for the fight. This battle has been a long time coming.

Williams doesn't leap up. Doesn't yell or threaten. Doesn't move.

I take a step closer, fangs extended, growling a warning. There's no response.

Is this a trick?

I morph back from vampire to human so I can better understand.

What I see is a human, eyes open, a slender spear of rebar piercing the center of his chest. As I watch, those eyes focus on me, then cloud over. His body writhes against the spike impaling him.

Williams never unleashed his beast.

*He's not dead,* Deveraux screams. *Get us out of here.*

I know he's right. If Williams were dead, if the spear had been wooden instead of iron, we'd be looking at a pile of ash.

Human instinct makes me want to help him. Animal instinct says I need to get Sophie to safety before he can do any more harm.

*Is she drugged?* I ask Deveraux, loosening the ropes at Sophie's wrists and ankles. When I pull them free, she sags against me.

*He gave her something in a cup of coffee. I never saw it coming.*

*But you're not affected?*

*Came to before she did. I guess it's a good thing. He was going to burn her. I read it in his head.*

I read it, too. It's what makes me want to get her out of here before he pulls himself free. He's no immediate threat. Even as a vampire, he'll take time to heal. When the beast emerges, though, it won't be pretty. I want to be gone.

I look back at the tunnel, wonder how I'll get her out.

Then I look up. The staircase is gone, but the landing one floor above is intact. This may be how Williams got Sophie here.

I scoop Sophie into my arms. She seems small and slight and utterly defenseless. Her vulnerability chases any inclination to help Williams right out of my head.

But before I carry her to safety, I do one more thing. I take the crystal bowl and fit it between her crossed arms.

Williams was right about one thing. Burke needs to die.

I flex my legs slightly, gather strength, leap upward.

I land squarely on both feet. The hall is dark and empty and smells of melted rubber and burned tile. The employee lounge? The twisted shells of their lockers and the remains of a refrigerator confirm. When I was here the first time, this wouldn't have led me to the front door. Now, with two floors compressed, I see light at the end of the hallway.

I carry Sophie toward it.

# CHAPTER 55

AS SOON AS WE GET TO THE COTTAGE, I CARRY SO-phie upstairs to the guest room and lower her onto the bed. She's still out, so I take a minute to shed my ruined clothes and pull on a T-shirt. The cuts on my back are already healed.

Sophie still hasn't come to. I figure she's in shock. She would be—from loss of blood if not from the terror of Williams' torture. Her pupils, when I check, are fixed and dilated. I gently loosen the torn fabric of her clothing so I can examine the wound.

She moans slightly as dried blood binds with the fabric. Despite my care, the cut reopens. It runs in a straight line from the neck of her shirt to her navel. Fresh blood oozes over my fingers.

I take a wet cloth and sponge the wound. It's about half an inch deep, eighteen inches long. Williams made the cut in one motion. Any deeper and he would have disemboweled her.

I swallow hard, appalled.

*She needs stitches,* I tell Deveraux. *I'd better take her to a hospital.*

*Aren't you forgetting? You can heal her.*

*She's lost a lot of blood. And she's a witch. I don't know if it will work.*

*She's human. You healed David.*

How did he know that? I sit back a minute, looking down at the girl but seeing something entirely different. A vampire. As real in his way as the girl. *If she dies, you do, too.*

A heartbeat goes by before he answers. *Does that make a difference in your decision to help her?*

No. I get to work.

I pull off Sophie's boots, strip her of her bloody clothes and let everything fall to the floor. I cover her lower body with a blanket. Ready myself.

I need the vampire. It isn't hard to summon her. Blood from the reopened wound does it. I don't need fangs to open a vein, just position myself over her body and let instinct take over.

I suck at the wound, beginning near her neck, gently at first, letting the smell and taste of Sophie's blood send those first shivers of delight through me. But this isn't arterial blood, I don't sense the pulse beat beneath my tongue. At first, it doesn't feel as if it will be enough. The beast awakens, demanding more.

I force it back, make it content to lap at what blood it can get, concentrate on healing rather than feeding.

Gradually, it happens. Sophie's skin responds, mending itself over the cut too shallow to have injured organ or muscle. I trail my mouth down the length of her body and up again, feeling the skin knit itself together. Feeling Deveraux beneath her skin. Feeling his pain lessen with the healing. Her blood is sweet. Too soon for the vampire, it's done.

ONE HOUR LATER, SOPHIE IS WIDE-AWAKE, SITTING up in bed, dressed in a pair of my sweats. She's showered and pulled her freshly washed hair back into a ponytail. She looks about fifteen. I have to keep reminding myself that she's not the helpless young girl she appears to be.

Every few minutes, her hands go to her midsection and she winces, as if reliving Williams' attack.

"You're all right," I reassure her. "You are completely healed and Williams can't hurt you anymore."

"He was so angry."

She says it as if she still can't believe what he did to her. She's calm, maybe too calm. Is she in shock?

I wish I could think of something to rationalize or explain Williams' action. Something to rationalize or explain what I'm about to do.

I sit on the edge of the bed, take one of her hands, rub it between my own. A simple human act of comfort usually denied me. The infusion of her blood heated my skin so my touch isn't corpse cold.

"Sophie, Williams is sick with grief. It doesn't excuse the way he hurt you, but I understand why he did it."

Something in my tone brings Deveraux to the surface.

*Uh-oh,* he says, *what are you going to do?*

Sophie is looking at me, her eyes wide. "You're going after my sister, aren't you?"

"I don't expect you to understand. Belinda is nothing like you. She set out to murder innocent women. She used some kind of magic to create a species of vampire whose sole purpose was to provide blood for her cream. She swore to kill my friends because I interfered with her plans. You were brave to come here and help us stop her. But it isn't enough. I have to finish it."

I wait for her reaction, expecting her to argue in Belinda's defense. Instead, she pulls her hand free of mine and intertwines her fingers, squeezing until her knuckles turn white.

"How will you find her?"

She doesn't know about the blood Williams collected. I don't want to tell her about it. "Do you have any ideas?"

It's unfair—asking Sophie to help me locate her sister so I can kill her. I backtrack. "I think there's a way. The same witches who helped me locate her before think they can locate her now."

Her expression reflects grave concern. "It would be dangerous, Anna. Belinda's magic may have been rendered ineffective here, but she's still powerful. You would be risking your life and for what? She won't be capable of hurting anyone again for a long time. Isn't that good enough?"

I wish I could say it was. But I think of Williams and how the depth of his grief drove him to attack Sophie. He and I have our differences, but he's not a monster.

Sophie watches my face, reads what she sees reflected there. "You need to think this through carefully, Anna. I don't know what you'll be facing. Belinda may be in her physical body—without glamour. An old woman. Could you kill her in cold blood? Are you capable of killing a helpless old woman?"

Deveraux pipes up. *You couldn't even kill Williams when you had the chance. And you should have. He's still on the loose, too.*

Sophie takes my hand again. "Deveraux is right. Williams was going to kill me. In a way, he's as dangerous as my sister. He is not your friend, Anna. You should be aware of that. He harbors great resentment toward you. Deveraux saw it. It's why he didn't make his presence known to him. He doesn't trust him. You shouldn't, either."

She is not telling me anything I haven't told myself. But it's not Williams that concerns me right now. It's Burke.

"Williams and I have had our differences. I know there will come a time when he and I will be forced to confront them. But at this moment, Williams is no threat. He was hurt today. Worse than you. He'll need time to heal."

She stirs and I anticipate her next words. I hold up a hand. "I know what you're going to say. That Burke is hurt, too, and no threat. It's different with Williams. I know his strengths and weaknesses. I know how to fight him. Burke showed me she could take away all my power. That she could hurt my friends and there wasn't a damned thing I could do about it. I can't let that go, Sophie. Not even for you. I'm sorry."

I pull back my hand, stand up. "I want you to stay here tonight. If you are serious about caring for the girls from the warehouse, I'll take you to them and fly you all back to Denver tomorrow morning."

Sophie studies my face, gauging, I suppose, if there is a chance she can talk me out of going after her sister. I wait for Deveraux to pop up with an argument of his own, too, but none is forthcoming.

After a long moment, Sophie sighs. "I think that will be best. I'll feel safer once I'm home. I have protection spells to put in place. And Deveraux will sense Williams if he tries to come after me."

*We'll be fine once we're back at the mansion,* Deveraux adds. *I still have contacts in the vampire community. Sophie will be well protected.*

It's decided. I leave Sophie then, go back downstairs, make sure the doors and windows are secure. I believe what I told Sophie, that Williams has been hurt too badly to be a threat. But why take a chance?

Especially since I'll be slipping away as soon as I know she is asleep.

# CHAPTER 56

WHEN I PEEK IN ON SOPHIE A HALF HOUR LATER, she's fast asleep. I wonder if Deveraux is, too, or if he stands as a kind of subliminal watchdog, ready to rouse her if he senses danger. I don't probe, though. I don't want him to know I'm leaving. Besides, the only person I can think of who wishes Sophie harm, Williams, could not have recovered this quickly from such a grievous wound. She'll be safe until I return.

And if I don't return?

I close the door softly leaving Sophie and that question behind.

Then I run downstairs and out to the garage. I'd already called ahead and arranged for the witches to meet me at park headquarters. They were expecting the call to come from Williams. I simply said there'd been a change in plans.

It's early evening, but a rising full moon and a cloudless sky bathe Balboa Park in a translucent glow. Shadows dance off the buildings and trees as if backlit. The only sounds come from the zoo nearby—the screams and howls of animals responding to some primeval urge to beg the moon for liberation. The animal in me responds, too. It stirs and growls and aches for the hunt.

The witches are waiting when I come off the elevator. It's quiet in the big anteroom that is the nerve center of the compound. Only a half dozen psychics are on duty. They pay us no heed when we disappear down the hall.

Once the door is closed behind us, Susan Powers speaks first, taking the bowl I hold out to her. "You are sure you want to do this?" She looks at the bowl with its ruby liquid—Sophie's blood—and places it on a table. "It is very dangerous. Once we get you to your destination, you have only ten minutes before we lose our ability to pull you back. After that, you will be on your own. Our magic will no longer be able to help you."

"Or protect you," Min Liu adds. "You will be a human with no powers on a ghostly plane. It's a foolish risk, Anna. We have no way of knowing what form Belinda has taken. Williams said she was hurt badly, but she survived what would have killed a lesser witch. We beg you to think this through carefully. There must be another way."

I draw a breath. "There is no other way. I can't afford to wait for her to get strong enough to come back. I've beaten her twice. Next time, she may strike without warning at people I love, at me. This is my only chance to strike first."

Ariela approaches, takes my hand. "Then if you're sure, we will prepare you for the journey."

I nod and let her lead me to the center of the room. She takes a brush and paints a circle around me with Sophie's blood. At the same time, Min dips her fingers into the bowl and dabs my face—forehead, cheeks, lips.

The blood neither awakens the beast nor excites it.

"Are you wearing the amulet?" Min asks.

I pull the charm from under my T-shirt and let it fall between my breasts.

She touches the amulet with the blood. "This will be your guide. It will lead you to Burke and after, back to us."

"What should I expect?" I ask. "What will this 'ghostly plane' be like?"

Susan has been at the table, first arranging candles, then mixing some kind of potion in a golden goblet. She looks up. "We don't know. None of us are powerful enough to attempt the journey."

She says it while holding my gaze with her own and with a kind of awe that makes my eagerness for what may come even more intense. I *want* to do this.

Min is still holding the bowl. "Give me your weapon. I'll anoint it, also."

"Weapon?" I repeat. "I have no weapon with me. I am vampire. I thought that would be enough."

Min's eyes widen. "I told you," she says. "You will be *human* on the ghostly plane. You will not be vampire. You can only pass through the portal as a human."

Susan frowns. "Williams didn't explain that to you?"

I press my fingertips against my eyes for a moment, seeing Williams on his back with that spear of rebar in his chest. "No. It doesn't matter. Weapon or no weapon, I've got to do this now."

The three exchange concerned glances. Ariela crosses to the table and picks up a dagger Susan had used to strip herbs from a slender twig. She touches the blade with the blood and brings it to me.

The dagger is about ten inches long, the blade tapering from a leather-bound handle to a fine point. Its weight lies heavy in my hand. I hold it up, watch light dance along the blade, nod to the witches. Ariela hands me the sheath. I secure it around my waist with a cord, slip the knife inside. Close my jacket around it.

"I'm ready."

The three move to the outside of the circle. Susan picks up the goblet, begins to chant. Smoke rises from the goblet, first white, then black. Min and Ariela join hands, adding their voices to the song, a simple phrase in a language unknown to me, a single rhythmic note repeated over and over.

I watch and listen, fascinated, waiting. I don't know what to expect—what will the journey be like? Will I fly? Will I sense movement?

A thrill runs through my body, prickly as electric current.

I am not afraid. I'm excited. Every cell in my body thrums with anticipation.

The smoke grows darker and denser. How could so much smoke come from that tiny goblet? The witches are a dim shadow lost in the haze. Their voices fade, receding as if it is they who are moving through time and space.

A tiny sensation. The floor shifting beneath my feet. A rumble of distant thunder. The room gone black as night. I close my eyes. For an instant.

When I open them, the world has changed.

# CHAPTER 57

I'M IN A ROOM. DAZZLING WHITE. NO WINDOWS or doors. Now what?

I touch the amulet.

It warms and begins to glow. As it does, shapes form out of nothingness. A table. A round globe in the center.

I approach it. I know what I'm supposed to do. Something deep in my subconscious guides me. I place both hands on the globe. Beneath my fingertips, it stirs as if alive. *Beneath my fingertips . . .* My physical senses are sharper. I watch, fascinated, excited, as clouds form in the sphere, then clear.

I see a room. A bed. An old woman lying still beneath a quilt of grass. She opens her eyes and looks up at me. Awareness blooms behind cataractous eyes. No fear. A smile. She beckons with a crooked finger.

A whirl of movement.

I'm at the bedside.

Belinda Burke is sitting up. She is bent with age and

stoop-shouldered. Her face is lined. She is squinting at me through lenses shrouded in the opaque film of age. But she recognizes me. Her bitter malevolence permeates the air like moisture after a summer storm.

"You came, Anna. Not Williams. But I shouldn't be surprised. Did you kill him?"

She shakes her head without waiting for me to answer. "No. Of course not. It's not in you to kill. You still fight the animal within. It will be your downfall, you know."

She stirs, one gnarly hand grasping the blanket as if to throw it off.

I move faster, grab that hand, still it.

She smiles up at me. "You have no power here."

"From what I see, neither do you."

A breath stirs the hair on the back of my neck. It's like the breeze from an open door. I whirl around.

The guy from the restaurant, the one I assumed was Burke's bodyguard, is behind me. He looks bigger than I remembered. He's dressed exactly like before, oddly tailored black suit. The only difference this time is his eyes. They are opaque like Burke's.

Her laugh is high-pitched, malicious. "You didn't think I'd be without protection, did you?" She waves a hand.

The man advances on me. He's snarling, snapping at the air like a dog.

I know I should be scared. In this place, I have no vampire strength or speed. And yet, I was a bounty hunter long before I got those powers. I'd learned to protect myself as a human. He's human, too. He's used to his size intimidating people. It doesn't intimidate me.

I step away from him. A side kick to the solar plexus catches him off guard. A follow-up elbow to the face and he staggers back. He shakes his head. Roars in outrage.

His hand moves to open his jacket.

Shit. Weapons *do* work here. I rush him. He's too big to get my arms around. He's male. The kick catches him square in the groin. It staggers him. But it's not enough. I put every bit of strength I have into a follow-up.

That works.

He gasps, doubles over, grabs at himself. Color floods his face.

My chance. I use the heel of my palm to strike the deathblow. An upward blow fueled by the pain and desperation of eighteen young girls. A blow that smashes the cartilage in his nose and forces bone into his brain with a satisfying crunch.

He goes down like a rock.

Now for Belinda.

I draw the blade from the sheath at my waist and show it to her.

Still, no fear. Her arrogance provokes a strange reaction in me. Not anger. Not resentment.

Confidence. I let the corners of my mouth tip up.

She frowns at the smile, waves an impatient hand in the direction of her fallen lackey. "It won't be as easy for you to kill me as it was him."

"No? Why?"

"You were defending your life with him. You won't kill me, Anna. I'm an old woman. Bedridden. Helpless. You pride yourself on being human. You think you know what you are meant to do with that humanity. Protect the weak. I have nothing to fear from you."

Even as I step close to the bed, her expression and tone don't change. She is unafraid, contemptuous.

"You are a stupid girl. Like my sister. You made a mistake coming after me. A mistake you will regret. I will rest here awhile. Then I will return. You will not see it coming. Either of you."

I move without thought, without hesitation. The knife slides in easily. Under the left breast. The blade meets no resistance.

I lean close, whisper in Burke's ear. "You made the mistake, old woman. You mistake being human for being weak. I will always protect those I love. Always."

I watch the surprise bloom and fade in dead eyes, watch life drain away. I keep pressure on the knife until I feel the last flutter of her heart, watch as her chest slows and caves with the expiration of her last breath.

When I withdraw the knife, the copper smell of her blood mingles with the waste released from a body already beginning to decay.

It is the smell of victory. The knife is suddenly weightless in my hand.

The amulet begins to glow again, but this time, for a different reason. I understand the message. My time is almost up.

Once again, instinct tells me what to do. I cup the charm in my hands. The room fades as my vision blurs. Night descends. Then, smoke. An odor. Incense. A sound. The song of the witches.

I blink and I'm back.

The witches' song stops. They gather round me, eager to know what happened, what the journey was like.

Words don't come. It's as if the last ten minutes belonged to someone else. When I replay it in my head, there is no feeling except one—relief. That I'm back. That Burke is dead. That Sophie and I are safe.

Susan frowns. "Are you all right?"

I shake my head, not in response, but in an attempt to clear it. "I think so."

Min takes the knife gently from my hand. Until that moment, I didn't realize I was still holding it. Burke's blood stains the blade. "She's dead?"

"Yes."

By my hand. I glance down. No blood there.

I look up and see how much the three want details. Their faces shine with excitement. It was as much their journey as it was mine. They deserve to be told how their magic worked.

I can't do it. Not now. My thoughts and feelings center on only one thing—I have to tell Sophie that her sister is dead.

When I leave them, it is with thanks for their help and a promise to be back. The concern for me in their eyes is like a mantle that sits heavy on my shoulders all the way home.

# CHAPTER 58

WHEN I WALK IN THE FRONT DOOR, SOPHIE IS
waiting for me. She's downstairs, sitting in the
dark. Shivering. She's twisted a blanket around her body,
tightly, protection against a cold she alone feels. Her eyes
shine in the light that filters through the windows. Unshed
tears make them shimmer and spark, glittering jewels that
reflect like mirrors the moonlight so bright it turns night
into day.

Her breath catches when she sees me.

I stop at the doorway.

She knows.

When I move to turn on a light, her voice, a ghostly
echo, says, "Don't."

I drop my hand. "I'm sorry."

"You're not sorry," Sophie says.

"Not for killing Belinda. It had to be done. I am sorry
for you."

Sophie's voice catches. "At least you're honest. But Belinda couldn't have hurt you. Not for a long time. You must have seen that."

What I saw was a malicious old woman already plotting to come after me—and Sophie.

What I see before me now is a grieving woman, mourning the loss of a sister. I wonder how she knew. I press the heels of my palms against my eyes. I've heard of twins having a psychic link. Perhaps sibling witches do, too? Did Burke come to her at the moment of her death? Did she make Sophie feel guilty because it was Sophie's spell that left her vulnerable?

It's easier to let Sophie direct her anger to me, to allow her to remember whatever good she can, than to shatter the illusion by telling her the truth. Burke was evil. If she had lived, Sophie and I both would have been targets of her revenge.

Fatigue washes over me.

"I need to sleep. Will you be all right?"

She doesn't reply.

*I'll take care of her.* Deveraux's voice is hushed, grateful. *I know what happened, Anna. I read it in your thoughts just now. You did the right thing. Eventually, she will see it, too.*

Maybe. Sophie is staring straight ahead, tears now spilling freely from her eyes. For once, I'm glad for Deveraux. Theirs is a bizarre relationship, but she's not alone.

Not like me.

I trudge up the stairs, my heart as heavy as my legs. For the last few nights I've slept in an unmade bed, with just a blanket wrapped around me. Now I pull a set of linens from the closet and tug, pull and smooth the sheets until the bed is made up. Tuck in blankets, fluff pillows.

I hope this simple housekeeping chore will relax me, remind me that my life is filled with more than monsters and killing. That it will prepare me for a good night's sleep.

But when I finally crawl between those sheets, it's not what happened today that banishes sleep from my mind.

It's what's going to happen tomorrow.

I'd almost forgotten.

Ortiz' funeral is scheduled for two o'clock.

# CHAPTER 59

I'M UP EARLY THE NEXT MORNING. I SHOWER AND dress, eschewing my usual jeans and T-shirt and choosing instead black slacks and a cotton blouse under a black blazer.

For the funeral.

Sophie is asleep in the guest room. She must have come back upstairs sometime during the night.

I make a quick run down to Mission Café. I order eggs Benedict and a fruit cup and a couple of cinnamon rolls and have it all packaged to go. I never keep food in the house—no need—but I know Sophie had nothing to eat yesterday. If she's hungry this morning, I want to have something ready for her.

Back at home, I place the eggs in a covered dish in a warm oven along with the cinnamon rolls and start the coffeepot.

Lance calls as I'm pouring my first cup. The sound of his voice warms me. He'll be on the first flight in the morning and asks if I want to pick him up.

He's coming home early. It's an unexpected gift. I'm so grateful I can barely contain my excitement. I jot down the time and flight number.

Sophie appears in the kitchen just as I'm hanging up.

Deveraux makes the first comment. *Boyfriend coming home?*

His tone is smug. Obviously he listened in to my conversation with Lance on his way downstairs. It's aggravating enough to make me want to snap back at him. But Sophie hasn't said anything, and I'm more concerned about her than irritated at Deveraux and his party tricks.

I point her to a place at the kitchen table. She drops into the chair, still without a word. I don't want to push. I busy myself setting out the food and utensils.

She watches me with dull eyes. She does pick up the fork, finally, but instead of eating, moves the food around her plate in small, unenthusiastic circles. After a minute, she pushes the plate away. "I guess I'm not very hungry."

I offer her a cup of coffee. She shakes her head. "You don't have tea, do you?"

Regretfully, I shake *my* head. "No. Sorry. I could run to the store, though."

She releases a sigh. "No. Don't bother. Water?"

I get a bottle from the refrigerator and hand it to her. She takes a tiny sip. "Thanks."

We lapse into silence. I don't want to bring up the subject, but there are still questions that have to be answered. Culebra and Frey are no longer in danger, but the women who were victimized by Burke and her miracle cream are.

"Sophie, what is going to happen to the women who used your cream? Will they get well on their own? Do the police need to track them down?"

She lifts her chin. "If they were given a strong enough formula, they'll go through a terrible withdrawal. They may even have the impulse to drink blood, so the police should be aware. With or without help, the women will revert back to their former selves within a month or so of their last application. If all of the cream was destroyed in the fire, there should be nothing more to worry about."

There's a hint of antagonism is her voice. Dark anger that I acted precipitously in going after her sister. She thinks the fire ended the threat.

But I know there are truckloads of the stuff out there somewhere. I saw them. Did Williams give the information to the police? So much has happened in the last few days, I don't know.

May as well broach the second subject. "Have you changed your mind about helping the—" I fumble for the right words. My first choice, the vampires your sister created, tortured and bled, seems too strong right now. She's grieving the sister, not the monster.

"The girls you told me about last night?"

Saved. "Yes."

"Of course I want to help them. Why would you think I'd changed my mind about that?" She pushes her chair back. "If you can give me a change of clothes, I'd like to get going."

I stand up with her and follow her up the stairs. She wants to get away from me as quickly as she can.

I suppose I can't blame her.

I give Sophie a pair of jeans and a sweater, a hairbrush and a toothbrush. She showers and is ready to go to Rose's in half an hour.

The ride to Rose's is quiet. Even Deveraux has lapsed into silence. Rose is thrilled when she meets Sophie and hears her plan. The girls, who think Sophie is their own age, go along happily, especially when Sophie tells them about the mansion that will be their home and how beautiful Denver is. One call to Jeff, and he says he'll have the jet waiting for them at the airport.

*  *  *

THE GIRLS HURRY ON BOARD THE JET, PROTECTED BY
billowing gowns that cover them from neck to ankle and
wide-brimmed hats. They chatter their good-byes to me as
they go, excited to begin a new life, hopeful in a way most
of them have never been before.

Sophie stands beside me on the tarmac after they are
safely inside.

"I'll keep you informed about the girls," she says.
"They'll be fine with us. They'll be protected."

I wish I could think of something to say to close the
chasm between us. I don't regret killing Burke. I'd do it
again. I regret not being able to ease Sophie's pain.

*She'll come around.* For the first time, Deveraux reaches
out.

No. She won't.

I lost a brother. I know. *Nothing* eases that pain.

# CHAPTER 60

I'VE SEEN IT BEFORE IN MEDIA ACCOUNTS BUT NEVER experienced the real thing. The funeral of a decorated police officer. Ortiz' funeral.

I arrive at the cemetery after the mile-long procession of police vehicles and limousines have already disgorged the mourners. Ortiz' empty coffin is on the grave site, draped in an American flag. A color guard is off to one side.

I stand in the back of the crowd, scanning for the presence of other vampires, on alert for Williams. I expect he'll be sitting with Brooke. He has great resources within the supernatural community. Resources that would have come to his aid yesterday and helped him heal. Knowing how he felt about Ortiz, I can't imagine he would not have moved heaven and earth to see his friend laid to rest. And yet I detect no other vampires—not even Williams. Is he cloaking himself from me?

I work my way through the crowd, but don't push myself to the very front. After what happened yesterday, keeping

him in sight while not exposing myself seems prudent.
I don't expect he'd try to retaliate here, but he may have
someone else do it for him. It may be the reason he's cloaking his thoughts.

When I reach a place where I can see the seated mourners, I get a shock. Brooke and her sister are together under
a covered awning. Alone. Williams is not with them.

The two sisters lean in toward each other, hands entwined. They are dressed in black, slacks, sweaters. Brooke
is listening to the police chaplain as he reads from an open
Bible. She has the weary, glazed look of one in shock.

I recognize the expression. It's one of the reasons I hate
funerals. No matter how long it's been, I'm transported
right back to the one funeral I'll never be able to forget.
The sharp anguish of losing a brother has not diminished
with time. The pain still gnaws at my gut.

There's an older woman seated to the right of Brooke.
She has an arm over the back of Brooke's chair, sits erect,
stares straight ahead. If she's listening to the police chaplain, she gives no indication of it. She appears more angry
than sad. Restless. Every few minutes, her eyes scan the
crowd, pausing on a face here and there, moving on. Who
is she looking for?

She finds me. There's no ambiguity in her reaction when
she sees me. It's nothing overt. She doesn't jump up or
point or yell in my direction.

She simply grows very still and stares.

As soon as our eyes meet, I know why. I recognize her.
From a night nine months ago when I was invited to a
party at Avery's. We were never formally introduced, but
I saw her in Avery's living room. She was there with her
husband.

She is Warren Williams' mortal wife.

For the remaining hour of the service, she doesn't take
her eyes off me. As it concludes, the color guard gives its

twenty-one-gun salute and the mourners file past the coffin to pay last respects.

Brooke and her sister are among the last to leave the grave site.

Mrs. Williams stands off to the side. I do, too. The sisters glance over at us but don't approach. When they've made their way to a waiting car, she turns to me.

"I know what you did."

Mrs. Williams is an attractive fortysomething, sophisticated, perfectly coiffed, attired in the proper ensemble for the funeral of a friend. Her tailored suit is charcoal gray, probably Versace, her shoes chic but sensibly low-heeled to handle the grass, her shoulder bag dark-grained leather. She wears a simple band of diamonds on her left ring finger, diamond studs in her ears.

What doesn't fit the polished exterior is her expression.

Anger burns through her eyes. It's a dark shadow on her face, a clenched jaw. She's human, but she's projecting enough animal hatred to make me take a defensive step back.

She closes the distance. "Warren is at home. He almost didn't make it. I had to pull that bar out of his chest. He might have died in that warehouse, and you left him there. You chose the life of a witch over one of your own."

There's no point in reminding her that her husband is a vampire and wouldn't have died. Or in asking her if she knew why he'd gone to the warehouse in the first place.

She's beyond the point of reason. She looks toward the car, turning her face away from me. "No parent should ever suffer the loss of a child," she says. Her voice is sad, haunted.

I don't understand. Is she talking about Brooke? Did Brooke lose a child? Certainly, it couldn't have been Ortiz'. Vampires can't reproduce.

When she faces me, I read the truth in her eyes. She's

talking about Williams and Ortiz. Williams sired Ortiz. I should have realized it sooner, recognized the bond between them. Ortiz was a son to Williams, the only kind he could ever have.

The moment of melancholy is gone in the instant it takes Mrs. Williams to wipe a tear from her cheek. Rage once again hardens her features.

"I told Brooke that he was so broken up he had to get away, be by himself. But Warren is strong. He'll get better. And when he does, he'll come after you. It isn't over, Anna."

She starts to walk away, stops, turns. "It didn't have to be this way. Warren had such high hopes for you. You were supposed to be the one to make the peace. Instead, you wage war."

She shakes her head, looking older somehow, sadder, as if the weight of her words is a burden she can't put down. "Warren said you have only a few months left to accept what must be. Instead, you continue this useless fight. And you know who will suffer?"

She lets her gaze travel to the car, to the girls staring out at us. "They will be the ones who pay the price. The innocents. Well, Anna, you want a war? You've got one. And it's a war no one will win. I hope you're satisfied."

# EPILOGUE

A WEEK HAS PASSED SINCE ORTIZ' FUNERAL. A week filled with wonderfully ordinary things that didn't involve witches or spells or veiled threats.

Lance came home and we had a few days to enjoy each other before he was off to his next modeling assignment. We took advantage of every moment. He listened to what happened, consoled and calmed me. I can't wait for him to come home again. I'm coming to realize how much I miss *Lance* when he's gone, not just the sex.

Two days later, David returned from his vacation and we went right back to work. Thankfully, a declining economy doesn't translate into a decline in the number of fugitives who need apprehending.

Sophie called once to let me know the girls were adjusting well to their new home. Her voice was strained and formal. It was nice to hear her voice, good to know the girls were doing well, but I doubt she'll call again. I killed her sister.

I talked to Trish on her birthday and, as luck would have it, caught her during the fireworks display my folks had arranged as a special treat. For a few minutes, I could pretend to be there with them oohing and aahing over exploding sky rockets and Roman candles.

Now that I have use of a jet, who knows? I may fly over to celebrate my mom's birthday in July.

But as hard as I try to pretend everything is back to normal, I know it's not.

Mrs. Williams' words haunt me.

She accuses me of waging war.

Her husband drew the battle lines. Not me. All I've ever asked is to live on my own terms.

In a few months, I will have been vampire for one year. Is that what she meant about having only a short time to accept what must be? That may be the biggest irony. Just when I decide to open up to the possibility that there might be something to this destiny thing, I have no one to help me discover what it might be.

Well, there's nothing I can do about that. I have my family, David, Daniel Frey and Lance. It's enough for now. If somewhere down the line a door opens and some mysterious destiny presents itself, I may hesitate. But in my head, in my bones, I know I'll walk through that door.

I'll have to see what's on the other side.